Home to Cypress Bayou

Home to Cypress Bayou

A Louisiana Romance

Susan Sands

TULE
PUBLISHING

Dear Reader,

With every book I write, something new and different is happening all around me. This book was written in the early days of the COVID-19 pandemic. My entire family contracted the virus and recovered while I wrote. We were lucky that our cases were mild and that we were healthy. So many others weren't as fortunate, and during this period, there was much fear and suffering. It's not over yet, as I type this, but the vaccine is showing great promise. My sincere condolences to those who've lost precious loved ones.

About this story: It's the very first book I ever wrote. The one most authors shove under the bed, never to be seen again. It's seen many iterations and suffered lots of rejection through the years. I could have changed the names and the setting so nobody remembers. But I didn't because I'm obstinate and possibly foolish like that. I love this story because it's the proof of my stubborn dedication to my writing journey. This story got me my first agent. But it didn't sell. I rewrote it between publishing my first four books. It got me my fourth agent. The agent gave up on it. But thanks to my editor, Sinclair Sawhney, who went to bat for me with this series, we've done the story and the series proud. Writers, don't give up.

The book is set in fictional Cypress Bayou, Louisiana, the actual Natchitoches, Louisiana, aka my college town. It's also the real setting for the movie *Steel Magnolias*, which was filmed my senior year of college. We were all consumed with the beautiful stars and movie making in our tiny town. Most places I mention in the story are real in Natchitoches. It is a special, historical town (older than New Orleans) that I hope you will research. Oprah even filmed a show once in Natchitoches, so...

A special thanks to those whose support I deeply appreciate: Christy Hayes, Laura Alford, George Weinstein, and Colleen Sands. Y'all are the ones I call when it's going well and not so well. Thanks to my mom for always being my first reader. Thanks to Doug, my husband, for his continued patience with dinner, or lack thereof.

All the best!
Susan Sands

CHAPTER ONE

Leah

I GOT THE call at three o'clock in the afternoon. The number on my screen showed a US area code. As an expatriate living in Paris, incoming calls from "home" got answered even when I didn't recognize the number—which I didn't.

"Is this Leah Bertrand?" the caller spoke with a slow female drawl, a dead giveaway to her Southern heritage.

"Yes. How can I help you?" I was at the gallery sifting through invoices while there were no customers. Getting a stateside call, one from the South no less, put me on high alert for lots of reasons.

"This is Georgia Jones from the National Bone Marrow Registry. I'm the transplant coordinator for the southern US region. We've got a patient here who's a match with your donor swab sample." Her molasses twang slow-slid across the ocean, sounding exactly like the people in my North Louisiana hometown.

Georgia Jones paused for a breath, then continued, "We're hoping you'd be willing to do further testing."

Her words caught up to me. *Wait, what?* Bone marrow? "O-oh, bone marrow testing? The registry. Yes, what do you

1

need me to do?" I began to catch on. It wasn't a call I'd expected. Obviously. I'd only recently signed up for the registry.

"The first step will be a simple blood test at the same place you did the original cheek swab to see if your tissue matches."

Georgia Jones had my full attention now. "Okay, I'm willing to have my blood tested." I switched the phone from one ear to the other and shifted feet. "The medical office is a couple blocks from where I work." This whole blood-drawing thing made my liver a bit lily-ish.

"That's convenient. I have that information right here in front of me. I'll send over the lab orders." She rattled off the street names, mispronouncing them badly in broken Southern French.

I almost corrected her. I didn't, but I cringed. Clearly, the woman didn't speak French.

"I see on our records that you're in Paris, France, so that could be a challenge, but you seem to be the only possible option for this patient."

My first thought was, *How sad for her.* But Georgia Jones didn't give me a chance to speak those thoughts. She powered ahead. "Since we've tried the US options for tissue matches and come up with none—" She paused. "How would you feel about an all-expenses-paid trip home?"

If I was a match, *I would need to go home...*or at least to the States.

Jake Carmichael's face briefly flashed before my eyes, as it always did when the subject of Cypress Bayou came up. Which is probably why I hadn't been back in quite a while.

"I—uh…" I tried not to choke on my past. "How soon would I need to travel?"

"This isn't a definite, but *should* you be a match, I'd say as soon as you can get your affairs in order to stay a couple weeks—maybe more if a marrow donation is necessary. Usually only a few rounds of plasma donations are needed, and the recovery time for the donor is less. We transport donations stateside but prefer not to rely on such supply chains internationally. Too many hours, and the possibility of something going wrong along the way is higher."

I sensed the urgency for this unknown person and imagined how scared she (I envisioned a woman) might be, wondering if this could be her last chance for a cure. "I'll go immediately and get tested." Gallery business was slow on this Tuesday afternoon, and Claude was available for clients who walked in or called.

"We'd certainly appreciate it. And if you are a match, I'll get in touch in a day or two and help expedite your travel. I can't thank you enough for your willingness to save a life."

"Where would I fly in to?" I asked the woman before hanging up. I figured I might as well find out all I could ahead of time. Just in case.

"Hmm, let me see." I heard some shuffling. "It looks like you'd have the option of Shreveport Regional Airport or New Orleans International Airport. Of course, I can't give you any patient information."

I knew it. Louisiana. "I thought I recognized your accent. You sound like the people in my hometown."

I heard a little laugh from across the ocean. "Yes. Born and raised. I noticed your name was Bertrand, which is a dead giveaway for almost anywhere in Louisiana." Georgia loosened up and went off script a little.

"Is it possible this is someone in my family?" The idea hit me hard.

"Oh, I don't think so, honey. The only search we've done in the registry has been for a donor match. Close family would've been tested first."

I dialed my sister in Cypress Bayou after I hung up. It was eight a.m. Central time in all of Louisiana, so Carly would've been up and heading out to whatever she had planned for the day. I never knew with Carly. "Hey there, Leah. What's up?" She sounded so cheerful. I missed her.

"Hey, yourself. I just got a call from the bone marrow donor registry about a possible match there in Louisiana."

"Bone marrow? Oh yeah, you told me about signing up." I could picture my little sister's puzzled expression. "Where in Louisiana? It's rare to find a match outside of family, right?"

"Not sure where. They won't tell me. I think it's most likely to match with family, but donors can pretty much come from anywhere, according to the literature packet."

"So, what do you have to do?" I could hear Carly multitasking in the background, maybe getting dressed for the day.

"I'm about to head down the street and get a blood draw."

"Hey, don't pass out, okay?" Carly knew me too well. "Because every time you think you won't, and then you do."

Not that I'd had my blood drawn that often, just on normal occasions. "I'll do my best this time." I paused a second. "We don't have any cousins who are sick, do we?"

"Mmm, not any that I'm aware of. I'll ask the women. They'll know."

"Yeah, they would know." Because they knew everything about everyone going on in Cypress Bayou and the surrounding areas. "Okay. I'll keep you posted." I figured putting Carly on checking into the health and well-being of the family while I was giving fluids made sense.

"I'll give Nana a call about it." Carly had graduated law school from Tulane last year and passed the bar exam. She was currently clerking at a law firm in Baton Rouge and volunteering her skills for women trying to rise from poverty.

"Good choice." We both laughed. Mom was rarely the first line of contact if it was possible to avoid because Mom was...difficult. And nosy. And difficult.

When one's mother was challenging, making fun behind her back was necessary to keep the bitterness at bay. None had ever been more Catholic than Karen Bertrand, which made her dogmatic in the way of martyrs. She attended mass daily. You'd have thought she'd been the one who'd died on the cross horribly; such was the woman's long suffering.

Nana seemed to be the only one who could straighten her up when Mom crossed the line from *whiny* to *not okay*. Thank God for Nana.

"Keep me posted on how this goes," Carly said.

"I'm heading out now, but I'll call after work."

Time apparently was of the essence for my bloodletting, so I found Claude, my business partner and co-owner of La Toile. He was bent at the waist and staring intently through a set of magnifying loupes at a tiny oil painting sitting on an enormous easel and looked up with the myopic gaze of one who'd not quite come back from where he'd been. "*Magnifique, oui?*"

I eyed the canvas and nodded. It was an old Italian artist's work. Not my favorite, but I refused to engage in debate as to why at the moment. Claude spoke perfect English, but he was a Frenchman and didn't hide his disdain for Americans. He wrinkled his nose at me, as he often did—like he smelled feet. "You have something?" He arched his perfect eyebrows.

"I'll be gone for an hour or so. Call if you need anything."

He waved me away turning back to his study.

Claude and I had an uneasy truce. A necessary one as co-owners of our recently inherited gallery. Alaine had been our glue, our bond that made things work. Claude and I were both still reeling from Alaine's recent passing. He was the reason I'd signed up for the bone marrow registry. To honor him. He'd died without a donor, without a possibility of a cure. No family and no matches. There hadn't been time to do a full search. His cancer had been quick and brutal.

Alaine had given me my first and best opportunity to succeed in my chosen career. Art wasn't just a job for me, it was a love of color, texture, and talent. I'd fallen in love with the many modalities during elementary school art classes. I didn't have a personal talent, but I loved the smell of paint and crayons, and I so enjoyed the creative process.

These days I craved discovering new talent and digging up treasures in unexpected places. Alaine realized early on that I had an eye for identifying what was special in a piece that was brought to our attention.

I owed Alaine for his belief in me and for putting me in a position to succeed in doing what I loved. He'd become my best friend on this side of the world. He'd devoted himself to my care when I'd been alone and hurting, and I'd done it for him when he'd gotten sick.

Claude and I had been—and still were—devastated. He'd left us everything. The gallery, his home (where Claude lived), and his money (which I didn't deserve). I tried not to judge whether Claude deserved it or not.

I still thought about Alaine every day. When I entered the gallery—his gallery—especially. So, getting this call, while shocking, made me feel like I maybe I could help someone for him. He would love that.

I made my way down the sidewalk, thankful the medical office was within walking distance. Georgia from Louisiana had told me what to say when I got there. Truth was, I got woozy when I gave blood. It was my not-so-secret shame. I was a grown woman, for heaven's sake. But I had to insist on lying down during the process and for a time after. They would roll their eyes at the stupid, squeamish American, but I was used to it.

I figured an hour would give me enough time to recover and get back to La Toile if I passed out.

HOME NOW FROM my harrowing near miss with death-by-needle-stick, I called Carly. I'd warned the woman at the medical office who'd come at me with a gleam in her eye that

I was likely to faint, but as usual they hadn't listened. Good thing the floor had been carpeted. I hadn't actually lost consciousness, but it had been a close call.

"Nobody's sick that we know of on our end," Carly responded to my earlier query.

"That's good to hear." I was relieved, and knowing the extended family was healthy reassured that slight question in the back of my mind about what strange providence this might have been. "So, how are *they*?" She knew of whom I spoke.

"*They* are how they always are. Mom thinks we're all going to hell because we don't go to mass every day, and Dad spends most of his day gardening and avoiding her, but boy, you should see the size of his zucchinis this year. And Nana is…resigned to it all."

"It's nice to know that nothing changes."

"So, you might come home, huh?" Carly moved to the bright side. "Finally?"

"I'll know soon enough." As I said it, Jake's face swam by again. "The patient isn't a match with anyone stateside, so I'm unsure why I would be. But who knows?" I'd poured a glass of my favorite red and was now in my usual after-work spot out on the patio overlooking my part of the city. My flat sat over a café and across from a flower shop. One couldn't get any more Paris cliché than that. But I loved it.

"What if Jake's in town?" Carly put words to my fear.

"What if he is?" *Did I sound childish?* "I can't control what he does." I definitely sounded childish.

Carly laughed at that. "Are you kidding? It's been two years. Either you're over him or you're not. Plus, he's rarely in Cypress Bayou from what I hear. It's unlikely you'll see him while you're in town unless fate strikes."

"Of course I'm over him. It's not like we had some big blowup. We just…didn't find our way back to each other." And I would be relieved not to see him in the flesh. Glimpses on social media were enough. "It's just as well he's not around. No use digging up the dead."

"Which is even more tragic, in my book. At least you had someone. I'm twenty-five and haven't had my big love story yet."

"You've had boyfriends. What about Joe in law school?" I remembered Carly sending photos of her with a cute guy at an event. And she posted often with guys on Instagram and such.

I could almost hear her rolling her eyes through the phone and across the ocean. "Joe had a crooked—"

"Wow, okay, too much information. It's pretty late over there—midnight, right? I'll keep you posted."

Carly was still laughing. "You're such a prude, Leah. I was gonna say he had a crooked big toe. And yeah, keep me posted."

I sputtered a little. "I'm not a prude. Okay, maybe a little bit of a rule follower, but I never know what's gonna fly out of your mouth, and it makes my face red."

"G'night, my sweet sister."

I frowned. Maybe I was a bit of a prude in some ways. Maybe that's why Jake had never circled back to me or tried harder. Why he'd lost interest.

Jake

JAKE'S PHONE ALERTED him to a new text.

Hey there. Got time for lunch?

Jake was in his office going over patient charts. Elizabeth Keller, MD was a childhood pal, medical school classmate, and coworker. They'd known each other forever. Since she'd been an overly tall, plain young girl. This likely explained a lot about her as a tall, model-gorgeous, highly successful surgeon who had quite an edge to her personality.

Elizabeth was a consummate professional when it came to her career. Most folks only saw the glamorous side of her. Some got the slightly snobbish side. Jake saw her as the insecure woman he'd always known, so he could forgive some of her more annoying behavior or comments that sometimes verged on rude or abrupt.

He checked the time. It was noonish, and he could eat. So, he replied: *I'll meet you in the cafeteria.*

It's a date

He winced a little. It wasn't a date. They weren't dating, though Elizabeth might've wished otherwise. But they *weren't* dating.

There'd always been someone else for him. Always. Leah Bertrand never strayed far from his mind, though she was about as far from Cypress Bayou as one could be, living in Paris, France.

The nudge from his phone that Elizabeth was waiting in the cafeteria spurred Jake into action and pulled him from his thoughts of Leah.

As he shrugged into his white lab coat, he shoved the ever-present stethoscope into his pocket. He never went anywhere without it while inside the hospital. An emergency could arise at any moment.

Jake Carmichael's job required him to travel around the state to different hospitals with his team of diagnosticians and handle challenging cases. He'd been referred to as a less abrasive Dr. House. The reference was to the television show he'd never taken the time to watch. It was long canceled but apparently still on Netflix or some other streaming service he wasn't familiar with. So, how behind the times was he?

But now that he was back home in Cypress Bayou, Jake might finally check out the show and take up golf like so many of his colleagues. He'd been working nonstop for almost ten years now, if he counted medical school. Surely he deserved a hobby aside from his job.

His phone *dinged* again.

He hoped meat pies were on the menu today. West Monroe, where he'd been just before here, hadn't had them as an offering. Louisiana was particularly food centric. Jake had his favorites in every hospital system, depending on which part of the state he worked.

In the southwest, the crawfish étouffée was amazing, but the muffulettas couldn't be beat in New Orleans, nor the oysters. The northwest provided perfect purple-hull peas and crumbly cornbread. Meat pies were a specialty of Cypress Bayou specifically. Some of the best fare could be had at a gas station off the highway that doubled as a diner.

As Jake rounded the corner, he caught sight of Elizabeth checking her watch as she stood outside. It was a clear sign of irritation. She raised a brow as if he should confess to something he'd done wrong.

"Sorry. I was finishing a chart." A lie. He never lied.

She didn't answer, merely strode into the fragrant, loud cafeteria where everyone seemed to be in a hurry.

They grabbed a couple trays and got in the line of mostly scrub-wearing souls who were on a quick lunch break from somewhere inside the hospital. A lab, a desk, or a nursing floor. Many would get to-go containers because of time constraints and budget cuts to their departments. Jake had worked hard for his lunch privilege, when he had one, but remained ever-cognizant of how difficult the mere act of finding time to eat a meal or even a small snack within a workday could be for those in the medical profession.

Elizabeth was busy questioning the food service employee about the freshness of the fish.

"Dr. Keller, this fish here is fresh as a daisy in springtime." The woman's tone didn't reveal any outward irritation at being interrogated regarding how she was doing her job. Her response was to be commended in Jake's opinion.

"Thanks, Hazel. I'll have the fish," Jake requested as soon as Elizabeth wrinkled her nose and passed on the catfish fillets stuffed with crab stuffing. "Looks amazing."

"Thanks, Dr. Carmichael. I know it's one of your favorites." Hazel grinned at him. What he wanted to say was *Ignore her, Hazel.*

Jake moved beyond the entrées to the desserts and snagged a chocolate pudding pie and joined Elizabeth at the checkout line. "The food here is second to none, and you know it."

Elizabeth swiped her staff card and paid her ticket, then

turned to reply. "It never hurts to keep the kitchen staff on their toes and let them know we're paying attention."

"Yes, but it's their job to handle the food. It's ours to be doctors." He left off *and it's rude.*

"Oh, stop being judgy." She waved her hand around as if she were swiping at a buzzing fly. "I'm glad you're back, by the way."

Elizabeth presented him her thousand-watt smile that reminded him how she could catch enough flies with her honey without losing more favor with her lapses of vinegar. "Thank you." Plus, she was a brilliant cardiothoracic surgeon so, mostly, her strong personality didn't matter to patients who were under general anesthesia.

They made their way outside to the patio seating area, which was a nice upgrade added in the recent renovation.

"How's the fish?" She eyeballed his plate like she regretted her choice of baked chicken and steamed veggies.

"Not on your life."

CHAPTER TWO

Leah

T HE NEWS CAME two days later in the form of an email. I
was a perfect blood and tissue match for the patient in
Louisiana. And that tingle of providence skittered up my
spine again. *Sometimes we shouldn't question things that just
are.* One of Nana's favorite sayings.

So, I worked with Georgia Jones to get me on a flight
Monday morning headed to Shreveport Regional Airport,
which was only an hour and a half by car from Cypress
Bayou After a quick stop in Dallas on the way, the flight
from Dallas to Shreveport was about an hour. I wouldn't
even have to deplane in Dallas, though I might wish by then
that I could.

I figured I might as well be with family while doing the
bone marrow thing. Home was a mixed bag.

I'd made the trip a couple times since moving to Paris,
but both times I'd left Louisiana at the end of my visit and
gone back across the ocean heaving a sigh of relief. The trips
home had been stressful and difficult, thanks to my mother—and to Jake.

My living in Paris wasn't supposed to be permanent. I'd
moved there for a post-graduate internship that had turned

into a fantastic job. Plus, I'd fallen in love with the city. The art, the culture, and the history. If Jake had truly wanted me to come home to stay, I'd have been living in Cypress Bayou right now, without a doubt. But time and distance had done a number on our relationship.

Now I would spend two weeks there, at least, with more needles and bloodwork (my least favorite things) and my sainted mother's attempts to re-Catholicize me. Thank goodness for Nana, Dad, and Carly. Wasn't sure if Jake would pop into the picture, but I would deal with that should it happen.

The idea of seeing him again in the flesh caused my brain to supply me with a fresh, full-color, smiling replica, barring no detail of his perfection. I hated my ability to do that. Because seeing his face forced other prickly and painful memories to the surface that I'd rather not have thought about.

But he'd not been perfect exactly. Because we weren't together now. A perfect man wouldn't have just let it slide— our relationship, that is. He would have worked harder to hold on to me and keep me. I could have tried harder— should have, probably. But that would have translated to my seeming more needy and desperate, which I refused to do. I was holding on to a hurt, a grudge. I'd refused to go to him, and he'd not come to me in any meaningful way. He'd not shown up. Texts didn't count.

Time did that, too, I guess. And miles. And other women who were accessible and convenient. And there didn't seem to be a shortage of those floating around Jake Carmichael.

So, I'd stayed in Paris and worked hard, helping Alaine run his gallery and feuding with Claude on occasion. Whenever Jake and I had spoken, there'd always been a reason he couldn't fly out and visit as promised. A conference, an important case that only he could handle. A life to save. And I'd gotten it. I had. But none of those things did much to bring us back together. I hadn't questioned the photos of him with his colleagues and administrators at benefits and hospital fundraisers on social media. The beautiful ones.

Jake had been my best friend and my first love. We'd bonded in middle school when my dog, Stinky, had been hit by a car. Stinky was a digger and had a habit of getting loose from my parents' backyard, no matter how strong the fencing. Jake, who I'd only known from school in passing, had been walking with a group of friends and had seen it happen. But everyone knew Stinky was my dog.

Jake had gently wrapped Stinky's injured body in his jacket and brought him home to me. I'd fallen in love with Jake's kind heart from that moment. He'd been a skinny tween at the time, and I'd still been in the awkward braces and glasses stage. But we'd shared something special. Stinky had died in our arms as we'd prayed for his recovery—together.

After that, Jake had sworn he wanted to be a doctor. I'd known he'd be a great one with his kind and compassionate heart.

When I'd moved to Paris, Jake had just started his residency at Tulane in New Orleans, so his immediate future would be busy and sleep deprived. An opportunity to work at a Paris art gallery was a dream come true for me and would make me a shoo-in for beginning my career as an art curator pretty much anywhere, especially in a town as small as Cypress Bayou. There were several galleries there even so.

We couldn't have fathomed at the time that the distance would be the death knell of our future together. We'd been solid. It always made me sad to remember, so I tried not to think of Jake.

I packed now for two-ish weeks, and if I had to stay longer, well, I'd figure it out. I packed for humid, eighty-degree springtime weather in northwest Louisiana, which would be hell on my hair, so I threw in some fabulous Parisian products. If I did run into Jake, my hair would look *magnifique.*

I worked to shift my focus away from Jake because I might not even see him. I *should* be planning how to ward off the carefully executed offense my mother had in mind to hogtie me and keep me in Cypress Bayou once my feet were back on southern soil. Mom was super tricky and made no secret of her intentions, but somehow we all underestimated her every single time.

I was determined to be vigilant to her ways while visiting. The passive-aggressive attacks meant to manipulate my emotions needed to be countered or outmaneuvered at all costs.

"When does your flight arrive?" Carly asked.

"I get in at four in the afternoon Monday."

"Can I pick you up?"

"Thanks, but I've rented a car to avoid being dependent on the parents, and I should be okay to make the drive from Shreveport." I hoped so anyway. It was hard to say when jet lag would hit.

"Hmm. I don't know. I'm wondering if you should plan to spend the night there and get some sleep before driving." Carly wasn't convinced.

I knew there was a good chance I'd be exhausted from the twelve-plus hours of air travel and the gaining of so much time, but surely, I would be fine on that last ninety-minute drive. "Tell you what: If I'm too beat to drive, I'll get a hotel room."

"Okay. Promise to call when you land."

I said I would, hung up, and dialed Nana's number.

"Hello there, my darlin', I've been waiting for your call," Nana said, her Cajun lilt like music to me.

"I'm calling with travel plans, Nana." I could have texted or emailed them to her, but as forward-thinking and modern as Nana was, she appreciated a phone call. So, I rattled off my arrival information.

"Where you gonna stay once you get here?" she asked, knowing exactly how things went with Mom and me.

"That'll be tricky as usual. I'll stay with you, if that's okay, but I have a feeling I'm not going to get away with it unless I spend a few days at Mom and Dad's before I make my getaway."

Some decisions were made with the lesser of two evils in mind. The fury and wrath of my mother if I skipped her house altogether wouldn't be worth the relief gained by not going there at all. Plus, she might refuse to make meat pies, which I'd missed and craved desperately since I'd been away from home. So yeah, I'd need to weigh these things carefully.

"Have you called your momma and filled her in yet?"

Nana asked, knowing full well that I hadn't.

"No. Not yet."

"Your homecoming isn't something she'll want to hear about secondhand, my dear."

I sighed. A deep, heavy outing of breath combined with a hard eye roll.

"I can see you through the phone. You've been doing that since you were a little girl." Nana knew me so well.

"Fine. I'll call her tomorrow."

"Better catch her before her cocktail hour," Nana warned.

"What?"

"Your daddy has been insisting she has a nice pre-dinner aperitif to relax her. I'm not sure how he managed to talk her into it, but somehow she's decided God's all right with it."

I shook my head in near disbelief. "Well, as long as God's okay with it and it chills her out, good for Daddy."

I could hear Nana's full-throated laugh through the phone. "Give your poor momma a little grace. Jesus drank wine, and that's okay with her these days."

"Maybe I should catch her after her drink if it chills her out," I said.

"She sometimes has two, so that isn't a great plan."

I laughed at that. "I'm behind the times, so I'll take your word for it."

"I'm so happy that you're coming home for a visit, even if it's for such an odd reason. I'll hold your hand while they take your blood."

Nana had always held my hand whenever I'd needed her. Without question or judgment. "I know you will. Thanks."

Jake

"OH HEY THERE, Dr. Carmichael. I've got something for you." Lurline Robichaud handed him a manila file folder from behind the main records desk. There was a pale-green patient sticker on the upper-right-hand corner with the name *Leah Bertrand* printed on it.

Jake automatically looked back up at Lurline in question before opening the folder. Her expression was one of gleeful anticipation as if she was awaiting his unfiltered response. "What's this?" he asked, working to control his physical response at the gut punch of seeing Leah's name.

"Well, I've just been asked to create a patient file for Leah Bertrand by the local bone marrow–matching branch. It looks like Leah's to be a donor for someone here in the state."

"But she's in Paris." He couldn't help mining the woman for more info.

"Not for lo-oong," Lurline singsonged. "Apparently, she's all set to come here to Cypress General for her prep as a donor."

Working hard to control his expression and reaction, Jake nodded curtly. This wasn't his specialty or his business. "Thanks, Lurline." He went to hand the chart back to her.

She pressed it back toward Jake. "Dr. Lalonde asked that we pass the file along to your team since you're in residence. He's going on vacation for two weeks. All the information has been loaded into the system and will also be available on your tablet." The hospital used both a hard copy as backup in addition to digital files.

Jake gripped the file and turned brusquely on his heel, nodding. "Okay. Thanks."

Once inside his office, Jake's heart rate was high as if he'd run up a flight of stairs. *Leah is coming back.* Any day now, if what Lurline said was true.

He flipped open the file and began to read. Maybe he shouldn't have, but it was sent to him from another doctor. White female. 29. Blood type: O negative. Weight: 124 lbs. BP: 118/70. There were other blood values that were measured for bone marrow—matching included in the report but they didn't signify without the recipient's information.

At least Leah appeared to be in good health. These stats were emailed and printed from a medical office in Paris. Of course, there wasn't any information about the recipient because it was all confidential and done through the labs. They would get more requests for specific tests in the coming days, he expected.

There wasn't yet any info about whether Leah would be donating stem cells or doing an actual bone marrow donation. That would depend on the recipient's needs, and if Leah was required to actually donate bone marrow, she would need to do so either in Shreveport or New Orleans since those were the surgical donation centers in the state.

At some point Leah would walk through the hospital's front door and return for several appointments for lab work and paperwork.

Since Dr. Lalonde, the local hematologist, would be on

vacation, it fell to Jake's specialized team, and his blood cancer specialist, to handle her case. Jake was more than qualified to do it himself, as an infectious disease specialist, but he would hand it over for personal reasons. Of course, he would oversee anything given to his team. But Leah would have to sign off on that since they had a personal connection. If she wanted him off her case, he wouldn't be involved.

He had mixed emotions about seeing Leah again. She hardly answered his texts anymore when he reached out. Of course, he hadn't done so as much in the past year. She'd been less than forgiving that last time he hadn't come to Paris as promised. He didn't blame her, as it had been the death knell of their relationship. But she lived in France. What had she expected?

They'd tried the first few years. Really tried. But she'd pulled back after that. Like something big had happened with her but he'd not been informed. The busier he'd become, life had marched on. It wasn't that he didn't think about her often. He did. But it was hard to stay together and committed across an ocean for such a long stretch of time.

They'd seen each other a couple years ago when she'd come home to visit her family in Cypress Bayou. But while they'd connected that trip, it hadn't mended their relationship. Every time they came together, Jake fell in love with Leah all over again, and every time she left, he had his heart ripped out of his chest.

So, knowing that she was due home any day created an anxiety that he knew would build until he saw her again.

"What's got you frowning like you lost your puppy?"

Jake looked up to see his brother, Tanner, standing at his door. "Who let you in?"

Tanner stepped inside and shut the door. "Don't try to deflect from the question. Spill."

Jake didn't want to get into it, but Tanner was as dogged when he knew Jake had something on his mind as he was when badgering a difficult witness in the courtroom. "Fine, Counselor. Leah's coming home sometime in the next few days. I just got word a few minutes ago."

Tanner plopped down into one of the matching chairs across the desk where Jake often counseled patients. "Oh man. I'm not sure if that's good news or not."

Jake shook his head. "Me, neither. I don't know how to feel about seeing her, especially after last time."

Tanner nodded. "How long's she gonna be in town?" he asked.

"A couple weeks, maybe more, I'm guessing. She's coming home for a medical procedure, and that's about all I can say. Not because she's sick, though. Sorry, you know how that is."

Tanner frowned. "That's not what I expected you to say."

"I know. It's unexpected." Jake hadn't had time to think about how odd it was that her match was in the state of her home.

"Well, brother, you know I'm here if you need me."

"I know you are." Jake gave his giant of a brother a grin. "You hungry?"

"Are you kidding?" As if that was the dumbest question ever.

They both laughed, and Jake shed his lab coat and grabbed his jeans and T-shirt. "Give me a minute to change."

CHAPTER THREE

Leah

I'D FORGOTTEN AGAIN. I always forgot. The smells, the humidity, the plants and flowers. No place was like Louisiana. After I'd navigated customs and made my way to the tiny car rental lot and grabbed a late-model generic gray sedan, I lowered the windows to allow the fresh air and sunshine to enter my body. How was it something as simple as the scent of fresh gardenias, growing at the edge of the airport's parking lot, could restore my brain's ability to function after such a long flight?

Maybe because it was the smell of home. And no matter how weird and stressful home could be sometimes, it was where I could find all the people who loved me. And I'd missed them all so much. Yes, even my mother.

When I'd called her to let her know I was making the trip, she'd behaved exactly how I'd expected. She'd ranted some, she'd prayed for my soul for a little while, and she'd even cried a few minutes. No worse and no better than anticipated. But I had wondered what it might be like to have a mother who didn't behave like she was in need of an exorcism.

I'd spoken with my dad for a few minutes, and he'd restored my good humor. He'd given me the update on the garden and all the things he was expecting to harvest in the coming weeks.

God bless that man.

I'd driven this interstate countless times, heading both north and south between Shreveport and Cypress Bayou since getting my driver's license at sixteen. Shreveport was the next largest city with a mall. Anytime we'd needed school clothes or anything more than just necessities, we'd hit the road headed north.

During the remaining miles to Cypress Bayou from Shreveport, I recognized the landmarks. I passed Landry's restaurant. My family nearly always ate there when we made a trip to Shreveport. Carly always ordered sweet tea with extra lemon wedges. Mom predictably had stuffed shrimp with cocktail *and* tartar sauces, and Dad ordered the rib eye cooked medium rare without fail. And while Mom would send her food back with the slightest provocation, Dad would eat his steak as overcooked as shoe leather and not complain.

Those things were as unchanged in my memory as the word *y'all*. My eyes teared up unexpectedly because it was all so *familiar*. This highway and this part of the country were seeping back in.

The wild clover bloomed bright red on the sides of the highway. While it wasn't intentionally landscaped, this part of the country was naturally and beautifully so.

Before I realized it, the female voice from the navigation reminded me I was one mile from my exit to Cypress Bayou. My heart sped up. I was going home for real.

My phone rang as I took the exit. I'd connected the hands-free cord, which allowed me to speak to a caller through the phone's speaker system. Such technology surprised me on the basic rental model. "Hello?"

"I'm on my way home. Where are you?" Carly's voice blasted through the car.

I'd forgotten to call her when I landed. "Oops. I was so ready to get on the road I didn't call."

"Are you staying awake?" She ignored my forgetting.

"I'm wide awake. The exhaustion hasn't hit me yet. Just exiting I-49 at Cypress Bayou now."

"You'll beat me by a half hour. I hit traffic coming out of Baton Rouge. Ignore anything Mom says. She'll be overcome with emotion at having you back, and that's never a good thing."

I rolled my eyes and sighed. "Yeah. Okay. I'll keep that in mind."

"You just rolled your eyes, didn't you?"

"How did you *know*?" I asked. Nana had said the same thing.

"You make that noise and huff out your breath when you do it. Better keep it in check around Mom, or she might forget you're a grown-up and pinch you in a soft spot."

"I'll pinch her back if she tries that crap. I'm turning thirty next month, and I'm done with Karen Bertrand's brand of intimidation."

"I'm kidding. She hasn't pinched in years." Carly laughed.

"I'm trying not to roll my eyes again. See you soon."

SINCE CARLY WOULDN'T be home for another half hour and I was starving, I decided to stop by my favorite restaurant and pick up one of my favorite foods. Today happened to be Monday, and Monday in most of Louisiana meant red beans and rice with smoked sausage. I didn't know of any other place in the world where a certain day of the week was specifically reserved for a certain food.

Red beans were served in nearly every restaurant in the state on Mondays. More so in south Louisiana, but it was an old tradition from back when Mondays were wash days and the ham bone from the previous night's dinner had been used to season the pot of beans left to simmer all day while the laundry was done.

The tradition remained, and I was happy for it. There was great rivalry for who could claim the best red beans and rice in every town. In fact, second to Cypress Bayou's crawfish cookoff, the red beans and rice competition that happened during the Christmas Festival of Lights was the most popular event in town. Folks here were serious about their food.

I stopped at Magnolia's on Front Street but had a heck of a time finding a parking spot. Finally, I slipped into one as someone pulled out. The original brick streets alongside the bayou reminded one of how old the town really was. As I stood, I stretched and yawned, almost forgetting how many hours I'd been traveling, and how far.

My exhaustion was put on hold as soon as the smell hit me. I could actually smell the smoked aroma coming from the restaurant. The bells on the door jangled as I adjusted my eyes to the darkened interior.

"Leah? Is that you?" I heard someone call my name about two seconds after I'd stepped inside the place. I looked over to my right, and sitting at a table were Lurline Robichaud and Honey Guidry, two women I'd known my entire life.

I smiled because that was what I should do and because sure, I was happy to see them, I guess. "Hi there." I moved over toward their table to greet them.

"It's so great to see you here. I was telling Jake we were to expect you just this morning—" Lurline's hand flew to her mouth as if she'd blurted out something she shouldn't.

Lurline cut her eyes at Honey and realized she'd need to explain herself. "I, uh, well, your name was on a chart at the hospital, as I guess you would know."

Honey stepped in then. "It's so nice to see you, Leah. You've been gone a long time."

I could only nod and try to smile as what Lurline said sunk into my brain. Jake. He was here. At the hospital.

Surely not.

"Oh look, Jake just came in with Tanner. What a *coincidence.*" Honey cooed this, as if it was something so delicious she could hardly help herself. They both stared at me as I turned to follow Honey's stubby finger pointed at the door where I'd entered not two minutes before.

Surely not.

My mettle was being tested. My jet lag found its opening at that moment, and I nearly dribbled down into a puddle on ancient the hardwood floor. I needed food. I needed sleep. I needed to get the hell out of there.

But the providence couldn't be denied, and as I caught sight of the one man I'd loved the most since girlhood, I couldn't control the gush of emotions that flowed through me. I wasn't surprised by it one bit. It happened every time.

He must've seen me about the same time. *Did he get a gush?* That was unclear. But Tanner, his brother, clearly read the situation immediately and came to both of our aid.

"Leah! So great to see you. Gosh, how long has it been?"

He wrapped me in a hug because we in Louisiana were huggers.

"Oh hi, Tanner. Um, it's so nice to see you," I faltered and stammered.

Once that was over, there was no avoiding Jake. He stared at me as if I was a ghost come back to haunt him. *Had* he gotten a mini gush at seeing me?

He stepped toward me and continued to stare at me. "Leah. I heard you were coming home." We did that awkward quick-hug thing where he sort of kissed me on the cheek. Just enough for me to get a quick whiff of him.

"Yeah. Lurline over there spilled the beans that she told you," I said for lack of something better.

"You look good." Those light blue eyes bored into mine, as if he was searching for some kind of answer. But I didn't know the question.

"You, too." Yes, he did. As he always did. Old NSU T-shirt from undergrad, faded jeans that appeared to be made by God just for him.

"Well, I'm sure I'll see you around while I'm here. Gonna just step over here and get a to-go order of red beans." I tried to make my getaway as smooth as possible so I could breathe normally again.

Jake's expression shuttered then. "Yeah. I guess I'll see you at the hospital."

I nodded and tried to smile again. "Bye, Tanner."

Tanner raised a big hand, not even trying to fix the awkward now.

They moved on toward a booth, and I somehow took care of ordering my food, which was thankfully ready in minutes. I got enough for Carly in case she'd not had lunch yet, either. Her drive was roughly three hours, so it was likely she'd just eaten breakfast around the time she'd left Baton Rouge.

Seeing Jake was like being thrown into the bayou head-first without any warning. A shock that left me sputtering and gasping for breath.

But I managed to wave at Lurline and Honey on my way out. No sense giving those two any further reason to spread their gossip far and wide through the community. Lurline had been a little hamstrung before by privacy laws at the hospital, but by seeing me here in the flesh—and witnessing my encounter with Jake—she was fully justified in firing up the phone tree now.

Jake

"YOU ALL RIGHT?"

Jake was staring at the menu as if he planned to order something besides the daily special. "Huh?"

Tanner pulled the menu out of his hands. "Dude. Get a grip."

"It happens every time I see her," Jake admitted to his brother.

"No shame in that."

"You'd think I'd be able to be a little cooler, though, right?"

"You'll get used to her being back here, and then you can try to figure out what's next."

"There's no solving anything with Leah. She comes, and she goes. Mostly, she goes."

"Maybe she's waiting for you to ask her to stay."

Tanner's words might have made sense a couple of years ago. Now, they only made things more confusing. Jake shook his head. "We're so far away from finding common ground, and it's been two years since we've had any kind of connection that I wouldn't even suggest it."

"Yeah, but look at you. You're a mess."

True. He was.

"Okay. No more squishy talk. It's lunchtime, bro. I've had my limit." Tanner saved Jake from further humiliation for now.

Jake was relieved by his big brother's willingness to have these discussions with him. Tanner was an alpha dog but had a soft spot for Jake, his only sibling. Since their mother was dead and their father had the heart of a shark and a snake combined, they were all each other had as far as family.

"Deal."

They ordered the Monday special, both likely wishing they could share a couple beers with their food but knowing neither of their employers would appreciate them coming back to work smelling like alcohol.

Jake would see Leah tomorrow at the hospital. He noticed she had an appointment with Dr. Lalonde in the afternoon for the initial workup. It was somewhat crappy that the doctor hadn't informed the patient that he would be out of the office once she arrived in town.

Leah

I ARRIVED AT my childhood home a shaking mass of nerves and exhaustion. Not the best way to face my mother. I noticed Carly coming down the shell-packed drive behind me, the willow trees curved in toward each other, completing an arch over our cars.

"Oh thank goodness," I said aloud to no one. Having Carly with me upon my entry would deflect some of the drama. My stop for food had made up the difference in our arrival times.

I pulled into one of the spots on the driveway pad reserved for visitors. Carly parked next to me. The first thing I noticed was how much longer her hair was. Unlike my own, Carly's hair was dark, nearly black. We almost didn't look like sisters. Except for the eyes. *Cat-ish* hazel, Nana always said.

Where *was* Nana anyway?

We both climbed out of our cars at the same time. "Well, look what the cat dragged in," Carly teased me, referring to my near-dead appearance, I assumed.

"You don't know the half of it, sister." I couldn't wait to fill her in. We hugged and laughed at just being together again, like always. "I ran into Jake at Magnolia's."

"*Get. Out.* I hope you brought me some beans and rice. I'm starving."

"That's all you've got to say?" I punched her in the arm.

"*Ow!* I'm kidding, you beast. I want to hear all about it—but not around Mom. And here she comes, so zip it." Sure enough, our parents were spilling out the front door heading straight for the two of us.

We both pasted on smiles then and greeted our parents.

"My Lord, I can't believe my eyes." My mother, with Dad in tow, rushed us, making me want to throw my sister in front as a human shield.

Mom grabbed at us, me specifically, and I was enfolded in a suffocating embrace. It was more punishing than loving, as she was a deceptively strong woman. "Oh, my girls. My daughters."

"Hi, Mom!" I said, my voice muffled as my face was shoved into Mom's armpit.

"Dear, maybe you should release Leah and let her catch her breath so I can have a turn," Dad said from somewhere nearby. Seriously, Mom was cutting off my oxygen.

"Proverbial chopped liver over here as usual," Carly joked, trying to draw fire her way, which I totally appreciated.

But Mom wasn't finished with me. "Let me have a look at you." Mom had me firmly by the shoulders now, frowning as she scrutinized my face for sins. Or at least that's what it felt like. "You'll do."

I was weak with relief as she passed me off to Daddy. "Hi, my sweet girl. We've missed you." He enveloped me in his strong arms, which seemed a little less strong than in the past, which worried me a little.

"Are you okay, Daddy?" I asked, pulling back and giving him the same scrutiny Mom had a minute ago. His snappy brown eyes were the same, and his smile could still light up a room.

"Of course, sunshine, why do you ask?" He appeared slightly confused by my question.

"No reason. Just checking. I've missed you so much," I said.

"I'll bet you haven't missed me so much," Mom said with her usual pouty tone.

"Of course I have, Mom." And I had. "Why are you upset?" I asked, truly baffled at her need to cause conflict when there was none.

She huffed and bristled, then pulled out of my arms. "I'm just trying to get the same kind of respect from you girls that you so freely give your father. Y'all know I'm the one who gave up my life and my youth to raise you."

And here we went.

Carly piped up then. "You want to talk about those C-sections, too?"

"Fine. Gang up on me like you always do. I'll leave, and you can all discuss how terrible I am and how I need to see a therapist for all my dysfunctions. The good Lord knows my heart. He loves me and forgives my sins."

She turned and stalked toward the house.

We all stared after her. What could you say to that?

"Well, girls, welcome home," Daddy said as he grinned at us. "Your momma's planning to make meat pies for dinner. Might as well go get freshened up. Leah, I'm guessing you'll want a nap after you have some lunch."

"Thanks, Daddy." I kissed him on the cheek. "I might want to plan for an alternate dinner since I might be banned from the table."

"Ah, she'll be right as rain in a couple hours," Daddy said.

Carly snorted. "More like a thunderstorm wrapped by a tornado."

"She made your homecoming a thrilling event in her mind, and it's not turned out to be how she'd planned, so let her reset a little while," Daddy suggested.

"It's never like she wants it to be because she starts that passive-aggressive shit and pisses everybody off," Carly said.

"True," Daddy sighed.

We unloaded my suitcase and tote bag, along with Carly's things from her car, and headed toward the front door. There was a large crucifix where most people might have a pretty wreath with flowers hung. Not my momma. Nope, she preferred the gothic reminder of Jesus dying for our sins in 3D to greet her guests as they arrived at her home. Such a fine welcome.

I no longer felt guilty about my anxiety at coming back here and knowing what I had to anticipate. Just one time, I'd like to be wrong about Momma.

CHAPTER FOUR

Jake

H E AGREED TO meet Elizabeth for dinner out of sheer desperation not to be home alone. Jake's roommate, Blake, a general surgeon, was working late tonight at the hospital, and Jake's inability to stop thinking about the encounter with Leah this afternoon was maddening.

She'd looked amazing. More than that, he'd made no progress in the past two or so years since the last time he'd seen her in getting over her. Wasn't it supposed to get easier with time?

"What in the devil has got you so down in the mouth?" Elizabeth demanded.

"What?" His head snapped up from checking a text on his phone about a change in his schedule for tomorrow. "Nothing. Just the hospital."

"Bullshit."

"I saw Leah today. She's back in town." Elizabeth would find out soon enough.

"Leah *Bertrand*?" Elizabeth's perfect lips curled with distaste.

Jake nodded. "She's doing a medical procedure."

Elizabeth's eyes grew frigid. More so than usual. "I don't

care why she's here. When's she leaving?"

"She'll be here a couple weeks, I assume. Not sure exactly."

"She doesn't like me much, you know?" Elizabeth smiled.

"You never gave her much reason to," Jake reminded her.

She swatted the air as if his words carried no weight. "I'll try to keep my opinions to myself."

"That's not reassuring, Elizabeth."

"I've never understood why you haven't moved on, Jake. Leah's been gone for years. Even now. I mean, look at you." She eyeballed him up and down with critical scrutiny.

"I admit running into her got under my skin."

"Is that why you're having dinner with me?"

"We're friends, Elizabeth. It's not unusual that we have dinner together when I'm in town."

She narrowed her eyes. "Yes, I know we've been friends since our daddies put us in the same playpen while they drank scotch and talked politics. But I was thinking we were working toward something more."

Since he worked out of town most of the time, he'd managed to avoid a situation that placed them together romantically or sexually—except that one time. And they'd both agreed it had been a mistake.

"Elizabeth, I care deeply about you, but I'm not willing to ruin our friendship to try to be something else. And you know how I've always felt about Leah." He hoped that would do it.

The look in her eye told him otherwise. In fact, it told him he might get his shrimp Creole dumped right into his lap. Or face. Elizabeth's shoulders stiffened, and when she spoke, her voice was shrill. "Next time you want to moon over your ex—who clearly doesn't want you—don't call me. Call someone who cares."

"Elizabeth, I'm sorry. I didn't want to lead you to believe that we were more than friends—"

She held up a hand to shut down his words. "Please stop before we make a scene. I'm going to walk out of here with some dignity." She then stood and didn't look back as she cat-walked her way to the entrance of the restaurant.

Jake knew Elizabeth had kind of a thing for him, but he'd hoped she would be satisfied with their long history of friendship. Unfortunately, the other element here was that she liked to win. And she and Leah had been what they called "frenemies" as kids. Everything was a competition—mostly on Elizabeth's part. Leah just plain hadn't liked Elizabeth once she'd stopped even pretending to be a friend and had tried to steer clear of Elizabeth once they were in high school.

Breathing a sigh of frustrated relief, Jake had both meals boxed to go since neither had touched their food, and he left the waiter a hefty tip. No sense letting great cuisine go to waste. He'd share with his roommate, Blake. At least Blake would appreciate it.

The issue was that Jake would still see Elizabeth at work. And Elizabeth didn't mind a little drama.

Jake had walked the two blocks to the restaurant since his apartment was so close. He and Blake had lived together since undergrad. Their apartment was owned by the elderly Mrs. Breaux, who lived down the street and had gobs of money. She'd refused to raise the rent as long as they mowed her yard once a week. They also looked in on her and made sure her house stayed in good repair because she had no family. Between the years of medical school and residency with one or the other living in town, he and Blake had managed to keep a close eye on Mrs. Breaux. Tanner had also helped with her estate and the mowing when neither Jake nor Blake were available.

Their large two-bedroom loft apartment sat above a storefront that overlooked the bayou. Now, it was considered prime real estate. Neither of them had seen a reason to move out before, so here they were all these years later, still room-mates…and still bachelors.

Leah

WE STAYED UP *so* late. Carly regaled me with some of her more entertaining stories about law clerking in Baton Rouge. "She insisted on bringing her support gator in *on a leash*!"

"Oh no. Did the gator have on a muzzle at least?" I asked, struck between fascination and horror at a client sashaying in with an alligator on a leash. I tried to picture it.

"We insisted on the muzzle, as Chewy was described by her vet as a 'fear biter.'"

"The gator's name was Chewy?"

Carly nodded. "And she wore a pink collar, and her nails were painted bright red. I swear I'm not making this up."

I nearly snorted the sip of water out my nose. "Where

was this woman from?" I asked because I had to.

"Down where they still speak a lot of Cajun French and there's as much water as land."

"Ah. I don't even want to ask what the lawsuit was over."

"Chewy bit someone who mistook her for their dinner. It's getting ugly."

Parts of Louisiana were still like no place else in the world. Down in the swamps in deepest southern corners, the old Cajuns still hunted nutria rats and alligators in their pirogues—pronounced *pee-rows*—not to be mistaken with the sandwiches.

It was like stepping back a hundred years from the rest of the country; the fishing shacks were no better than lean-tos without reliable plumbing or electricity. Forget the internet. These people still spoke Cajun French like their ancestors with a few words of English thrown in and didn't drive cars.

Dental care meant you pulled a tooth if it got to hurting too bad, and you traded with your neighbor for what you needed. Unless, of course, somebody was going into town.

But I could appreciate culture of almost any kind, and it was fascinating to hear the stories Carly told about these people. They made things with their hands. Nets, boats, food from their catches, and art. Art was my thing. Especially folk art.

I had a personal collection of folk art, so when I came home, I visited local shops and galleries and was always on the hunt for new artists or new pieces from old artists, which was another reason I was excited to be back in town. Louisiana was rich in local folk artists, both known and unknown.

I was trying to figure out what to do with my recent inheritance from my dearest friend, Alaine. He'd been my boss first but quickly become family after I'd moved to Paris. Glad to be able to help someone else when Alaine couldn't be saved, I felt a sense of satisfaction at being a donor match for someone else. I would use his money to do good as well.

"Did I lose you?" Carly brought me back from my wandering.

"I'm gonna be dead for a week if you don't let me sleep," I'd said, unable to control the huge yawn that escaped me then. Jet lag was no joke, and I'd tried to outrun it by spending time with Carly.

"I know. I'm just so happy to be here with you," Carly said. "You mind if I just stay in here?" She'd snuggled down beside me in my old bed.

"I won't even notice you." I reached over and turned off the old lamp on my bedside table.

This was so familiar. We'd often ended up in the same bed throughout our childhoods. Carly was three years younger than me, but at the end of the day, we liked being together. For some reason that irritated Momma instead of pleasing her. She likely thought we were scheming against her.

More likely we were giving solace to each other for whatever happened that day because of her.

"DIDN'T YOU SAY you have a ten o'clock appointment at the hospital?" Carly's words were muffled. My face suddenly became cold as she yanked the pillow off my face.

"Go away!" I just needed another twelve hours of sleep, and all would be well.

"Nope. Sorry. You made me promise to drag you out of bed no matter what threats you made," she said, her tone way too cheerful for my taste.

I scowled but refused to open my eyes. "Coffee?"

"Momma's been up for ages. Smells like bacon so you'd better drag your skinny butt out of bed and do it justice."

I finally made the effort and sat up. "Okay, fine. I'll do it for bacon."

We made our way downstairs to the smell of coffee, bacon, and what might've been French toast. Momma showed love with food, which I could so appreciate right now.

Instead of French toast, there were blueberry pancakes with real butter and maple syrup. "Wow, Momma. This looks amazing, and I'm starving."

Her face softened for a moment, and she smiled. An unguarded rarity. "You're always starving in the morning."

I poured myself a cup of strong chicory coffee and added a good-sized dollop of heavy cream while Momma heaped a plate of the good stuff for me and set it on the table. Carly served herself and plopped down beside me. "Looks great, Momma," she said.

"Where's Daddy?" I asked.

Momma just pointed out the back kitchen screen door. Of course, we all knew what that meant. He was in his garden. His happy place.

"The blueberries are awesome," I said.

"Those are from the freezer. The new crop won't be in until early June." Momma and Daddy kept us in fresh fruit whether it was in season or not.

"We've got some fresh strawberries there on the table; your father picked them just this morning."

There was a dish of ripe, juicy red berries in the center of the table. "Oh, score!" Carly plucked one of the strawberries immediately, as they were her favorites.

The Bertrand family had lived farm-to-table my entire life. We didn't keep any live animals besides a few laying hens in the coop at the back corner of the property, which made for delicious fresh eggs for all the baking and breakfasts.

"What's your plan today, Leah?" Momma asked as we finished our breakfast.

"I'm heading over to Cypress General in an hour for my first appointment."

"Make sure they understand how squeamish you are about needles and such." Momma had learned the hard way about my needle phobia the first time I'd gone in for a vaccine as a young child and fainted dead away on the doctor's office floor.

"Don't worry, I will."

"And I heard that Jake was back in town. Will you be seeing him today?" An edge creeped into her voice.

"I'm not sure. I ran into him and Tanner yesterday when I stopped at Magnolia's." A mental image came unbidden to mind whenever Jake was mentioned.

She narrowed her eyes at me but didn't respond.

I controlled the urge to say, *What?*

"I'm guessing he'll be sniffing around here soon enough." Momma made a distasteful face.

"I'm only going to be in town a couple weeks, so I don't think Jake's going to be around." I didn't say that I planned to go to Nana's house in a day or two...or as quickly as I could get over there.

"If you'd have come home before now, he'd have married you, you know." She meant, *Too bad you missed your chance.*

"Let's not rewrite history, okay? Jake and I didn't work out, so I'm going to leave it at that for now." I couldn't even imagine myself married to Jake—or anyone for that matter.

"Why on earth someone approaching your age would want to live alone in another country instead of near family makes no sense to me."

I said nothing because there was nothing to say that wouldn't bring unwanted opinions and censure on my head from Momma. I could tell her that I loved the city, with its cozy cafés, French music, visual arts, and culture. That it was a unique and special place to live. Those things would be true.

But getting into why I didn't live here in Cypress Bayou was another matter entirely. I'd been hiding out in Paris, that was true enough. But coming home to a place where every single corner reminded me of what I'd lost was still too hard. No, Momma wouldn't understand that.

We helped tidy the kitchen once we'd cleaned our plates, which went without saying.

"Well, I for one have some things to take care of." Carly changed the subject. "I'm working remotely for the next few days so I can be here with you people."

"Thanks for doing that. I'm so glad you're here." I really

was glad she came home for me.

"We're only missing Nana," Carly said, then turned to Mom, who was wiping down the table and asked, "Mom, where's Nana? We haven't seen her or heard from her since we've gotten into town."

"She's been out at Melrose volunteering for the art festival over the weekend. She should be back sometime today."

"I thought that was in the summer." I was sorry to have missed it. Melrose showcased some fantastic artists and their work.

Mom shook her head. "They changed it because of the heat these days. It's gotten to where it's so hot at the end of June."

"I'll give her a call later today." I missed Nana and couldn't wait to see her.

"I'm surprised we haven't heard from her. She knew you girls were coming in yesterday," Mom said.

Nana was the most independent soul I knew, and she was busy as well. So, she would call as soon as she was free of her commitment at Melrose. Melrose being a historic house museum that preserved the legacy of Cane River Isle Brevelle Creole of Color Community. It was part of Nana's commitment to the Natchitoches Parish Historical Society. Melrose history was important local history.

The art that came from Melrose over two centuries told stories of slavery, heartbreak, and triumph and were some of my favorite pieces I'd collected. So, I had a special fondness for the events held at Melrose. I couldn't wait to hear about this year's arts festival.

"I'm sure we'll hear from her at some point today." I

moved to the bottom of the stairs. "I'm headed up to get dressed."

I showered quickly, careful not to let the time get away from me. The last thing I needed was to be late for my first appointment.

CHAPTER FIVE

PULLING INTO THE parking area, I appreciated the fact that the parking lot was now an actual asphalt parking lot rather than a packed-white-shell one. The front entrance had been updated, and the entire structure appeared freshly painted, which was far better than in the past. I'd heard from Nana about the hospital's upgrade to a Level III trauma center a while back. Since Cypress Bayou pulled patients from a large geographical area of smaller towns, it was much needed in this area.

As I'd driven through town, I'd noticed new landscape projects and several beautifully renovated and restored homes since my last visit. Growing up here, I couldn't think of any progress that had happened during that time. It had always been the same. Lovely, but old. Now, it seemed a little fresher, as if the history was more appreciated now than back then. I was glad to see it.

I took a deep breath as I entered the double whisper-quiet automatic doors. Yes, I was nervous. Wasn't sure how much of it was because Jake Carmichael was sure to be inside the building and how much was the anticipation of needles and blood. My blood. There was both, for sure.

As I approached the front desk, I recognized Lurline Robichaud most recently from Magnolia's restaurant and run into Jake and Tanner there. Had that only been yesterday? I needed a nap.

"Y'all, it's Leah Bertrand," Lurline called to the ladies working in the back office.

"Hi, Lurline. Uh, it's—great to see you again. I'm here to—"

She laughed and swatted my words away with a hand. "*I* know why you're here. And I think it's a noble thing you're doing."

I wanted to tell her that I didn't require her approval but kept it to myself. Living in Paris had cured me of my patience with busybodies. "Where should I go?" I asked instead.

"Oh yeah. For this, you'll have to go to Oncology. That's the *cancer* wing." She did a dramatic stage whisper of the *C*-word as if saying it out loud might spread the dreaded disease to us all. "It's on the second floor. Take the main elevator there, and you'll see Becky at the desk. She'll have your paperwork." Lurline winked at me as if we were in this together.

Before I could turn and head to the elevators, a middle-aged woman with graying hair approached from a back office. "Hi there, Leah. It's so great to see you."

"Oh, hi, Mrs. Theriot. How's Jennifer?" It hit me that I hadn't called my hometown best friend to let her know I was coming in town. "I meant to call her, but this all happened so suddenly. She's gonna kill me, isn't she?"

Mrs. Theriot's mouth quirked into a knowing smile. Jennifer was a feisty young woman, and they both knew what an understatement that was. "Might want to give her a call before word gets out that you're back." She was standing slightly behind where Lurline sat, and I received the signal loud and clear that "word" meant Lurline's big mouth.

"I will. Please put in a good word for me," I said. After all, donating bone marrow should've bought me a little grace.

Mrs. Theriot nodded. "I'll make sure she knows you're on a mission of mercy."

I thanked her and headed upstairs to sign in, kicking myself for not calling Jenn. How could I have forgotten? She really was gonna kill me.

Jake

THE INTERCOM ON his phone desk beeped, and the floor coordinator announced, "Dr. Carmichael, you have a patient checking in at Oncology."

He assumed they'd asked for him specifically, since he wasn't an oncologist. But this wasn't a huge hospital and Oncology here covered more than just cancer. "Thanks. I'll be right down." His office was on the third floor, with a small conference room adjacent for his team to gather when they were in town.

Most of the hospitals in the state made it work for them, but not all had such a nice space. Since Cypress General was their home base, they'd accommodated him during the renovations. He'd agreed to spend at least one week a month here, so the hospital made it worth his while. Cypress

General drew from many smaller towns in the area, and they were booked out well ahead of time during his scheduled week. Sometimes they saw patients, and sometimes they met with other healthcare professionals from smaller hospitals about cases.

He'd only recently decided to stop traveling so much and try letting them come to him. It was becoming chaotic. This week, covering for another physician, when Jake thought he would have a little downtime to settle in, frustrated him.

He grabbed his lab coat and headed to Oncology. At this point, he would go where they called him. No sense having his entire team following him around unless they were needed. He could call in a specialist if required.

When Jake stepped off the elevator, the gut punch of seeing Leah's name on the chart again caused a momentary pause.

Even though he wasn't actually required for this, he was the temporary replacement for the physician who would oversee her care. So, protocol called for his greeting her at least until he turned her care over to someone on his team.

He knocked on the treatment room door before stepping inside.

Her eyes widened when she saw that it was him. "I didn't expect you."

Jake tried not to take that as *I wish you weren't here*. But clearly his presence made her uncomfortable, same as when he'd seen her at the restaurant. Fair enough—he supposed he did owe her some explanation as to why he was here instead of the physician she was expecting.

"I'm covering for Dr. Lalonde while he's on vacation. I

just found out when I got in town. Sometimes the hospital administrators throw things at us because it's convenient for them. I'll have one of my team be your point of contact moving forward until he returns."

"N-no, it's—fine." Except it plainly wasn't fine. "As long as I don't have to take off my clothes." She obviously regretted her choice of words the moment they'd been uttered, as her face flamed.

"You don't." But she had said the words, which reminded him of when she had taken off her clothes and he'd been in the same room. Was his face flaming red, too? God, he hoped not.

"What do I have to do?" she asked. "I barely got started on all the papers."

"So, you'll have to finish that first. Then, we'll need to draw some blood, of course. Still squeamish?" he asked because he remembered that she was more than squeamish.

She paled and nodded.

"Okay, you've got the clipboard and a good pen. Finish filling out the forms, and we'll get the best phlebotomist in the place to do the rest for today."

"Thanks." Her voice was low.

"Oh, and Leah…" he began.

"Yes?" she asked.

"I'd like to get together while you're in town. It's been a long time, you know?" he said, trying to keep the slightly desperate edge from his voice. "Maybe we could get dinner?"

She frowned, or maybe she narrowed her eyes. "I'm not sure that's such a great idea, Jake."

"Think about it, okay?" he asked.

"I will." But her frown hadn't disappeared.

"Okay, I'll leave you to your paperwork. You can go out into the waiting area if it's cramped in here."

"Thanks."

Leah

I DID GO to the large open waiting area instead of sitting in the tiny room that still smelled like Jake. Smelled like him in a good way, I guess. Because he never smelled bad, he just, well, smelled like Jake. Too familiar for my senses.

Just as soon as I'd gotten settled and begun answering what seemed like an invasive amount of questions about myself, I heard the clicking of high heels. It was a unique sound that I'd gotten used to in Paris, so I didn't take much notice. Until the clicking stopped right next to me and I saw the expensive nude heels. Those were Manolos.

Dread gathered in the pit of my stomach. Only one person I knew here in Cypress Bayou had the money and the cheek to wear those shoes in a town where Keds sneakers were considered name brand.

"Are you going to pretend I'm not standing here?" Elizabeth Keller demanded in a slightly piercing tone.

My eyes traveled up her lab coat, opened to reveal a flesh-toned wrap dress that hit her figure in all the right places and just above the knee so that her legs were displayed to their best advantage. Of course. As always. She wore gold jewelry and an expensive watch.

"Hello, Elizabeth." I kept my tone flat but not unfriend-ly.

She smirked at me. We'd known each other since child-hood, and Elizabeth and I had a complicated history. We'd been friends. Sort of. At some point I'd realized she wasn't my friend and begun avoiding her. I still never knew how an encounter with her would go.

"Jake told me you were back when we had dinner last night." Her perfect white teeth were the same shade as a toilet bowl.

The swiftness of the verbal punch came without warning. But I dared not show that she'd drawn blood. "Yes. I'm here for a visit. Nice to see you." Hopefully that would suffice.

"Looks like you're filling out some serious hospital pa-perwork there."

I halted my pen for a moment and looked her in the eye. "I'm doing the paperwork because I'm a match for the bone marrow registry."

"Wow. Good for you. Well, don't let me keep you." She turned and clicked back the way she'd come. I refused to watch.

I'd seen a few photos of the two of them together, and yes, it had bothered me. Elizabeth had always had the hots for Jake, and I knew it, but until now, she hadn't actually made a play for him. Or, if she had, I'd not heard about it.

Elizabeth had likely seen me as a rival since the yearly spelling bee in elementary school, at which I'd gotten the big-ass trophy and she'd settled for second place after misspelling *hemorrhage*.

She and Jake had maintained a friendship throughout

medical school and their careers, so I hadn't ever thought much about his dating her. He never went much for the drama, though. But clearly, Elizabeth hoped I thought they were dating.

I spent the next half hour focused on completing my paperwork and trying not to think about today's events. When I turned in the clipboard finally, I was directed to the hospital's lab, where Beverly—the phlebotomist extraordinaire—ensured I was reclined with rails on either side of me before the torture began.

After two glasses of orange juice and a tuna sandwich from the cafeteria, I was fit to drive myself home. Fortunately, neither Jake nor Elizabeth were anywhere to be found.

WHEN I CHECKED my phone back in the car, I had a missed call from Nana. *Finally.* Her voice mail said she would be at Mom's waiting when I returned.

I still needed to contact Jennifer to let her know I was in town, though it was highly unlikely she hadn't heard by now. I would figure out a way to make it up to her. But Jenn did hold an epic grudge, so it would have to be dinner at the Marina, her favorite.

Instead of heading straight home, I decided on impulse to swing by Jenn's house to see if I could catch her at home. It had been quite a while since we'd spoken, so I had no idea what her schedule was. Fortunately when I pulled up, there was a car in the drive. I assumed it was hers since her husband, Brad, had always driven a giant four-wheel-drive truck.

I killed the engine and approached the house on the sidewalk, but before I got to the front door, I heard the God-awful caterwauling, which frightened me for a moment, until I realized it was someone singing. I tried to find the source and had to trace it around the side of the house to the flower bed.

A brown-haired, ponytailed woman in cut-off jeans shorts and a sleeveless white tank kneeled on the edge of a flowerbed. Wearing headphones, she did a squatting kind of dancing and sang off-key within the confines of her position to whatever jam she listened, heedless to innocent bystanders. Yep, that was Jennifer, all right. Never cared a whit what anyone thought. A small abandoned bike sat a few feet to the left.

I hated to sneak up on her, so instead, I stepped around behind her and almost into the flowerbed where my former best friend was briskly weeding. The caterwauling made me cringe inwardly, as did the bizarre squatty dance moves, but they also made me want to laugh out loud. Memories of my friend's antics throughout our childhood and teen years bombarded me. It all brought back such great times.

Jenn became very still, her gaze traveling slowly up my casually well-dressed form. Jenn stood, ripping the headphones from her ears, and narrowed her eyes.

"Are you shitting me?"

I grinned at her. "Um, no."

"What the hell?" she demanded, gardening gloves on her hips. "What? No phone call? Not even a text?"

"Aren't you a little glad to see me?" I might have been slightly miffed.

"Of course I am, but you should've called so I wouldn't have been caught squatting in the dirt like my sharecropping ancestors while you slide into my line of vision looking *like that*." She pointed at me with her flowered gloved finger.

"What?"

"Oh, you know. All Paris-y. Hair done in your dressy clothes. I mean look at those fancy sandals." We both looked down at my flat leather sandals. They were nice but nothing so fancy.

"Hey, just because I'm not in gardening wear doesn't mean I'm fancy. These are regular clothes. They aren't Paris-y."

"They are for Cypress Bayou," she accused.

It was my turn to narrow my eyes at her. "Should I have come to town and worn my camo?"

Jenn snorted. "Touché."

"I would hug you, but I'll wait until you're showered. No offense." I might have wrinkled my nose at her to be funny.

She lunged at me, but I anticipated it and sprang back laughing. "Oh hell no, sister. Get cleaned up, and I'll take you out to dinner at the Marina. To make up for the lack of notice."

We were both laughing now. "Okay. Deal. I'll see if Momma can watch Joey. Brad's working nights."

Brad was Jenn's husband, who'd also grown up with us. He'd been the star of the football team back in the day. "Where's Joey now?" I asked.

"He's at school."

"I can't believe he's old enough to go to school. It seems

like he was a toddler just yesterday," I said, truly marveling at the rapid rate of little Joey's growth.

"First grade now at St. Mary's. I wanted to send him to the lab school over at NSU, but Momma wouldn't have it. She bleeds blue and silver. Go Tigers, right?"

The Northwestern State University campus was in the heart of Cypress Bayou, and it was an excellent education college for teacher training. The laboratory school had a fully functioning elementary and middle school right on the university campus.

"It's nice you have good options for schools for Joey."

"Yes. So far, St. Mary's is working out, and my parents insist on paying the private school tuition. Otherwise, he would be a lab-schooler all the way."

"I've got some things to fill you in on." Of course I did.

Jenn pulled off the gardening gloves and swiped at her dirty knees and shorts. "It's been a while since we've talked, so I'm guess we both have some catching up."

"Should I pick you up?" I figured Jenn was most likely to drink more than I was.

Jenn nodded. "Seven okay? I'll feed the crew first. I don't think it'll be a problem for Momma. She's always asking to watch Joey. He'll go to bed around eight, so she might even want him earlier."

"I ran into her at the hospital today."

"Why were you at the hospital?"

"One of the things we need to catch up on."

Jenn frowned with concern. "Everybody okay? You okay?"

"Yes. Everybody's fine. We can talk later over dinner. I

need to get home to Mom's. Apparently, Nana's waiting for me. I haven't seen her since I got back yesterday. Was it yesterday? I'm jet-lagged and can't keep my days straight. I hope I don't fall face first onto my plate."

"I promise to keep you awake. See you this evening."

CHAPTER SIX

S OMETHING INSIDE ME calmed at the sight of Nana's old black Mercedes wagon sitting in the drive. Her gentle presence was a balm to my soul. A shroud of protection against my mother's constantly hurled prickly barbs. "Death from a thousand cuts" happened quickly when the cutting came so hard and fast.

Nana was the one person who could slow the process and make it less painful. As I entered the house, it was, as always, a mix of *home* and of *trepidation*.

I found the women at the kitchen table sipping tea from my great-grandmother's china cups. Mom and Nana both looked up at my arrival. "Hello, darlin'. It's so good to finally have you back." Her smile was so warm and genuine, I knew it would all be fine.

I leaned down and hugged her. She smelled like lavender. "I've missed you," I whispered into her ear.

"What took you so long?" Mom asked, a little crossly.

"I stopped by Jennifer's house to let her know I was in town." I tried not to sound defensive.

Mom wrinkled her nose. "I ran into her at the soap store the other day. Put on a few pounds, she has." For a Christian woman, Mom spared no one her most brutal opinion.

I ignored that. "We're having dinner at the Marina tonight."

"Well, that'll be a treat, won't it?" Nana said. "I've always liked Jennifer. She's got some real spunk, that girl. How's her little boy? Joey, is it?"

"He's fine. In first grade this year, if you can believe it."

"Did you see Jake at the hospital?" Mom cut off our train of conversation.

I ignored her rudeness and answered the question. "Jake is filling in for Dr. Lalonde while he's on vacation, so yes, I saw him."

"Oh, how did it go?" Nana sounded concerned.

I turned to my grandmother and answered her directly. "As it turns out, I already ran into him on my way home from the airport, so it wasn't the first time this trip. But, as usual, it's like seeing a ghost. Hard to get used to."

"Sit down and join us for tea." Nana motioned toward one of the empty chairs.

I nodded. "I'm hungry, and I think they took at least a pint of blood. I had a half a sandwich at the hospital, but it wasn't quite enough."

"You need more than cucumber sandwiches, then," Mom said and stood, heading toward the refrigerator. "Let's get some protein in you. I've got just the thing."

"Thanks, Momma." I appreciated her wanting to take care of me. She did have her moments.

Nana poured me a cup of tea and added sugar and cream, just how I liked it. Somehow, she'd always done it better. "Thanks."

Mom came back with some cold boiled and peeled shrimp, rémoulade sauce, and a boiled egg. "Looks delicious."

"You get your bearings and tell me all about the gallery—and what that naughty Claude's been up to lately." Nana changed the subject from Jake. She knew I would fill her in later.

I relaxed, ate, and regaled them with my most recent stories of Claude's strange and eccentric behavior. Both Nana and my mother laughed out loud as we all relaxed. It was a pleasant hour spent, and I was feeling back to my old self by the end of it.

Carly breezed in carrying bags from doing some shopping on Front Street—Front Street being the downtown area of town along the bayou where there were shops, cafés, and bars reminiscent of New Orleans, only Cypress Bayou was actually an older city than New Orleans with equal history in its architecture and culture.

"Ooh, what did you find?" I asked.

"That darn soap store is a treasure trove. I can't pass it up no matter how I try." She handed me a bag. "Smell that and see if you don't make a beeline for it next time you're downtown."

The heavenly aroma reached me before I opened the bag. It was a lemony, clean scent with a touch of almond, maybe? "Hmm. So yummy. Yes, I need to go there." It was called The Soapery and was a tourist favorite as well as a local one.

"There's some bubble bath from there in the bathroom upstairs." Mom pointed toward the staircase. "I think everybody in town shops there."

"I love the honey-pear scrub," Nana said. "Makes my old skin smooth as a baby."

We all laughed at that. Though I had to admit, Nana's skin was freaking awesome for a woman her age. I could only hope to age as gracefully into my seventies.

I wanted to move over to Nana's house as soon as I could manage a semismooth transition without Mom throwing a tantrum. Right now, she was pretty mellow, so I wouldn't risk it. I'd not unpacked my clothes for that reason. Carly would likely go back and forth from Mom's to Nana's as she visited regularly, and it wouldn't be such a big deal to them where she stayed. Plus, Carly couldn't give a hoot what Mom thought about her actions.

I was more of a pleaser and hated rocking the boat, so to speak. Less so these days, but still, if I could keep Mom somewhat happy, I supposed I should. But I refused to stay at her house for most of my visit, where I would have to walk on eggshells the entire time and wonder when her next outburst of disappointment would come.

Timing would be everything. Plus, Nana lived in the coolest house ever. It was what one would consider an ancestral home. Old as could be, and filled with ghosts of the past and history of generations of family.

Old houses absorbed emotion. At least that's what Nana swore. That's why some were harder to live in than others. Unless it was purged regularly with the burning of herbs and prayer. Nana swore by sage and a few others. I wasn't certain about all that, but she didn't kid around about it, so I never argued the point.

I figured bringing up the subject of moving to Nana's house for the rest of my visit in front of Carly and Nana would yield the most support. Maybe I wouldn't go all in.

Just ease in.

"Nana, is it okay if I come to your house for a few days?" No reason. No explanation.

"Of course, darlin.' Your room is always there for you."

Momma's head snapped around. "Why? You just arrived."

"I'm splitting my time." Nothing else. I didn't want to sound like I was explaining. No sense going into why. That would be bad. Though I wanted to tell her that her house was a tense place where I couldn't relax because of her behavior.

"I guess that's what I should expect. You stay here two days and head off where it's more *fun*."

"She goes where you're not complaining about everything she does, most probably," Carly said calmly. "Momma, if you want us to hang around, you should try not to badger us so much."

Our mouths all dropped open, including Momma's. Momma sputtered, her face turned beet red, and she glared at each of us. "Y'all are ganging up on me, is that it?"

Carly seemed prepared for this fight. "No, I think you know what I said is true. You use your harsh words and extreme behavior to keep us in line, Momma. We're all grown-ups here and would like to be treated as such."

More sputtering by Momma. Nobody but Nana ever said this kind of thing to Momma.

"Karen, dear, it seems that Carly has found her voice. I've been telling you for years to calm down or your girls would rise up and hurt your feelings." Nana's voice was calm and quiet. Soothing almost.

This was happening so fast, I could hardly keep up. We were being *honest* with our mother? I didn't know how to do that. The little girl in me almost ducked to avoid a slap or pinch I knew was coming. But it didn't come. We *were* grown. All-the-way grown.

This was a *reckoning*.

"I don't know what's gotten into you, Carly, but I don't appreciate being spoken to like this in my own home."

Carly's body language told the story. She stood tall and proud without any signs of backing down. The least I could do was not be a ninny and to back her up.

So, I waded into the conversation. "So, Momma, I've got to agree with Carly. We've all been intimidated by you our whole lives. I won't go into some of the things you did when we were kids that might have caused that…but I tend to avoid calling you sometimes when I would like to talk to you because of how you speak to me. I wish that wasn't the case."

"So, now, after all this time, I'm supposed to change, is that it?" Momma's voice was harsh.

"Darlin', I know you feel cornered, and yes, we're unintentionally ganging up on you, I suppose." Nana stood and put an arm around Momma, whose posture had gone from defensive to defeated. "Think of this as an intervention. I know you haven't gotten to this point in life without realizing there was a disconnect between you and the girls."

A tear ran down Momma's cheek. She often behaved like a child, so it made sense that she would now as well. "I—I know I wasn't easy as a mother, but y'all know I tried my best. It's not like you girls were cooperative."

"I didn't like getting pinched in the soft spots for whispering in church," Carly said, frowning at Momma. "Or spending hours on my knees in the corner for not cleaning my room."

I had to agree with those things and so many more, but I decided bringing up too many points at once, the message might get lost.

"How else was I to teach you right from wrong?" Momma asked. "Neither of you came with a manual."

"I have a feeling this won't be solved today, but maybe today is a good start, yes?" Nana said.

"I do think you were harsh with us. We weren't bad girls, but you made us feel like we were beyond naughty. And no, we didn't come with a manual, but you've continued to treat us like we're wicked. But we're not. We're grown women, and we turned out okay." I couldn't let this golden opportunity pass without saying what I'd wanted to for so many years. Even if it didn't penetrate, at least we'd chipped away at her defenses. It was a start.

It felt unkind, yes, to gang up on her. But if anyone ever deserved this kind of *intervention* that might move her toward a better relationship with her family, it was our mother. And for us with her.

And I knew my father would be less conflicted should we make some headway with this, though he might not admit it. And, come to think of it, where was Daddy anyway?

I'd guess out in his garden, so I decided to not actually ask the question aloud in case it sparked a new and different debate. Daddy's role in Momma's parenting methods was to step back until she crossed a hard line. She was pretty careful to wait until he was out of the room to pull her real nasty stuff. I had to give it to her, she was slick when it came to waiting until nobody was watching to dole out the rod.

Had it been abuse? Yes. Had we understood it at the time? Not really. Parents did things differently in the Deep South back then—and especially ones who'd been nutty with their religious leanings. Daddy hadn't had the heart to spank us or even shout loudly. Momma always said since he was weak, it was up to her to be twice as strict.

I didn't think either Carly or I had spent any real time analyzing how far beyond the pale Momma had gone with *discipline.* But we both understood something wasn't quite right with her. Nana didn't discuss Momma's mental health directly with us. She mostly sighed and said she wished she'd done a better job with her as a young woman.

"None of us can change the past, but it's important to discuss how we might all get along better now. Because now is all we have," Nana suggested.

"You all have waited a long time to decide that I abused you girls. And now, I'm so horrible that you can't even stay more than a couple days of your visit, Leah." She was pointing and very red in the face.

Nothing was going to be solved today so I tried to end the conversation. "I'll be here as much as at Nana's house, Momma. I spent half my childhood there, so it won't be any different. It will be less stressful for you if I stay there any-way." She started to speak, but I held up a hand. "I'm headed upstairs to change and going for a quick run around campus before I shower for dinner."

Being a grown woman had its perks. As in, I could do whatever the hell I wanted.

I turned and left the room without looking back. I heard the sharp intake of breath that could only be Momma's outrage for my obvious disrespect.

Families. What a disaster they could be.

CHAPTER SEVEN

Jake

WHEN THE TEXT came from Elizabeth, Jake wasn't in the mood to deal with her. He was currently on a run around the NSU campus, approaching mile two. They hadn't spoken since she'd ditched him at the restaurant, and normally, they didn't even speak that often, but an apology was in order on her end.

Elizabeth: *I ran into Leah at the hospital*

Well, hell. They were going to do this.

Jake: *Okay*

Jake didn't like the direction this was going.

Elizabeth: *I'm sorry for leaving you at dinner last night*

There it was. Jake wanted this over and done with, so he replied, *You're forgiven.*

Elizabeth: *Let me make it up to you. Can you join my parents and me for dinner tonight?*

Jake had plans with Tanner tonight. *Sorry, I've got plans.*

Elizabeth: *Fine.*

Just as soon as he'd gotten back up to speed, he noticed a woman running toward him. He recognized her gait and her body. And those legs. It was Leah. He remembered she'd liked to run here, too.

She saw him; he could tell by the stutter in her step and the way she'd tensed up the minute she'd realized it was him. There was no avoiding each other. That would be silly anyway.

They both paused in their running, labored breathing in different rhythms. Judging by Leah's expression, she was not thrilled at having her run interrupted. "Hey there," Jake said, for lack of something smoother.

She nodded. "Hi."

"How far have you gone?" he asked. It was a legit question.

She pulled up her wrist and consulted her smart watch. "Almost two miles. You?"

"Just over two."

"Want to join me?" he asked and indicated the way he'd been traveling with his hand.

"I'm headed toward the lake. Wanna join *me*?" she asked and indicated the opposite way he'd just come from.

The whole area was a loop around campus, so either way they could end up in the same place. He grinned at her. "Sure."

So, they headed off at a good clip. Obviously, his strides were longer, but he matched her pace. She'd always been a strong runner, and long ago, they'd run together. Felt like old times—sort of.

"When will my bloodwork be back?" she asked.

"A couple days. They're trying to determine if the patient will require a PBSC donation or an actual bone marrow donation. So, there are results the doctors are waiting for that'll decide the next steps for you."

"I read about that. Does it mean I'll have to stay longer if I have to donate bone marrow?" Her words came out in huffing breaths, her cheeks slightly flushed from exertion.

"Yes, most likely. It's a surgical procedure as opposed to a plasma donation, which would be a series of blood donations. Definitely marrow donation is more invasive with a longer recovery."

Leah was quiet for a minute as they ran, their shoes pounding the pavement. It was the middle of the afternoon, and there weren't many people around. Only the occasional passing car, bicycle, or jogger. There were always students sitting on the banks of the bayou.

"I'd hoped to only be here for two weeks."

That figured. She came and she left. It was how things had been since she'd moved away. "That will depend on the type of donation, for sure. I'm guessing they told you that from the start."

She nodded. "I just didn't ever think it would happen."

Changing the subject, he decided to get it out of the way. "Elizabeth said she ran into you at the hospital."

"Running into Elizabeth didn't feel like an accident." Leah's tone was filled with derision.

"What happened?"

"Typical Elizabeth. She made sure I knew the two of you

had dinner together last night."

That sounded exactly like something Elizabeth would say to Leah. "We're not dating, Leah." He wasn't sure why it was so important that she knew it. "I'm sorry she behaved that way. You know how she can be sometimes."

"Ha. Sometimes?" She laughed in a not-funny way. "It doesn't matter. You can date anyone you want. It's none of my business."

Her words pierced his heart. He pulled her arm gently to slow her down to a stop. "Leah, can't we sit down and talk? About us?" This wasn't how it had used to be between them. They'd used to laugh together and had an easy comfort that he'd not felt with anyone since.

They were both winded by the pace as their speed had increased during the course of the run. Leah shook her head. "There's nothing to discuss, Jake. You haven't seemed to make much of an effort over the past few years. I've seen the pictures. It doesn't appear your life has slowed or stopped."

Ah, social media. "You can't tell anything about my life or how I feel from across the ocean."

"No, I can't, can I? Because you've canceled any plans to see me. Something has always 'come up,' hasn't it?" She used air quotes.

"Oh come on, you know I had important reasons to cancel our plans. Lives were at stake." It sounded lame, and he knew it, even though at the time it had been true.

"Yes, well, our lives have moved on, haven't they?" Her face was red with heat and maybe anger now. "I'll see you around."

Leah sprinted off before he had the chance to respond.

And he sure as hell wasn't going to chase her down in the middle of campus.

Leah

DAMN JAKE CARMICHAEL! Why did he always get to me? The moment I'd caught sight of him in Magnolia's, I knew there would be no way possible to avoid him, but it seemed everywhere I went, there he was! I didn't appear to be able to have a civilized conversation with him no matter how hard I tried or no matter how hard I worked at being the adult I supposedly was.

I sprinted toward where I'd left my car without slowing down, checking behind me every few seconds. Of course he wasn't following me. That would be ridiculous.

I was completely out of breath by the time I made it back to the giant gnarled oak I'd parked beneath. The leaves were beginning to fill out the branches now that spring had returned to Central Louisiana. The flowers were blooming now, and everywhere I looked, there was beauty and life. I'd been moving so fast since my return that I'd nearly missed it.

Not to mention the fact that I'd been so distracted by Jake's and my family's antics. I couldn't believe I'd been back almost two full days and hoped to come and sit beside the water and take in the beauty as soon as things slowed down. The bayou here was more of a chute lake shaped like a finger. It was fed by a tributary from the Cypress River. Maybe it had been a flowing bayou at some point, but now it was a long, narrow lake that was enjoyed by residents and visitors for water sports, fishing, and boating.

As I climbed into my rental car, I was glad I remembered a towel. Between the humidity and the exercise, I was a sweaty mess. I'd run harder and for longer than planned after encountering Jake. Why hadn't he gotten horseshoe hair or soft in the belly? It might have been easier on me if I'd found him less attractive. Or maybe not. He'd still be Jake.

And I was still stuck on him just as he was. Or would be, I was afraid to say. His eyes were the same, and so were his lips. I grabbed my water bottle and chugged.

I did love my hometown, and I would've returned here to be with Jake once he'd come back from completing his residency. Our plan had been to take the best opportunities to land us in our career futures, then make a life together here, where our families were. Because there was no better place than here.

Nana was gone from the house when I got back, but Carly was upstairs in her room working on her laptop. She appeared to be on a call with headphones in, so I mouthed a hello and proceeded to get ready to go out with Jennifer.

Neither Momma nor Daddy had been downstairs when I came in, so I figured I'd gotten off easy in that respect. Daddy was mostly easy unless he was trying to be a referee between Momma and me.

I'd noticed decorations on the dining room table when I passed through the foyer and remembered that Nana had mentioned they were in the middle of planning the annual crawfish boil for the Cypress Bayou Preservation Society. It was a long-standing event that included nearly everyone in town and surrounding areas, and Nana hosted it at her property every year, the Saturday after Mother's Day. This was still quite a ways away, but planning began months in advance.

I hadn't made it to a crawfish boil in four years. And since it was always a highlight of the year, I had so many memories of our family sharing better times together at Nana's house while the whole town gathered. We had scrapbooks filled with photos commemorating the event throughout the years.

My stomach growled just thinking about it. Well, my stomach growled because I'd run off the lunch I'd had earlier with the women. I was feeling no ill effects from the blood draw, and for that I was thankful.

I couldn't think of anything more cathartic than spending the next few hours spilling my guts to someone who'd known me since kindergarten and who'd shared the braces, zits, and boyfriends stages of our development. Jenn was that person, and I looked forward to it.

She would definitely keep my mind off Jake and bone marrow transplants, at least for the evening.

THE MARINA, OUT on Breaux Lake, had been around as long as I could remember and sat on pylons, overlooking the water. I'd made a reservation as soon as Jenn confirmed she was available. Even though it was Tuesday, the place got crowded at dinnertime. The food was always delicious, and diners drove in from miles around, especially on the weekend.

For Cypress Bayou, it was a somewhat pricey restaurant and boasted an impressive menu. The Marina was an oft-chosen venue for milestone celebrations but also for dinner on a regular evening.

"I've been craving the hell out of some stuffed shrimp with crawfish sauce," Jenn said as we drove into the parking lot. "I love this place. I'm so glad they finally reopened."

"Reopened?" I asked. "When were they closed?"

"They'd shut down for a while when the ownership changed."

"I hadn't heard about that," I said, truly taken aback. Nothing much happened in Cypress Bayou without somebody from home telling me about it. "Not sure how that went down without my hearing it."

Jenn looked over at me and rolled her eyes. "I guess things get lost between here and France, huh?"

"I guess so."

"So, what are you in the mood for?" Jenn blessedly didn't pursue the subject of my long absence further.

"Catfish, actually. Fried, for sure," I said. "Maybe with that Pontchartrain sauce on top. And some broiled oysters. God, I've missed the food here."

"You had me at Pontchartrain sauce."

Pontchartrain sauce was a creamy sauce made with wine, shallots, garlic, and butter, among other things. Sinful and delicious, it somehow enhanced the fish without overwhelming its flavor.

We checked in with the host, whom I recognized as Jeff, a high school friend, whose eyes widened when he saw us.

"Oh, I saw y'all's names on the list, girls. I'd give you a big hug if I could, but I'm supposed to be *professional*."

We both snickered at his expression as he said the word. "It's great to see you, Jeff. How are your parents?" It was a usual question in a small town, and I'd asked it as one did.

"Yeah, are you still sneaking around with Paul?" Jennifer whispered dramatically and gave him an elbow to the ribs.

Jeff's eyes grew wide and round in shock. "Jenn! Hush your mouth, girl." But his mouth quirked up on one side as if he couldn't keep his joy inside. "I'll tell Paul you said hey."

Then, as we arrived at our table, he turned to me and said, "Momma and Daddy are fine, Leah. Thanks for asking. Your server will be here shortly. Enjoy your dinner." His step was light and happy as he retreated.

We had a fantastic view of the lake and sunset since our table was beside the window with no other tables between. "This is nice." Jenn pretended she hadn't just spoken to Jeff like that.

"Did you have to out Jeff like that?" I fussed at Jenn.

"Jeff's been out for years. He just pretends to be shocked when somebody points it out. It's his game. His parents have known since high school. Remember when they caught him and Paul together after homecoming?"

I nodded. "I'd forgotten about that." It was tough being gay in a small Southern town, unlike Paris, where nobody even blinked at same-sex couples.

The server stopped by our table then. She smiled and handed us giant menus. "How're y'all doing tonight? I'm Lainey, your server."

"Fine, thanks," we answered in unison.

Lainey proceeded to fill us in on the specials that were many and varied, which made me question my earlier plan for tonight's entrée choice.

Once we'd ordered a bottle of white, the server moved on, and we pored over the large laminated menus. "Wow, there are too many choices. So different than in Paris."

"Well, you're not in France anymore, are you, Fancy Pants? Here in Louisiana, we come to restaurants to eat large quantities and unbutton our top buttons when we're full so we can eat some more. Got it?" Jenn took no prisoners when she saw what she believed to be snobbery, which, of course, I hadn't intended.

"Got it. Not everybody in Europe is a snot, you know?"

"Maybe not, but I'm reminding you how we do things here. You've been away too long, in case you were wondering."

I heaved a sigh. "Yes, I know, but it's hard to get back now that I own half an art gallery in Paris." A very successful one.

"I guess that puts a different spin on things, huh? It's not just a job anymore, is it?" she asked. "Sorry to hear about your friend, by the way."

I figured word had gotten around about my inheritance. Momma didn't mind letting folks around town know what was happening in our lives. "Thanks. Alaine was my dearest friend since I moved to Paris."

"Sounds like it. I can't think of a single friend who'd leave me gobs of money and a cash cow of a business if they died." Jenn was nothing if not direct in her words.

"Alaine didn't have any family, so Claude and I were his

nearest and dearest, according to his will."

"I can't imagine not having any family at all. Sounds lonely."

"Me, either. If he did, I didn't know about them." Alaine had been gay and had had no children or significant other. I thought that he and Claude had been an item at some point, but that must have been years ago because I never saw anything that led me to believe they'd been involved during the time we'd all worked together. Both Alaine and I had been alone, so when I took the job there, we'd clicked like Will and Grace.

"Have you ladies decided on an appetizer?" Lainey popped by with her order pad.

"I'm still fixated on the broiled oysters. Could we get a dozen, please?" Jenn nodded in agreement.

"Great choice. The oysters came in fresh from the Gulf this morning."

Lainey had also brought their bottle of Chardonnay, of which she'd quickly poured us each a generous glass. We put our entrée orders in and relaxed.

We thanked her and stared out the window for a few minutes sipping our wine. A large pelican perched on the edge of the pier in search of her dinner. Cypress trees lined the bank, throwing shadows over the edge and making the water appear black.

Breaux Lake was small as far as lakes went, with houses sitting on its banks and a tiny island with a few trees in the center. We'd water-skied here throughout our teen and college years with Tanner, Jake's brother, driving the boat most often. So many memories everywhere I went.

"So, you really think you'll never come home?" Jenn mused but didn't look at me.

I hadn't honestly given in to the thinking about the "forever consequences" of never coming home to live. "I honestly don't know what will happen. Paris doesn't truly feel like a forever place for me. But honestly, I never saw myself here in Cypress Bayou without Jake, either. Whenever I pictured the future, it was with the two of us here together."

"I've heard he's been seen out with Elizabeth Keller, but I'm not sure they're dating." Jenn stared at her wine.

"He gets to choose who he dates." Her words hit me hard, though. Picturing the two of them together almost spoiled my appetite. Almost.

The scent of garlic, parmesan, and hot, sizzling broiled oysters hit me before I saw them. A welcome distraction from the topic at hand. "I've been craving these almost as much as Momma's meat pies."

"Y'all enjoy!" Lainey placed the tray in the center of the table, and we didn't delay in helping ourselves to them. Next to Drago's in New Orleans, these were hands down the best broiled oysters I'd ever had.

French food was amazing, no lie, but Louisiana food was my favorite. It was home. So, for the next ten minutes, my best bud and I gorged ourselves on broiled oysters.

When we came up for air, we stared at each other and burst into laughter. It had been like nothing and no one had existed until the platter was empty. "I hope nobody was watching that." I peered around surreptitiously. Fortunately, there wasn't a soul nearby whom I recognized.

"Well, I feel better; you?" Jenn patted her belly.

"I'm not rabidly hungry anymore but nowhere near ready to call it a night."

Fortunately Lainey had the good sense to show up at that moment with our dinner entrées. I'd gone with my gut and ordered the catfish Pontchartrain, and Jenn got the less heavy grilled snapper, which had been one of the dinner specials.

As we worked through our fish, we caught up on the happenings in Cypress Bayou. What our classmates were doing, the local gossip, etc.

"So, tell me why you're home. I know you didn't just decide it was time for a visit." Jenn impaled me with a glare.

"Um, no, I didn't—though it was time for a visit, I admit." I wiped my mouth. "I'm donating bone marrow, or maybe just plasma, for a patient here in Louisiana. You know my friend in Paris who passed away? Well, he died from blood cancer, so I signed up for the registry in his memory."

"How benevolent. But why is there someone in Louisiana who needs your plasma or bone marrow? Isn't that strange?" A repeating question, same as everyone else had asked.

I went through the spiel with her as I had the rest of the askers. "So, yeah, just coincidence."

"And Jake's in town, I hear. So, no avoiding him either, huh?" Jenn asked.

"He's a magnet to me. No matter where I go, he seems to be there, which really stinks." I was downplaying my reaction to seeing Jake at every turn.

"I'll bet it more than stinks. The two of you are like two freight trains headed for a collision. You can't fool me with your calmness. You forget, I know what happened, even though Jake doesn't."

Yes, she did. My secret had remained mine, with a plan to share with Jake in person, should he have shown up as scheduled. But he hadn't. And that cancellation had pretty much ended any chance of a future together.

"Are you ever gonna tell him?" Jenn asked, taking a sip of her wine.

"I doubt it. There's no real reason to now." Why dredge up old tragedy? It would only serve as a way to hurt him. Nothing would change what had happened.

"Hmm. I don't know that I would be above it for punishment," Jenn said, frowning. "But that's just me. You're a kinder soul."

CHAPTER EIGHT

Jake

J AKE AND TANNER did what they did every year on this
date, the anniversary of the death of their sainted mother.
It had been six years. Six years since she'd lost her battle with
breast cancer. She'd been the best mom that ever was, despite
the fact that she'd loved their father. Well, she'd loved him
until he'd made it impossible. Until he'd proven beyond a
doubt what he was and that he was incapable of loving
anyone but himself.

True narcissism was the one thing that couldn't be
prayed away. Judy Carmichael was proof of that. Carson
Carmichael was the ultimate proof of that.

"I wonder if Mom ever stopped thinking Carson could
change?" Tanner asked to the darkness.

"Doubt it. Still sticks in my gut, the years she wasted on
him." And they'd begged her to leave him. They'd provided
every opportunity for her to separate from him and lead a life
independent from Carson as he'd sucked the joy from her
each day. But she'd believed in the vows she'd made and in
their family. Plus, he'd been a powerful manipulator.

He'd never abused her physically that they knew of, but
the hell he'd put their mother through should've allowed her

instant entrance into heaven, no questions asked.

And an instant and questionless access straight to hell for Carson. Neither Tanner nor Jake had called Carson "Dad" since they'd been kids.

Now, they sat on the dock that led over the water on the bayou. The old homeplace their grandfather had bequeathed directly to the two of them after learning the true character of their father. Their mother had quietly blessed the decision years before she'd died. But the house had burned down not long after Poppa had passed away. So, the beautiful land with mature trees remained along the bayou, ready to build on should they decide the time was right. And Jake had been rolling that around since he'd moved back to Cypress Bayou.

Now, under the stars, they toasted their mother with longnecks.

"To Mom."

Fortunately, the mosquitos weren't out yet, as it wasn't late enough in the season, so the evenings were warm but without the annoying bugs. "I'm thinking about breaking ground on a house on the property. What do you think?" Jake asked Tanner. This seemed as good a time as any to bring up the subject with his brother.

"That's fantastic, man. What made you decide to do it now?" Tanner asked with a slow smile.

Jake stared at the dark water. "Since I finally realized things aren't gonna play out the way I'd planned. Or hoped."

"Yeah. Well, I should probably break ground right beside you, and we could be confirmed bachelors since I got nothing going on, either. I hate it that you and Leah didn't work out, but I don't think you should give up on her yet."

"I wish I shared that optimism. Every time I try to speak to her, she cuts me dead. It's like something happened that I don't know about."

"If you weren't there, how could that be?" Tanner asked.

"It couldn't. It's just a feeling I get. I'm sure it's the time and the miles. And those damned pictures on the internet."

"What pictures?" Tanner asked. "You got something going on I don't know about?"

"Nah. Just normal stuff taken at hospital functions and benefits. But they look like I'm going to prom with other girls in them."

Tanner's laugh was a low rumble. "Girlfriends don't like that."

Leah

I'D ONLY HAD a glass and a half of wine to Jenn's three, so I felt confident driving us home. I dropped her off around ten a little tipsy but not so much that she couldn't get her key into the lock.

As I drove from her house, I headed toward the water for some unknown reason and parked alongside the bayou. Just to sit for a few minutes before heading home. Then it hit me: today was April 17, the anniversary of Jake's mom's passing. I'd always called or texted him on this day to let him know I was thinking of him and Tanner, even since we had stopped seeing each other.

I quickly sent a message: *Thinking of you and Tanner today* ☺

The little dots jumped up and down immediately, as did my heart as he typed a reply: *Thanks. We're having a beer on the dock. Join us*

The dock. The one at the site where we'd planned to build our dream home. Where we'd spread a blanket and celebrated Jake's passing his medical boards. The one where we'd—

I don't want to intrude
Tanner says come have a beer like old times

I couldn't refuse, could I? Or maybe I was feeling nostalgic and didn't want to…

See you in five

I drove the mile and a half to the far end of the bayou where the property sat. There were four acres right on the water and the edge of town, which was unheard of these days. But it was an old property with huge ancient oak trees. Two acres belonged to Tanner, and two to Jake. Enough for each of them to build a nice house and have a large yard and barn, even, if they chose.

I turned into the downward-sloping drive that wound toward the dock. I knew it by heart.

My headlights hit two trucks: Tanner's large one and Jake's only slightly smaller one. I could see the two guys silhouetted out on the dock in folding chairs. I knew they did this every year, and it touched me deeply how they'd kept the tradition alive, along with the memory of their mom, Judy.

Thankful not to have consumed more wine at dinner, I navigated the dock over the water quite a ways before reaching the guys. The moon was high and bright, which was a good thing since it was pretty dark otherwise.

Tanner broke the ice. "Hi, Leah. Glad you could join us to toast Mom." He held up a longneck beer in welcome.

"I'd just dropped off Jenn, so I was in the area. We had dinner at the Marina."

"How was it? I haven't been since the new owners took over," Tanner asked.

"My catfish Pontchartrain was awesome, as always. I noticed some items on the menu were more globally influenced than in the past."

"I read in the *Times* that the new owners had traveled extensively and were planning to reflect that in the menu." Jake read the newspaper in print form every morning with his coffee, or at least he always had. It was such an old man thing to do. It made me smile to think he still did.

"I hope that goes over well here. You know how people are about keeping things the same. The Marina has been an institution for ages." I thought back on all our many dinners there together.

"So far, they seem to have a busy parking lot every time I pass by, so good luck to them." Tanner flipped open the small cooler at his feet and pulled out a beer and held it up toward me.

I took it. "Thanks. Here's to your mom. She was a lovely woman."

We all held up a bottle in tribute.

I dropped a hand onto Jake's shoulder because I was feeling sentimental. "She would have been so proud of you both." The skin under his shirt was warm, but I felt him tighten at my touch.

Neither answered aloud, presumably because they were likely a little choked up. Instead both took a swig of their beers and nodded in response.

When the moment passed, Tanner said, "So, Leah, did Jake tell you he was planning to break ground on a house here?"

I nearly fell off the dock into the water and likely would have if Jake hadn't grabbed my arm, which pulled me off balance toward him, dumping me right into his lap. Where I stayed a moment too long because landing in his lap invariably had his arms coming protectively around me. And for just a moment, I was completely short-circuited and unable to move.

I inhaled him. His warmth and his scent knocked the good sense right out of me. Then I felt his erection, and I hopped up so fast that it was a good thing he still had a hold on me or I would certainly have gone into the drink.

"Oh, uh, sorry." His voice was a mumble.

So awkward. But I was so stupidly turned on that my crimson face would have given me away if it hadn't been for the cover of darkness. A blessed concealment.

But then it hit me what Tanner had said. Jake was building our dream home without me. *How could he?* Tears sprang to my eyes.

"I guess I'd better go. Karen will likely call the sheriff if I'm out too late." Using my mother did come in handy when I needed a bad cop.

Jake stood and moved to follow. But I held out a hand to stop him. "No. I'm fine."

But he followed anyway.

"Leah, I just told Tanner tonight that I was thinking of building on the property. I had no idea he was gonna say anything to you."

His hand was on my arm. I shook it off. "Jake, it's your land. You can do whatever you want with it."

"It's my land, but it's always been our dream." His words might as well have been flaming arrows through my heart. *Our. Dream.* Before I could recover, he pulled me gently into his arms.

I wanted to resist, but I couldn't. I'd already been exposed too closely to him tonight. My resistance was weak. I would permit myself this moment.

"Jake—don't." I'd said the words.

"Don't what? Don't try to talk to you? Why, Leah? Why can't I try? Why can't *we* try?"

"Because it's too hard. It hurts too much."

"Yes, it does. But if we both still hurt so much, there's got to be something there worth trying for," he said. He touched his forehead to mine, our breath intermingling— beer breath. I'd always weirdly loved his beer breath.

"I live in Paris," I reminded him.

"You don't have to live in Paris," he reminded me.

"I own an art gallery." That was important.

"So, sell it."

That woke me up. Wasn't it just like a man to expect a woman to give up what was most important to her for him? "Um, no. I don't think so." I pushed him firmly away. "Nice try, Jake. Maybe if you'd shown a little more interest in me and what I cared about the past few years, you'd be in a better bargaining position."

He blinked as if coming out of a fog.

"It's easy to touch me and make me vulnerable. Works every time, doesn't it? That was never our problem."

CHAPTER NINE

Jake

J AKE LIKED TO think that privacy laws within the medical community worked for everyone. Patients *and* physicians. They prevented humans from making terrible decisions. Or feeling like they had to. So, when he received a text with a photo of a woman in a hospital bed who looked exactly like Leah—more like Leah a decade older—Jake was dumbfounded.

It read: *I hate to bother you, but could this woman be related to Leah?*

The number wasn't in his contacts, and whomever sent the text didn't include the woman's name or the name of the hospital. So, theoretically, he or she could have gained consent for the photo.

Jake's palms began to sweat. This had to be Leah's marrow or plasma recipient. And a close relation.

How to answer the text? The sender clearly knew him and knew Leah.

A knock at the door caused him to startle.

"Come in."

"Yo-ho, mate. Why so glum?" Blake, his roommate, stuck his head inside. Blake wore green scrubs and a surgical mask around his neck. His spiked and highlighted hair stood at full attention.

Jake motioned him inside. "I'm not sure what to do."

"Uh-oh. Sounds like a morbid deal."

He turned the text toward him.

Blake leaned in and had a quick look. "Yikes. That's some weird shite. Leah doesn't have an older sister, does she?"

Jake shook his head. "Her recipient is supposedly a complete stranger who's not a blood relation."

Blake pointed a bony finger. "That lass is *blood*-y related."

"Without a doubt."

"Yikes. Problematic deal, for sure."

"I still don't know how to reply. I'm worried about the confidentiality of it." Jake stood then and got out from behind the desk. The tightness of his office surrounded him. He led Blake toward the connected conference room where there was more space.

The windows stretched along the wall of the room overlooking the newer part of town. And by new, I meant not in a good way. More like, forty or fifty years old and due for some updating. Not the best view. Jake stared outside anyway.

"Maybe you should ask the sender what the deal is."

Jake again looked at his phone and frowned.

Several scenarios came to mind: What if Leah had a sister she didn't know about? What if that sister didn't know about her own family? A hush-hush adoption before Karen had married Bob? Did Nana Elise know about it? On the other hand, did Bob have a secret daughter with another woman that nobody knew about? Or maybe they did know and didn't tell anyone.

It was obvious this woman was older than Leah and Carly, and she was obviously ill, so that didn't put her in her best light. It was all too much of a coincidence. And he'd learned there weren't nearly as many coincidences in the world as books and movies would have us believe.

Oh, the questions.

"What're you going to do?" Blake's question reminded Jake he was still in the room.

"I'm gonna find out who she is before I do anything."

Blake stood. "Welp, good luck. My lips are sealed like a sucker fish." He made a face that might only be that of a sucker fish. A born comedian, even when he didn't try. Blake was a Brit from someplace in the wilds of England. Some shire or ford. How he'd gotten here, Jake had never heard the same story twice. But Blake was good to his bones and had proven it over and over through the years. He could be trusted. And since he was within the medical sphere here at Cypress General, Blake was bound by his oath to stay silent regarding any patient info.

"I'll keep you posted."

"Right."

Jake replied to the text: *? Yes, it appears so. Your number isn't in my contacts.*

Oh, sorry. It's Charles Thibodeaux down here at Tulane.

He'd gone to medical school with Charles at LSU in Shreveport. Jake decided this was best discussed on a call, so he dialed the number.

Leah

"DARLIN', WE'RE GONNA work on decorations for the crawfish boil today if you'd like to help, or just come visit and keep us company." Nana swished into Mom's kitchen wearing an ankle-length printed caftan over black leggings.

I was halfway through my scrambled eggs and sausage balls. Living in Paris, I'd missed sausage balls so much. "Sounds like fun. What time, and where?"

"We're going to Mother's house at noon since that's where the event will be held." Momma began the kitchen cleanup before I finished eating. I swore she did that to make me hurry and finish my food.

"Oh, okay. I've got a few work calls and emails to make, and then I can join you." I'd noticed some correspondence from Claude had come in overnight. Some things he couldn't handle without my input.

"I'm guessing your sister will join us as well at some point after she's finished her work."

Carly wasn't in the kitchen at the moment. I'd left her upstairs working with a cup of coffee.

Still out of sorts this morning after last night's run-in with Jake, I finished eating and rinsed my plate. I made my escape from the kitchen before the women peppered me with questions about my evening. I was feeling especially fragile this morning and knew they might sense my weakness and yank details out of me without much fight if I let them.

I couldn't get Jake out of my head this morning. After falling in his lap and nearly kissing him senseless, he'd found his way in again—in my senses, in my soul. Just like he always had. I wasn't surprised I'd dreamed about him, but it had been so real. I could see the house. The one we'd planned years ago that overlooked the water. Every detail. All the way down to the baby's room.

The thought made me want to puke up the breakfast I'd just inhaled.

In the family, only Carly knew about the baby I'd lost, and of course, Jenn. Not Jake. Why would I tell him? He didn't come visit in Paris during that time when I'd thought I might die. Something or someone else had been more important. That canceled visit had been the killer of our relationship, and he hadn't even known it.

Because I'd needed him, and he hadn't shown. No matter that he hadn't known about the miscarriage. He'd put me last again. And God, had I needed him to be there.

So, our growing apart hadn't been so gradual, as Jake believed. Yes, we'd had sex on my visit home and I'd gotten pregnant, and three months later, I'd miscarried. And it had been the last time we'd seen each other. The last time he'd held me—until last night. Though last night was a nothing. A tiny sliver of nothing. But it was enough for my soul to respond to him. Dammit. Maybe I should let my mother re-Catholicize me. Then, I'd be eligible for an exorcism of Jake.

A purge. That's what was required. Or a new start, which was out of the question. Too big of a bridge with too much dirty water gone under. Truth was, I couldn't trust him to be there for me. Because he hadn't for too long.

So, today I was raw and in need of time spent with my female family. But not yet. First, I would run and sweat, and if I saw Jake, I wouldn't stop this time.

I DIDN'T RUN into Jake, thankfully, but everything here in Cypress Bayou had his fingerprints on it. The memories. There wasn't a piece of this town we hadn't explored together at some time during our teen years or beyond. That's the thing about a small town—one of many. It belonged to us both. We'd both grown up here. We shared friends. Our triumphs and tragedies weren't our own.

I didn't run into Jake, but just as I checked my watch to calculate my distance, I sensed someone approach. I didn't hear them because I had my earbuds in. My head jerked up as a shadow came over my line of vision. Like a storm cloud. Darkening my day.

The man could darken Satan's day, for sure. "Hello, Leah. I heard you were back here slumming with the commoners." Carson Carmichael was a shithead. His being Jake's dad mattered not at all. I was so thankful to have the father I did. Jake and Tanner got a supershort straw. In fact, they might have been better with a different straw altogether.

He stood too close, so I stepped back. "Yes, I'm home for a visit." I was standing in the public parking lot down the hill from the Front Street shops. It sat directly overlooking the bayou. "Can I help you?" So far, he was just skulking.

"I thought I would say hello. I'm meeting the mayor for lunch." He pointed a long bony finger upward toward the general direction of several restaurants.

Of course he was meeting the mayor. Had to keep his minions under control. "I'd better get moving. I have a meeting." I tried for a smile. It didn't happen.

"Please give your family my best." His smile made me cringe a little. Carson could be best described as "cartoonishly evil."

I quickly unlocked my car door and slipped inside to avoid any further conversation. Certainly to avoid any exchange about Jake. Yes, it might have seemed rude the way I'd treated Carson. But his deeds over the years more than warranted it. Nobody wanted to speak to Carson for longer than necessary.

Jake

CHARLES ANSWERED ON the first ring. "Hey there, Jake. Man, this is a strange deal, huh?"

Jake didn't know what it was exactly. "Yeah. What's the deal with the woman in the photo?"

Charles let out a low whistle. "Her name is Allison. I wouldn't have said anything because of confidentiality, but she's asked me to help her find her family. It seems she's been searching for a while and landed down here in New Orleans when she got sick."

"What do you mean about her searching for a while?" Jake was beyond curious.

"She's shared that she found out she was adopted when

her mom died. It was a closed adoption without much information. She came here from Missouri, apparently. But she's got a birth certificate from New Orleans with her adoptive parents' names."

So, no confidentiality issue if the patient was sharing information. "I don't know how to do this without stirring up a hornet's nest." Jake could feel beads of sweat pop out on his lip.

"I'm thinking whoever Allison's donor is must be her biological sister. I mean, what are the odds she's not?"

Yeah. What are the odds?

"I hear the donor is there in Cypress Bayou," Charles pushed a little then.

Jake figured that wasn't too hard to find out. "I can't say anything about that. You know I can't, Charles."

"She's here, and she's alone. And she's pretty sick. Don't you think her family, if she has one, would want to know about her and help?" Charles put the sticky stuff out there.

Jake knew Leah's family well. The answers were yes and yes. Weren't they?

"I can't break laws for this, Charles. Losing my medical license isn't an option." Jake had worked too hard for too long. He'd lost too much for his career. He'd lost Leah.

"I know. I don't blame you." Charles whooshed out a hard breath. Sounded like he was invested at this point.

"Did you tell her who she resembles?" The thought occurred to Jake then.

"No, but that's not a bad idea. Then, she could continue the search on her own and nobody would be on the hook." Charles sounded hopeful then.

"I think that would put you in the category of being on the hook," Jake warned him.

"I'll give it some thought."

They hung up, but Jake was in no way satisfied that this would end well for any of them, least of all Leah and her family. He couldn't imagine introducing a new family member at this point in time to them. This would throw their world into chaos unless they already knew about her. Allison. *And if they knew about her, why isn't she part of the family?*

Somebody knew about her.

Which meant *somebody* had a gigantic secret. Or more than one somebody.

And this information could not come from him.

Leah

I MET MOMMA and Nana out at Nana's house, which was also called Plaisance House because it'd had historical significance during and after the Civil War. All the extremely old houses had names. Plaisance House was originally built in the late 1700s, but it had burned during the war and was rebuilt later in the Greek Revival style.

The house was listed on the registry of historical sites and was opened to the public once a year, at the Cypress Bayou Annual Crawfish Boil. So, a deep cleaning and refreshing of all the rugs, floors, furnishings, and draperies happened in anticipation of the event, so things had stayed in pretty good repair throughout the years. The house was…impressive.

There were so many named houses and sites in Cypress Bayou because it was so old. As in *older than New Orleans* old. The French, Spanish, African, and Native Americans had all left their mark here in the architecture, art, and people. We were an eclectic bunch of folks here. Diverse. Interesting.

I entered Nana's house, inhaling the scent of beeswax and history. And shrimp gumbo maybe? Gosh, I hoped so. Nana made the best.

I could hear the women arguing before I made it as far as the foyer.

"How do you know for sure it's not her?" Momma's shrieky tone was more shrieky than usual.

"Darlin', don't you think we would know by now if it was?" Nana's calming manner didn't seem to be working.

"But what if it *is*? This would ruin *everything*." There was a quality to Momma's voice that I hadn't heard before. She sounded scared.

I stuck my head in. "Y'all okay?"

They jumped like I'd caught them smoking something illegal and day drinking by their expressions. I might have laughed if they hadn't appeared so shaken.

"Oh, Leah. Did you just arrive?" Nana smoothed her hair and turned to stir something on the stove.

"We were…discussing whether or not to include Judge Breedlove's wife, Cynthia, in our planning circle. She's an annoying woman. A *Southern Baptist*." Momma made a face. As if the woman being a Protestant wasn't bad enough. But something was off. Momma's face was puffy, like she'd been crying.

But I'd play along for now. "Is that why she's annoying?" I couldn't help myself. "Because y'all sounded more like you were arguing whether or not to cut her head off."

Momma waved my words away. "You're being silly. Cynthia thinks we need to take turns praying out loud before and after every meeting." Momma was all about praying, don't get me wrong. But competitive prayer, not so much. She preferred her silent rosaries, rote meal blessings, and the cool quiet of the mass, where nothing was done too loudly or off script.

She turned to me and explained. "Cynthia is…how shall I say…a bit of a blowhard."

"Ah." I nodded. Competition.

"I know what you're saying without saying it. She's got dreadful taste. And we've done this crawfish boil every year. It's about quality and discernment. Not orange plastic all over the place."

The women had managed to find a balance between a messy outdoor food event and keeping it classy, it was true. Fortunately, the tours of Plaisance House were held the week before the actual crawfish boil so there were no concerns about anything being ruined by stinky hands.

"Is that shrimp gumbo I smell?" I changed the subject as my stomach growled.

Nana grinned at me. "Why yes, it is. I've got the potatoes on to boil for the potato salad, too. It should be ready in about an hour."

I looked heavenward. "I love you so much."

"The feeling is mutual, of course, darlin'."

And yet, I was still convinced the argument I'd inter-rupted was about something more important than the judge's wife's involvement in party planning. The tone of their voices felt *important*. I'd never known them to keep a secret from either Carly or me. I sensed a serious cover-up.

This didn't sit well with me, but I would wait it out and decide how to proceed after I discussed it with Carly, who was due anytime now.

"Leah, dear, can you grab the rice cooker from the cup-board under the microwave, please?" Nana asked. While Nana's kitchen was as old as the oak trees in the yard out front, she'd had the kitchen updated in the sneakiest of ways to enhance the beauty of the home. Nothing of the modern kind was missing. The countertops were marble and soap-stone, and she'd had a giant farmhouse sink installed that held more dishes than I owned. The stainless fridge took up an entire wall. If someone wanted to open a bed-and-breakfast here at some point in the future, the place was outfitted to feed an army of guests.

The house itself was pretty huge, so turning it into some-thing like that made sense. Nana's living here alone made sense to her but no one else. It was a lot to keep up. But she adored this house and had never shown any desire to make a move. This place had been our childhood playground, so we obviously adored it.

I always breathed a sigh of reprieve when I walked through the front door. It was a refuge. Until today, when I'd caught the knife-edge of tension between the women upon entering. There was something in the air here. Now. Something besides the aroma of gumbo and garlic bread.

Even now, I caught them exchanging glances when they didn't think I noticed.

"Oh, hey. Sorry I'm late." Carly bustled in carrying a couple bottles of wine. Her dark hair gleamed. I might have been a tiny bit jealous of how gorgeous she was. My sister. So lovely and spirited. Unafraid of anything or anyone.

"Hi, darlin'. Just put the wine there. Pop us a cork, would you? Glasses are on the bottom shelf." Nana pointed to the butler's pantry.

So, we *would* be day drinking. Well, fine. I guessed a little wine while we worked wasn't the worst thing. Maybe it would loosen up the women enough to spill the terrible thing they'd been arguing about when I came in.

"Hey, Leah. You okay?" Carly set a glass in front of me at the table.

"Huh? Yes. Just thinking about old times. Lots of memories here." This was completely true, even though my mind wasn't on them at the moment.

Carly sighed. "Yep. We had great times ripping through here as kids, didn't we?"

I felt something brush my ankle. Something soft and warm. "Oh, hey, Beau." Nobody knew exactly how old Beau the Cat was. He'd shown up one day about fifteen years ago and made himself at home here at Plaisance House. His Persian fur combined with calico markings made for a gorgeous combination.

I scooped up Beau and settled him on my lap. He purred loudly like always. "Some things don't change." Carly reached over and stroked Beau's head.

Momma and Nana were arguing whether or not to string

lights on the outside of the tents during the crawfish boil or just in the trees, so I took the opportunity to mention what I'd heard as I came in. I spoke quietly because I knew the women were distracted.

"Who do you think they were talking about?" Carly made a show of petting the cat.

"I don't know, but whoever it was, Momma was frantic. Nana was doing her best to calm her down, but they definitely did a one-eighty when I walked in. Made a humongous show of covering up their conversation with a whopper of a story."

Carly frowned. "That's weird. They usually tell us everything."

CHAPTER TEN

CARLY AND I decided not to press the women on whatever it was they were hiding—yet. If they'd gone to that much trouble to keep something from us, it must be something big. So, for now, we'd keep our eyes and ears alert for anymore weird conversations or signs of secrecy.

I'd finally moved my belongings into Nana's house and gotten past the loudest of Momma's protests about the subject. Beau and I were now sharing a room.

Today was my follow-up appointment at Cypress General. It had been almost a week since I'd arrived from Paris and I was finally back on Central Standard Time. I would find out the results as to whether or not I would need to donate stem cells or actually have the bone marrow donation surgery. The odds were in my favor for stem cell donation, as that was the most common kind of donation.

I was waiting in a small treatment room in Oncology, similar to the one when Jake had surprised me the first day. But when the door opened, it wasn't Jake who entered. I had to admit my mild disappointment.

"Hello, I'm Dr. Derbonne," a middle-aged man with sandy-blond hair and a nice smile greeted me.

"Leah." We shook hands. "It's nice to meet you."

"I've got good and bad news, I'm afraid."

"Oh?" I waited for his response to see what that meant.

"The good news is that everything matches up perfectly. It's as if you and the recipient were closely related. The bad news is the patient will require an old-fashioned bone marrow harvest." Dr. Derbonne frowned. "And we don't do those here."

"Wait. What?" I didn't get the gist right away. "Where would I need to go for that?"

"Tulane would be the optimal place since they have the newest state-of-the-art donation harvesting facility. You could do it in Shreveport at LSU-S, but we are recommending Tulane."

Tulane was in New Orleans. That was four hours away. "How long will I need to stay to do the bone marrow donation?"

"It depends. The patient will begin conditioning treatments ASAP with chemotherapy and radiation, which can take a couple of weeks, so as soon as their white-cell count is at the optimal low, we can transplant the harvested cells. But you won't need to go to New Orleans until a few days ahead of the donation."

This was not the two-week trip I'd hoped for. I realized that was the shortest possible time frame, but now, if I understood this doctor, it might be upwards of a month's stay. I couldn't back out now. *Could I?* No, that would completely go against my entire reason for getting on the list in the first place. In Alaine's memory. To honor him.

Plus, it had been made clear to me that whomever I was donating for, it was his or her last chance. They would likely die if I up and skedaddled back to France because I didn't want to stick it out here. I couldn't live with that on my conscience.

"So, real surgery, huh?"

"I'm afraid so. But it's not terribly invasive, and the recovery is quick." Dr. Derbonne smiled, like he wanted me to feel good about this. "What you're doing is heroic."

"Heroic. Hmm. I don't think it's so heroic. It's only heroic if I'm putting myself at risk, which isn't the case. I'm only putting myself at a pretty large inconvenience and maybe some serious fear of needles and such."

He laughed. "Well, it's an awfully kind thing you're doing, and not many folks would be willing to do it. How's that?"

"I'll take it," I said. "So, what now?"

"Now, you plan for a longer stay than you likely intended. We'll let you know when you'll be needed for donation surgery, so if you'll be available on a couple days' notice for surgery, we'd appreciate it. Also, you'll need to sign a form committing to the process so the recipient can count on your donation. The team at Tulane can't begin the chemo and radiation until we're a hundred percent sure there's a donor."

I nodded. "I'm committed." The seriousness fell on my shoulders like a heavy cloak.

Dr. Derbonne handed me a multipage, printed, and stapled form attached to a clipboard. "Okay, then. Read through this, and initial and sign the highlighted areas."

I took the clipboard from him, along with the pen he offered. "Thanks." I noticed the logo of the bone marrow donation service I'd signed up with initially. It was an official thing.

"I'll serve as witness, and Denise at the desk is a notary public. Sorry it's such a process. It's so people don't pull out at the last minute."

"I understand. Someone's life is at stake, and I don't take it lightly." And I didn't. After watching dear Alaine suffer from the disease as he had, in desperate need of a donor, I wouldn't allow someone else to go through that because of me, despite my moment of panic.

"I'm so glad you understand the gravity of your generosity."

I WAS RATTLED. Shaken. This was more than I'd bargained for. Literally. More time away. More travel. And I was nervous about having surgery.

The doctor suggested strongly that I go to New Orleans. I loved New Orleans. But I hated New Orleans because it filled me with intensely beautiful memories of Jake and me together. Our best memories.

"Oh, hey there, Leah." Jake popped into my line of vision as I stepped from the elevator on the ground floor. He wore hospital scrubs and a lab coat, like something out of a television medical drama, where all the doctors were insanely good looking.

"Oh, hi." I tried not to sigh like a lovesick fan. But wait. I was pissed at him. I might have narrowed my eyes then.

"You don't look so good. What's up?" His concerned stare made me want to throw myself into his arms—just like in a television show.

"I just found out I've got to do a real bone marrow donation instead of the plasma thing. I also learned that it can't be done here. My options are Shreveport or New Orleans. You might have told me."

Guilty. Dead busted. His body language said it all. "I figured there wasn't a need to add that to your worries unless it came to pass. Normally, the plasma is all that's required."

"Now I have to make arrangements to travel. But not until they let me know with only a day or two notice." I knew I sounded pissy. But I was getting pissy.

"I'm sorry for not telling you." His blue eyes were sorry. I could tell. But I wasn't having it.

"Yeah, well, maybe you can find me a nice last-minute hotel near the hospital in downtown NOLA," I flung at him.

"Done. I'll even drive you down if you want."

Is he serious?

"I'm serious."

"Thanks, but I can't imagine this won't happen without my family entourage. Can you?" I laughed a little then, my irritation almost gone, but it was true. Momma wouldn't be kept from the action.

"Leah, I would like to help with this. Tulane has a new state-of-the-art facility for organ and tissue donation. I know it's farther and more expensive, but it really is the best option."

"I don't think you need to be in on this. Dr. Derbonne seems perfectly capable."

"I want to be with you because I care about you and I can help during the process. I have surgical privileges at Tulane, so it might come in handy to have someone beside you who can navigate things from both sides, even if I'm not handling things as your doctor."

Someone beside me. "It would've been a big help if you'd been beside me when I needed you." I couldn't help myself from blurting this out.

He stepped back like I'd struck him. "What are you talking about?"

I glared flaming daggers at him. "Not a single damn thing. Forget it."

We'd made our way through the front door of the hospital and had fortunately stepped outside during the course of our short conversation. I'd ignored the people passing by, so I had no idea if we'd been overheard.

I turned and marched off toward my car in the parking lot. Jake called my name, and I ignored him.

It seemed we were destined to end our encounters this way. Or maybe it wasn't destiny. It could've been my inability to put out there what was sitting so heavy on my mind. The hurt and anguish I'd endured. My refusal to do this made me run away when emotion overtook good sense.

Jake

WHY DOES SHE *always do that?* Fling zingers at him when he had no way to defend himself. It was maddening. Leah was clearly referring to something, and today it was something more crystalized than in the past. An event he'd somehow missed by not showing up.

Before, Leah's comments about his canceling that last trip to Paris had been less specific. How she'd not been able to count on him. How he'd canceled because she'd not been important enough. How he'd put others ahead of her.

This time had been more emotional. Jake should have followed her and insisted she tell him to what she'd referred. It had sounded important to her. Jake understood that once he'd not shown up in Paris that final time, it had been the proverbial straw in the overload on the camel's back. But it had been something more. An inciting event.

As sorry luck would have it, Elizabeth stepped out of the elevator as he waited to board. "Oh, hey there, stranger." They'd not spoken since the last time when she'd asked him to dinner and he'd refused.

"Hello, Elizabeth." He wanted to step right into the elevator to avoid a conversation with her right now. He wasn't in the mood. But he also didn't want to be overtly rude.

"So, did you tell Leah what happened between us?"

Jake just stared at her. "How did—"

"I was up on the second floor taking a call by the window and saw her tear out of here. When I got downstairs, you were still staring after her. I put it together that maybe she found out about our little oopsie."

"No, I didn't tell her about that…night. And why would you think that was about us?"

One night when he was lonely, Elizabeth had been kinder than usual. He'd drunk more than he should've at a hospital party. And they'd…spent about an hour together. An hour he'd never get back.

Of course, Leah had been in Paris. Like she'd been for

the better part of four years at that point. But Jake had been sad and moody that night. He'd been supposed to visit Leah, but he'd canceled the trip to work on an important case. One where he and his team had spent weeks trying to figure out what disease process was killing a woman. They had figured it out, but not in time. So, in the end, his canceling the trip had made no difference.

And Leah had broken up with him after he'd canceled his flight. Told him not to bother rebooking the ticket. She'd said they were over. Jake had tried to reason with her, but she wouldn't call him back.

Tanner had been out of town, as had Blake, which almost never happened. And Jake had dipped low that night, running on a combination of booze, loneliness, and failure, which led him to almost make the worst decision he'd ever made.

Jake hated to say she'd been waiting for her moment. Still, not her fault. But he hadn't actually had sex with Elizabeth. But it had been close. Too close. They'd made out. They'd even shucked off most of their clothes. His body had responded, which, in itself, was a betrayal. So many other men he knew would've gone through with it and not looked back. But Jake's heart and body had belonged to Leah.

Does it still? Maybe so, but he'd not tested the theory yet. He supposed that was weird in today's world.

"Are you going to tell her?"

"Nothing happened. Why would I tell her?"

She studied her nails. "I wouldn't hate being a fly on the wall to see her reaction."

CHAPTER ELEVEN

Leah

"WHAT DO YOU mean you can't do the bone marrow donation here?" Momma was irked that I would need to travel south to do this. "Is the woman in New Orleans?"

"The woman?" I looked up from my computer.

Momma batted my words away with her hand like she wanted them to stop. "You know what I mean. The *person* who's getting the bone marrow."

I didn't know the answer to that. "I'm not sure. Maybe. Probably. But we're not allowed to know who it is. There's supposed to be no contact between the donor and recipient for at least a year, and then, only if both parties agree and make arrangements through the registry." I might have recited the brochure verbatim. I'd read it all so many times.

"So, you don't even know if it's a woman?"

I shook my head and returned my attention to my screen. But something paused me.

"Is everything okay?" I stopped writing the email I was working on and looked at her closely. Something about "the woman" and how she'd said it.

She feigned an innocence I knew wasn't sincere. "What?

Of course I'm fine."

We were at Nana's house. Momma was working on some party stuff, and I was catching up on gallery business.

"Where do you plan to stay in New Orleans?" Momma sounded casual and uncommitted as she pulled out a length of silver ribbon.

"I'm not sure yet."

"Well, if you're having surgery, you know we'll want to be there." *Snip. Snip.* She used Nana's large black-handled sewing scissors to slash the ribbon, the sound emphasizing her point. Those scissors were at least as old as me.

"You realize there's almost no risk involved with the donation surgery, right?" I wanted to offer my parents the opportunity to *not* crowd me during this process. Of course, I'd hardly seen Daddy since I'd been home. Momma had been so stirred up during my visit so far that he'd retreated to the backyard from sunup to sundown. I'd have loved to spend a little time with him without all the stressy stuff swirling around. Meaning: Momma.

"Nice try, Leah, but surgery requires prayer. And I don't see anybody else around here willing to put the time in on their knees." She arched a brow in silent personal judgment of her family's lack of Jesus.

I decided not to share that prayer could be executed from a safe distance. Or from far enough away that travel and lodging weren't required.

"And what was Jake thinking, not telling you about this? You should have known from the start that you couldn't have that donation surgery at Cypress General." *Snip. Snip.* More ribbon fell away.

"I agree completely, but he apparently was trying to save me some stress on the front end." I hated defending Jake, but Momma haranguing on him didn't sit well.

"Well, now we've *all* got to make arrangements."

No, you don't. "It's your choice whether you decide to travel, Momma. Really, it's something I can do on my own." I dared to rebel. "It will be last minute because there's an optimal window to transplant the bone marrow. I'll have to go in a few days before the transplant to prep for surgery and do final bloodwork. So, if you're going, you should wait until the actual surgery."

"I know you don't want me there." Mom did that little sniffing thing.

I rolled my eyes then. I couldn't help it. "I just don't see the necessity."

I saw the enormous inhale that would certainly precede a tirade. I tried not to duck.

"Hello, my dears. Have you warmed up the gumbo yet? No, I see that you haven't." Nana must have either sensed the conflict or overheard us as she entered the house. Or maybe she'd even eavesdropped for a minute or two. Either way, I was ready to kiss her for her timely interruption.

"Where have you been?" Momma asked her.

Since Nana carried several tote bags with the Super1Foods—Brookshire's throughout my childhood—logo emblazoned on them, it was more than obvious. I hustled over and took the bags from her.

"Just leave the butter out on the counter, darling. I'm gonna make a pound cake and need to let it sit at room temperature."

I would require a longer than usual run today if Nana was baking a pound cake. "Mmm. Sounds yummy. Lemon?"

"Lemon, if that's what you want."

"You spoil those girls too much." Momma seemed to have forgotten to scream at me for the moment.

"Probably would've done lemon anyway, but I'd rather make what'll get eaten the fastest. Doesn't hurt to make others happy." Nana called it spoiling with love as long as it didn't hurt anybody else.

"Did you hear she's gonna have to donate bone marrow in New Orleans?" Momma snipped another length of ribbon as she informed Nana of my news.

Nana put a hand on my shoulder where I was standing with the refrigerator door open placing the milk inside. "Oh, Leah. I wondered when you'd find out how it would all happen. Do you know when?"

I shook my head. "Not yet." I described the scenario Dr. Derbonne had laid out to me. The timing and factors involved. I shut the fridge and gathered the grocery bags.

"That's got to be unsettling for you. The waiting and wondering." Nana was gentle and comforting in her reaction. "How long will you have to be in New Orleans?"

"That's a little unclear. All told, maybe a week or so until I get back here. I'm not sure how long until I go back to Paris."

"So, you'll need a place to stay in New Orleans while you're there when you're not in the hospital."

"Looks that way. Momma and I were just discussing that I won't be in any danger, so there's no need in my having an entourage in tow for this." I eyeballed Momma. I figured we might as well go ahead and get this over with.

"And *I* strongly disagree with your granddaughter." Momma glared back at me.

Then I said it: "Jake says he'll handle a place for me to stay. I don't know what the demands on my time will be." I said it because I hoped it would help me set a boundary. If I officially had someplace apart from the family to stay, away from my mother, then she couldn't insist we all use this as an opportunity to have every meal together and spend every moment in one another's company when I wasn't being poked with needles.

But now I'd need to take Jake up on his offer. And hope he didn't get the wrong idea.

Maybe now would be a good time to have that run.

Jake

JAKE HARDLY GLANCED at his social media these days. Most of what he saw there was political ranting or his friends and former friends posting or tagged in perfect life stories. So much of it was probably phony. Because he knew them and was privy to all the dirty backstory of their not-perfect lives. A place like Cypress Bayou dug up the ugly stuff like a garden tiller, purging fact, innuendo, and rumor and spitting it into the town collective for all to contemplate. Truth might take a while to sift through, but the pages on social media with the absence of any ugliness was laughable.

But something made him click on the icon with all the

red notifications. Friend requests, comments, and group invites. The friend requests showed several former med school classmates, friends from all grade levels here in Cypress Bayou, and several he didn't recognize. But there was something alluring about peering into others' lives. And wrong.

Jake moved the cursor to close out the page when he noticed a stranger's friend request. A woman. He sucked in his breath.

Her name was Allison Miers. Date of Birth: 12/25/1985. Hometown: Naperville, Illinois. No education to show or work history. No family information.

Allison Miers was a dead ringer for Leah, except her hair was darker, more like Carly's. A little older, but so much alike.

Shit. This was being laid at his feet. Not through medical channels. Jake and Allison had one friend in common. His friend from medical school, Charles Thibodeaux at Tulane. Charles had clearly made a few suggestions to this patient with regard to finding her family.

Jake's first instinct was to blast Charles by text about his irresponsibility. But when Jake thought about this woman, this likely sister of Leah's and how she must be suffering from cancer alone, Jake sighed. It sounded like Charles might be in a medical/personal pickle himself.

What would Leah want him to do? What was legal? What was *right*?

This could change lives. Ruin lives. He needed more information before bringing this to Leah. If he told her about this woman now, there would be more questions than answers.

Jake stared at the blinking cursor.

Instead of accepting the friend request, which Leah might see in the unlikely event she was stalking him on social media, Jake clicked on the Instant Message icon next to Allison's name, which opened up a chat window. Since she'd requested his friendship, it seemed he was able to freely communicate with her.

Careful with his words, Jake composed a message: *Hi, Allison. Charles, a mutual friend, has suggested you are looking for family in the area. Could you fill me in on your situation?*

Now, hopefully, he might get some information about this woman.

Three dots danced in a wave almost immediately, startling Jake. Within a couple minutes, he had his answer.

Leah

"WOW, YOU LOOK snazzy. Where are you headed?" Carly and Nana were curled up sipping tea and watching some documentary about giraffes.

"Yes, darlin', you do look pretty. Do you have a date?"

"*No*. It's not a date. I'm meeting Jake. He wasn't specific but wants to discuss something. I'm assuming it's about planning an itinerary for the trip to New Orleans, but he wouldn't say." I shrugged. "So, I'm meeting him at Laborde's."

"Text me if you need a rescue." Carly grinned into her

teacup.

"I can handle Jake Carmichael." I said this with large confidence.

"Mmm-hmm. I'll be here all night, just in case."

"I can have a problem if you want," Nana offered. "We senior citizens are believably prone to such things."

Carly and I laughed at that. "Not likely, but I'll keep your offers in mind in case I need an exit strategy."

I drove the two miles into town and parked in Laborde's parking lot. The restaurant was locally famous as a "meat pie kitchen." The only one of its kind in the area. Jake knew it was my favorite. Always had been. I didn't like the optics or the talk our meeting after hours would cause.

But he'd sounded strange on the phone, which was one reason I'd agreed to it. I knew him so well, and he was rarely anything but his usual chill self. He'd sounded worried maybe. If his worry had something to do with my medical situation, I knew I should hear it immediately. I had my hesitations about meeting him. Too much history. Too many old feelings. But I had my own reasons, too.

I had to give him the green light to make a plan for my lodging in New Orleans. The bone marrow registry would cover any expenses, but Jake insisted he had inside info on someplace to stay near the hospital on short notice. The truth was, he and I had spent time together in New Orleans during and after college. Our memories there were…intimate and special.

So, going back to a place where we'd shared passion and memories and where we'd envisioned a lifetime together sounded pretty weighty. Combine that with my having surgery, and I was convinced too much togetherness would be a bad idea.

As I entered the restaurant, I noticed Jake waiting for me in the foyer area. Laborde's was a small family-owned place and was filled with memorabilia from the town and with years of photos documenting the people, the celebrations of family, Christmases, and food.

Jake smiled when he saw me, his blue eyes catching mine. But I saw the unease I'd heard in his tone earlier.

The host, likely an NSU student, led us to a booth in the back. I didn't blame her for the admiring glance she didn't bother to hide when she caught sight of Jake, even though he was probably a decade older than her.

We sat down, and I asked, "Everything okay?" I hated dancing around whatever bomb he was about to drop.

"I need to show you something." He didn't waste any time with platitudes but pulled out his phone and opened up Facebook. "I needed to do this when we were alone."

"What is it?" It wasn't like Jake to be surreptitious.

"I got a message from a woman in the hospital at Tulane. I've been trying to figure out what to do about this. I decided that it's not my secret to keep."

I frowned as I tried to catch up. "Show me." I put my hands over his and pulled the phone toward me. I somehow knew this was something I couldn't unsee.

But he hesitated. "This came to me in an unorthodox way, initially through someone who knows us both. He suggested to this woman to track you through social media via me."

"*Show me.*" Something about his babbling made me

want to scream at him.

I stared at his screen. The woman had dark hair but could have been me. Kind of. "Who is this?"

"Her name is Allison Miers. She's looking for her family here in Louisiana."

I looked up. Jake was staring into my eyes as if he wanted me to understand something. "I don't understand."

"I think you're her family. You and your family."

I shook my head. "How is that possible? I don't know her." I was fighting against something. Something descending onto me. Something invisible that threatened me and my family.

"She is getting a bone marrow transplant."

My head snapped up from staring at the photo of Allison Miers. The older me.

"My recipient." The something settled into my pores and my bones. It suffocated me.

Jake nodded. His expression told me he was sorry to break this news to me.

"How did you find out?"

"She—Allison—was starting the search for her family when she got sick. She landed at Tulane with blood cancer. Someone recognized her as looking like you. Someone who knows us both. That someone reached out to me."

"Was she adopted?" I asked, a buzzing in my head almost knocked out my hearing. I hardly noticed the sounds of the other diners in the restaurant. "I don't understand. How?"

Jake pulled the phone back and tapped on the screen. A message box came up. His eyes caught mine. "Leah, I reached out to her when she sent me a friend request. I had to know who she was."

My fingers were shaking as I read the message in response to Jake's questioning her.

Hi, Jake. Thanks for reaching out. Yes, I do look like Leah and maybe Carly. I was told that I do by a doctor here at Tulane. I also understand that you are or were involved with Leah. I know this might be upsetting to the family, so I thought I would start with you. My mother passed away recently, and I found sealed adoption records. I've always known I was adopted but was told the adoption was closed. Now that I'm alone, I want so badly to find my birth family. My birth certificate led me to New Orleans, but it had only my adoptive parents' names. It was a starting point. But I got really sick while I was here, and someone called me by Leah's name and swore I was her, so I told him my story. That's how this all started. So, I'm hoping you can help.

I looked up at Jake. I didn't want this. But I had to know. "How could she be related to us? Momma? Daddy?"

"I guess either. But she looks an awful lot like that wedding picture of your momma on the wall at your house."

Jake had a point. She really did. "But *how*? Before Momma met Daddy? She would've been so young." I thought about Momma then. We'd always known her as a little batty and overzealous. But I'd never thought about her as a young woman. Before she'd hardened. Maybe even a scared pregnant teen. A Catholic one.

That was something I could relate to. I hadn't been a teen when I'd been pregnant, but I'd been scared and pretty much alone at the time, which made me squirm because Jake was staring at me so intently.

"Are you okay?"

I nodded to keep him from reading my mind.

Then it hit me. I recalled Momma and Nana's weird argument and how they'd hushed when I came in. Momma being hung up on the idea that my bone marrow recipient was a woman. Nana would've known if Momma'd had a teen pregnancy and a closed adoption.

Parts and pieces that weren't enough for a puzzle but enough jagged ones for something broken. I had to tell Carly. I had to ask Nana. I couldn't bring this to Momma or Daddy unless it was confirmed. I had to get confirmation before Allison burst into our lives and caused the kind of mayhem that couldn't be righted.

"I need to tell Carly."

"How do you want me to answer Allison?"

I hadn't really thought much about Allison. Until now. *How do we handle her?* She wasn't an invader, though that's what it felt like. An invasion into our family. And she was sick. Maybe she was dying. But I might save her life. And then she would invade our family.

"Leah?"

I'd almost forgot Jake was there. A first, for sure.

"Tell her to focus on her health and not to contact any-one in the family yet. Put her off. Stall." I slid out of my side of the booth without sparing Jake another glance.

CHAPTER TWELVE

"YOU'RE BACK EARLY." Carly was in her bedroom curled up with Beau watching Netflix when I got back to Nana's house. Nana was most likely in bed watching one of her "programs" she'd recorded. Or an old Western. We'd never met our grandfather, as he'd passed away when Momma was a young woman, and Nana hadn't ever remarried, so she was pretty set in her ways.

I slipped inside Carly's bedroom and gently shut the door. "We have to talk. Turn up the volume a little. I don't want Nana to hear us. Let's go into the bathroom."

Carly frowned in question but picked up the remote and upped the volume several notches.

I grabbed her laptop off the bed, and we tiptoed into the tiny adjoining bath and shut the door.

"What the heck, Leah?"

"Remember the argument between Nana and Momma I told you about the other day?" She nodded. "Well, I think it had something to do with what Jake told me tonight."

"I don't understand."

"Log into your Facebook, and do a search for Allison Miers. Miers with an *i*."

She did it, and the result came up almost immediately. "She looks like you."

I nodded. "Jake says she's waiting for a bone marrow donation at Tulane *and* she's looking for her family. Closed adoption."

Carly stared at the photo again, then she looked back up at me.

I stared at Carly, and she stared back. "Is that what's wrong with our mother? She had a secret baby?" Carly whispered this.

"My thoughts exactly."

"But she would've been so young."

I nodded.

"Nana would've had to know."

I nodded.

"Daddy doesn't know."

I shook my head.

"We have a *sister*."

I nodded. Both of us had tears in our eyes. One slipped down my cheek. I wiped it away.

Then we laughed for a minute and held hands. It was a weird kind of maniacal laugh like we didn't really think anything was funny but didn't know how else to feel.

Regaining composure, we went back to problem solving. I threw out, "What will Momma do when she finds out we know her secret? She's kind of unstable during the best of times." The idea that this was for real was beginning to sink in. And now the consequences of this were beginning to sink in.

"So, now what? Do we go to Nana with this? Or do we reach out to Allison Miers?" Carly's mind shifted into lawyer mode. Because there was a whole host of legal stuff that might be attached to a new sister. "Do we make her take a DNA test?"

"Hmm. Let's not lead with that."

"Maybe not, since she's so sick."

"I think we can trust Nana not to tip off Momma that we know her secret, don't you?" That was my suggestion. Though I knew that Momma and Nana were close, all things considered.

Carly seemed to consider the question for a minute. "Yes, definitely Nana. But we can't wait too long because it doesn't sound like Allison is going to wait too long as sick as she is."

"Can't blame her for that, can we? Especially if she believes her birth sister is her donor." I really didn't blame her for that. I wouldn't want to be going through cancer alone in the world. Though how could she know how we would respond to her?

What a terrible pickle she was in. No remaining family, and the possibility of her birth family rejecting her outright because it might cause them trouble. I can imagine she was researching the heck out of us now that she'd figured out who and where we were.

"What are you thinking?" Carly's stare was intense.

I answered carefully. "Imagine how Allison must feel. She's alone. She's sick. And she has no idea how we'll react to her butting into our family out of nowhere."

Carly nodded. "We can't know where Momma and Daddy stand until we find out from Nana who knows what."

"And the scandal. Can you imagine?" I rolled my eyes at the thought. Momma was all about her reputation in the community. As wonky as she behaved with her family, she managed to keep her boat afloat around most folks in town.

"We're gonna have to get in touch with Allison soon, Leah. To keep her from contacting Momma before we've figured out the history on this. This is happening whether we want it to or not. And this has the makings to be bigger than any one of us can fix."

"Seems like Momma rolled a grenade into our family tree before we were born. Allison just showed up to pull the pin." Maybe we could keep things from exploding too bigly and badly.

"Let's hope we can keep too many branches from getting blown off. I'm hoping Daddy knows about Allison. I'm praying he does." Carly clamped her hands together and held them toward the ceiling, reminding me of our mother.

Jake

JAKE PACED. THIS helpless feeling was paired with a terrible guilt. Had he just blown up Leah's family? His career? After hashing it out with Tanner, he'd come to the conclusion there was no way to keep Allison from climbing over him to get to them. That sounded harsh, he knew. The poor woman's life was at stake.

Should Leah contact the bone marrow donation organization? There were very strict protocols about privacy, so he didn't know if they would pull their support and funding if the procedures weren't followed to the letter. Regulations in the medical field sometimes put patients at risk when the legalities weren't followed. It all had to do with liability.

Should Jake need defending, Tanner would have his back legally. But more important was the necessity for Leah to donate bone marrow and for Allison to receive it. The procedures, hospital stays, lab work, and other medical costs were upwards of a million dollars, all said. And nobody involved could take on that kind of financial responsibility.

All of this had to be taken into consideration as they moved forward with communication with Allison and with her medical care and treatment. He thought she should keep quiet for now for her own benefit. Jake hated secrecy and, more than anything, wanted everyone to do things aboveboard.

But he was also worried about Leah. About Karen and Bob and how this all might affect their marriage. Secrets were terrible. His family had plenty of their own, and he hated them. Having a corrupt political figure for a father made Jake work tirelessly to be transparent in every part of his life. So, this muddy water situation tore at him.

Leah's anguish last night when he'd seen the understanding dawn in her eyes tore at him. The inability to comfort her also tore at him.

They first had to save Allison's life. Beyond that, they would slog through all the secrets toward a new normal. But none of it was going to be easy.

Next steps meant he had to do as Leah asked: Tell Allison as kindly as possible to stand down and buy the Bertrand family some time to get the facts about how or if there was a firstborn baby girl who'd been secretly adopted out before

Karen married Bob. It would be easy enough to find out but hard to know.

Now, while he worked on charts and before he did rounds for the day, Jake composed a message to Allison.

Hi, Allison. Thanks for your response. I'm sorry to hear about your illness. Yes, I'm still in contact with Leah and her family. I shared your message with her, and she has asked that you wait before you try to make any further contact with the family. She needs a little time to get some information from her mother and grandmother, if indeed you are related. This is a very sensitive thing, and Leah wants to confirm there was an adoption before moving forward. She sends her best for your full recovery. Also, on another note: Be cautious about sharing too much information with the bone marrow registry due to their stringent privacy policy. I'm concerned about the funding for your procedure. Best, Jake.

He pressed Send and closed out the page. He hoped this would give Allison enough hope that the family was open to meeting her but also give her pause while the difficult way forward was chiseled ahead of her possible arrival on their proverbial doorstep.

Leah

MOMMA THANKFULLY HAD a lunch scheduled with the mayor's wife today. Yes, the one she didn't particularly like. That's how we got Nana alone out on the sun porch with cucumber sandwiches, mimosas, and cheese straws.

Carly made notes so we wouldn't forget details. Not that we had a whole lot to work with at this point. But we couldn't have her sliding out of telling us something important.

"So, girls, what's got you darting your eyes to and fro on this fine spring afternoon?" It was a fine afternoon. Perfect, in fact. The windows on the enclosed sun porch were open, and the cool breeze moved the air around with a hint of gardenia riding on a wave of that breeze.

My eyes did dart to Carly then, but I knew we had to get this settled before Momma returned. "It's a bit of a setup, Nana." We sat on heavy wicker furniture with thick cushions laden with accent pillows and cotton throws. There were area rugs upon the painted wood floors. It was an inviting space that lent itself to truth telling.

Nana's dark brows lifted. "Oh? Oh dear. That sounds rather dramatic."

Carly dove in headfirst. "Yes, it's come to us that we might have an older sister. That maybe Momma had a baby and put her up for adoption before either of us was born."

Nana paled and placed a hand over her heart. "Well, you should have warned me we were about to embark on this journey." Her voice was breathy, and it was obvious she hadn't been expecting our question.

We both sat beside Nana. I was on the sofa next to her, and Carly sat in the chair at a right angle. "I'm sorry we had to do it like this, but we figured you would be the one to tell us the truth. *Did* Momma have a secret baby?" I asked this question.

Nana looked back and forth between us as if to check for a way out. Then she sighed, her face crumpling. "This isn't my secret to reveal, but I'm afraid it's already out if you're asking about it. So, the answer is yes, Karen had a baby before she met your daddy. We put that sweet darling up for adoption to avoid Karen's ruin. Her reputation, I mean."

Carly and I looked at each other across Nana as we got our confirmation.

Nana continued to speak now. "But, girls, you must understand how it was back then in this town. Having babies out of wedlock meant your momma would've been ostracized and likely couldn't have married a respectable man."

Carly brushed past the defending of Momma's honor. "Well, all that aside, we've got a more immediate problem. Maybe more of a situation. The 'sweet darling' Momma gave up is looking for her family, and she's waiting for Leah to donate bone marrow to her."

Nana wrung her hands. "Oh dear. Oh goodness. We all thought that was quite a coincidence, didn't we? Leah's match being right here in the state? Karen has wondered all along if it might be her child. Though not a child any longer. Older now than Leah, yes?"

"We needed to confirm this with you because we can't keep our sister from reaching out to make contact with our family. But it's important that Momma knows it's coming." I stood and stared out the window, then asked the question that was burning inside my gut. "Does Daddy know?"

"No. He doesn't."

"Okay, wow. That complicates everything." Carly stood now, too. "How could she marry a man and not tell him she'd had a baby with someone else?"

"Because it wasn't his concern. It was your mother's business. And it was before his time and their time together.

I know you girls think full disclosure is the thing, but when a woman has a trauma that will alter the course of her life because of how society—and men, mostly—view her, then she should be able to decide and control her own narrative. You mother suffered greatly with this decision. And it's the one thing that changed her."

Nana's tone was pure steel. And she'd clearly been in full support of Momma's decision to help her daughter move forward without bearing the weight of her past. Maybe giving up the baby had been driven by Nana.

Carly and I stared at each other. I shrugged. I wasn't one to judge secret keeping.

"So, how do we tell Momma about Allison?" I sat back down to ask the question.

"Allison? Her name's Allison?" Nana's voice broke with suppressed emotion.

I nodded.

"Do you have a photo?" Nana wanted to know.

Carly pulled Allison's photo up on her iPad and slid it in front of Nana.

A tear slipped down Nana's cheek. "She's a spitting image of your mother at this age. And you girls. She has your hair, Carly, and your facial structure, Leah. Karen can't deny this is her daughter."

"How do you think she'll take this news?" Carly asked.

"She's already obsessing about it. Troubled about it. Down in her heart she knows Allison has come back. It might relieve her to know for certain that it's come to pass. I'm concerned about how Bob will react to this. He's such a stoic man, and he's put up with so much from Karen throughout their marriage. I'm not sure how he's gonna take this news."

"Poor Daddy. I wish we could break it to him." I figured we could do a better job than Momma.

Nana pressed her lips together and shook her head. "Though I supported Karen's decision at the time from her end, I do believe it was her choice whether or not to tell, and this kind of news has to come from the one who caused the hurt. Bob will likely see it as a betrayal of trust. Karen's decision to leave him out of that part of her life might seem as if she tricked him into marrying him by not telling him about her past and not giving him the opportunity to decide whether or not to take her on with such a background."

"It sounds archaic. Like something out of a period novel. Not the twentieth century." Carly was a modern woman if ever there was one.

"The small-town South thirty-five years ago hadn't yet come into the digital age, my dear. No internet or cell phones. We weren't there yet. And the values *were* still quite antiquated. If you got pregnant, you got married. Period. Unless you got pregnant by a boy whose family wouldn't have you. And that's all I'll say about that." Nana snapped her mouth shut as if she were afraid she'd already said too much.

But she now made me desperately curious about Allison's father. Momma's baby daddy.

CHAPTER THIRTEEN

Jake

HE'D JUST BEEN forwarded an email informing him that Leah would be needed at Tulane for preliminary tests within the week, which concerned Jake a little. Only because things must've been moving swiftly with Allison's condition. He knew that sometimes they fast-tracked the chemotherapy and radiation to prepare the recipient when the patient required the transplant quickly.

So, while he was very concerned with how things were going with Leah and Carly working to discover their family history and how it might involve Allison—or not—now Jake had new concerns about Allison's health. This put an edge of urgency on everything.

While Leah hadn't given him the green light to find a place to stay for both of them, he also realized she was distracted by all the other things happening right now. She would have to put up with him in her orbit. Unless she came up with a better idea. If so, more power to her.

But as soon as he began searching hotels for accommodations within the window they'd require, he noticed flexibility was going to be an issue. They would need a place to stay for a few days before Leah's going into the hospital while the pre-op tests and results were finalized and then a place to convalesce for a few days after the surgery.

Jake checked with his normal places he stayed while working in New Orleans, but since he hadn't booked weeks ahead like he normally would, there was particular a lack of availability during the upcoming dates they required. There must be some kind of event in the city. The bone marrow registry paid for lodging, but New Orleans was tricky depending when that lodging was needed. And location was key.

He sighed. There was always the Bergerons' place. But Leah wouldn't like it. If it came down to it, he would discuss it with her.

He hated to bother Leah now while she was in the middle of this upheaval, but he knew they should finalize plans to get her down there and settled for surgery.

Jake's phone buzzed beside him on the desk. The caller ID said *Carson.*

His father. If Jake didn't answer, he'd continue barraging with voice mails, texts, and emails. Then, Carson might show up at the hospital.

So, Jake answered, "Carson? What's up?"

"What? No *hi, Dad, how are you*? You'd think your momma raised you boys better than that."

The mere mention of their mother on his lips riled Jake. "I've got a busy day. What can I do for you?" Jake felt a pounding in his temples as his blood pressure rose.

"I've got a mole. Can you have a look? Might be cancer."

Jake rolled his eyes. "Make an appointment with a skin specialist. Dr. Cobb on Second Street is excellent."

"I'll have my assistant, Imogene, make that appointment."

Jake was silent. Carson was silent.

"So, I ran into Leah the other day. Did she tell you?"

She hadn't. But now they were getting to the real reason for his call. Not the mole. "No. She didn't."

"Hope you're not getting back on that train." It was a warning. Carson despised Leah. And her family. Jake hadn't ever asked exactly why because that would thrill Carson, but he'd surmised it had something to do with Nana from years past.

"What train would that be, Carson?" Jake's voice was cold and bored.

"You know how I feel about that family." Carson enjoyed using his menacing voice to try to strike fear into him like he had when they'd been kids. Back then, it had worked. They'd been children, and Carson had been Satan.

"Mind your business, Carson. I can't think of any reason you'd have to call me and try to stick your nose into who I date. Or anything I do. Better check on that mole. Those things can kill you."

Jake hung up. His heart was pounding. His head was pounding. All the blood he had pounded everywhere. Fathers weren't supposed to be compared to Satan.

Leah

I GOT A text from Jake as I bit into a slice of cantaloupe.

> **Jake:** *We should meet. New information about timeline for your surgery. Can you meet me on the riverfront under the big tree at noon?*

I checked my watch. It was seven thirty. Jennifer and I were doing a Pilates class at eight. She'd contacted me a few days ago to accompany her on her new fitness adventure. Jake was suggesting a lunchtime meeting.

> **Me:** *Okay. Should I pick up some food?*
>
> **Jake:** *No. I'll get po'boys from Mama's Oyster House. Shrimp for you?*
>
> **Me:** *Sounds good. Thanks*

I tried to calm the butterfly anticipation at meeting Jake in one of our *places*. I wondered if he'd done that on purpose. To dredge up memories of fun times together. The big tree was an ancient oak on the bayou at the edge of campus and had been a make-out spot in high school. We'd laid down a thick comforter that Jake kept in the back of the cab of his truck. We'd stared at the stars. Made plans for our future.

"Mornin'." Carly shlepped in, her black hair a messy mane.

"Good morning. You okay?" She was generally more chipper this time of day.

"I didn't sleep much. I keep thinking about our intervention with Nana. Where is she, by the way?" Carly pulled a cereal bowl from the cupboard.

"Hmm. Haven't seen her yet." It was still pretty early, so I hadn't thought much about Nana not being downstairs yet.

"So, when do you think we're going to hit Momma with the truth?" Carly poured milk into her cereal.

Nana had asked that we give her a little time to decide on a strategy. I assumed she meant hours, not days. "I'm meeting Jake at noon to discuss my surgery. Something's come up apparently."

"Oh? I wonder what?"

"I don't know. I knew I'd have to wait and see about timing. So, I guess he's got updated information now."

I thought maybe I should call Georgia Jones from the bone marrow registry about lodging in New Orleans, but she'd hinted it would be better if I found my own place to stay and they would reimburse. I figured I could bring it up with Jake today.

"I'm off to Pilates with Jenn." I brought my plate to the sink and rinsed it. I hadn't eaten much, knowing I'd be contorting my body shortly.

"Sounds like fun stuff." Carly grabbed yesterday's *Natchitoches Times* from the center of the table and rifled through it. Nana still got the local daily paper.

I'd hold off on expectations for now. But Jenn would be entertaining, as she always was. "It's her new fitness journey, so we'll see."

Carly looked up from the paper. "Ah."

"Tell Nana I'll be back in an hour. Text me if you get any new info."

"Will do."

As I grabbed my bag, water, and towel, I worked to keep my thoughts on the moment. If I allowed them to move ahead of now until even a little later today, I could feel anxiety creeping up on me like the shadow of a frog on a fly. And I was just as helpless to escape.

A little Pilates might be just the thing.

Jennifer was climbing out of her SUV just as I parked at Warehouse Fitness, an old warehouse that, years ago, had been turned into a fun multipurpose community gym. Over time, the Warehouse had added different modalities and classes as trends in fitness evolved. Memberships were low cost, and I'd kept mine current since high school. I guess I'd always figured I'd end up back here someday.

"It's been a while since I've worked out here." As usual, I got a nostalgic punch at entering the place. Also as usual, it was mostly because of the many, many times I'd come here with Jake. Upon entering, the whiff of the old warehouse mixed with the usual gym smell triggered memories. Mostly fun times of our much-younger selves.

I wondered if Jake still worked out here.

"We're back here in the studio." Jen pointed toward the back corner that used to be unfinished space.

"They have a studio now?"

She nodded. "Progress in this small town. Ain't it great?"

We met up with some of the locals. Some I knew, a few I didn't. Towns like Cypress Bayou didn't get a lot of real turnover. There were quite a few founding families. The ones whose names were on the buildings and law offices in towns. I guess my family was one of those. The industries nearby were multigenerational. The chicken plant, the paper mill, and the university. But there was some turnover with the university. New untenured professors and their families came and went over the years, so there were always a few new adult faces around. And of course, the students, of whom there were several thousand at any given time.

There were reformers in the Pilates studio, which I knew how to use thanks to my former experience with them in Paris, but today's class was a floor class. We grabbed hand weights, mats, and stretchy bands. Our instructor's name was Wendy, whom I'd not met. She was wildly fit, which made me wish I'd been running more and faster lately.

As Wendy brought us through the different stretching and toning exercises, I tried to control my snorts of laughter at Jennifer's barely controlled grunts and noises, some of which came out more like, "Are you effing kidding me?" I'm pretty sure she called Wendy a psychotic bitch at some point during the class.

But we managed to prevail until the end without getting tossed out of the class. Wendy didn't smile and wave at us as we exited like she did at the others, though. Not a great sign.

"You might want to try to *not* tell the instructor where she should stick her dumbbell next time."

Jennifer cut her eyes at me.

I held up my hands as if warding off an attack. "It was just a suggestion."

She shrugged, then changed the subject. "What's the latest with Jake?"

"I'm meeting him at noon for an update about my donation surgery. Says there's an update, but I don't know what." I hadn't yet filled Jenn in on the latest family drama.

"That's not what I meant, and you know it."

My turn to shrug. "We aren't really talking about anything besides the medical stuff. He keeps trying, and I keep shutting him down. I can't get past the past, I guess. Plus, what's the point? I live in Paris."

"Don't you miss it here?" Jenn looked around. This wasn't the prettiest part of town, but I didn't think either of us noticed. It had always been *our* town.

I did miss it here. Living in Cypress Bayou left nothing to want. "Sure. But I've got strong ties in Paris still, even without Alaine."

"If you did live here, would you give Jake another chance? He obviously still loves you."

We were sitting on the porch of the Warehouse, dangling our feet and watching cars go by as they bumped over then dipped as they crossed the railroad tracks.

I thought about Jenn's question. If I lived here, could I make peace with Jake enough to follow my heart? "I don't know, honestly. I've been holding a grudge for a long time."

"Yes, but you love him—it's so obvious. I know you."

"I honestly can't answer that question. And it isn't relevant because I don't live here and don't see myself moving back, certainly not in the foreseeable future."

"You are wasting precious years. And your biological clock, whether you want to admit it or not."

That slapped me in the face. "What an *un-feministic* thing to say. Nobody says that to men." Which drove me nuts. "And you know my thoughts on this subject, especially where Jake is concerned."

"Yeah. So, sue me. I know you're sensitive about having a miscarriage. I had one last year, and it still stings. But I'm planning to try again. Don't use that as your basis for not moving ahead with life and relationships, no matter who they're with."

I tried not to tear up. Jenn could be terribly insensitive at the worst times. But she could also be right in those times. "It did stop me in my tracks."

"It's not meant to be easy, and it probably seemed like losing Jake's baby was a final way to lose Jake. But you haven't lost Jake unless you want to. That seems like it's up to you."

Jenn put a hand on my shoulder.

My tears fell. Right there on the porch of the Warehouse with cars bumping over the railroad tracks in front of us.

"You've got to tell him about the baby. And you've got to tell him how you still feel about him. The two of you may never get back together, but maybe you'll be able to move forward."

I nodded, wiping the wetness from my face. I rarely cried. I'd learned early as a child that if Momma got tears from us, she'd claim victory.

"I'm sorry for the tough love, but you seemed stuck with the whole Jake thing. Stuck is a bad way to be, Leah."

"Yeah, I've been stuck, for sure." We picked up our bags and walked toward the parking lot on the side of the building. "There are some things happening with the family that I need to tell you about. Some wildly unexpected things. I don't have time to discuss it now, but I'll call you sometime later today or tomorrow, okay?"

"Wow, now you've got me curious. Call me later, for sure."

I nodded and waved. "Thanks for bringing me along. Let's do it again."

Jenn snorted. "I'm thinking yoga next time."

I smiled. I noticed a little of the weight had lifted. Not to say there wasn't still weight because I had plenty I was carrying around that had nothing to do with Jake. But maybe Jenn had allowed a little light into the cracked parts where he was concerned.

I noticed a text had come in from Carly while I'd had the sounds turned off on my phone during our workout and mini therapy session.

Carly wrote: *Nana went out early this morning to meet Momma.*

That could only mean one thing: Nana was giving Momma the heads-up about Allison.

Me: *I'm on the way home now.*

Who knew how Momma would react to the news that her secret baby had come back to haunt her and expose her hypocrisy to the community and to her husband—our father. Because, if we were being honest, Momma was a hypocrite in the first degree, even before this humdinger.

Most folks probably rolled their eyes behind Momma's back, secretly glad they weren't her target on that day. Momma maintained a standing in the community because of who her family was mainly. She did a ton of community service, worked on committees, and went to church—a lot. Who cared if she was a little over-judgy and shrill?

This wouldn't be a small thing, though, here in Cypress Bayou when it came out. A secret baby—no matter when it happened, simply because it was kept a secret—made for delicious gossip. And who knew who the father was? Maybe everybody when they thought back about who Momma dated thirty-five years ago. This would be a truly scandalous revelation.

CHAPTER FOURTEEN

Jake

JAKE SPREAD THE old comforter beneath the tree on the gentle slope beside the water. It was slightly overcast, and the air wasn't as humid as it might have been in late April. He'd bought the po'boys at Mama's and gotten the cocktail sauce on the side in a little container like Leah always had.

She'd texted to say she'd be five minutes late, which gave Jake a couple extra minutes to get things set up. Their conversation might be tense, so if he could make her comfortable, then he would do so. Leah was a creature of the familiar, whether or not she liked to admit it.

Jake stared out at the water. It hadn't changed in his memory. It was the one thing he could count on to calm him during stressful times.

"Hey there, sorry I'm late."

Jake turned to see Leah a few feet away, making her way toward him down the embankment. Her arrival, as always, was like a wave of renewal for him.

"No problem. I hope you're hungry." Jake indicated the spread.

"Wow, it looks amazing. I'm starved." She grinned as she noticed the food and blanket.

"Then we'll eat first, then talk."

They sat cross-legged and opened the food. Jake always got the muffuletta with extra olive salad. Leah hated olives. But she loved a shrimp po'boy.

"Mmm, this is exactly how I remember. So good," she said between bites. "God, I've missed this."

Jake hoped he might be a small part of "this" but knew better than to say it. "I wondered if you'd had the chance to have one yet since you've been back."

She shook her head and made a negative sound because her mouth was full.

They crunched their Zapp's chips and sipped Abita root beers. It was a uniquely Louisiana lunch that Jake mostly took for granted.

But Leah didn't. He could tell by how many times she sighed and closed her eyes in pure appreciation. "They don't have these in France." She held up the bag of chips.

"I'll bet not." Jake laughed at how hard she worked to get every last crumb from the bag.

After they'd finished and cleaned up, Leah flopped down onto her back. "I can't believe you still have this old comforter."

"You'll be glad to know that it's clean these days and has been stored in the linen closet at my apartment instead of behind the seat of my truck."

Leah laughed. A real laugh that rolled through him. The first one he'd heard from her since she'd been home. "That's good to know."

She appeared relaxed and he hated to be a downer by bringing up unpleasant subjects, but he had news she needed to hear. "So, it seems you'll need to travel to New Orleans in a few days. They've been prepping Allison for the transplant with radiation and chemo."

"Is she okay?" Leah sat up.

"I don't have her medical records. I only know your end of things. They've sent word that you need to get to Tulane and be ready for transplant. They only tell me what I need to know about the recipient as it applies to the donor."

"Can you find out her condition?" Leah was frowning now, clearly worried.

Jake shook his head. "I'm not supposed to breach that protocol. If Allison tells us how she's doing or gives permission through a private person, then we can find out."

"What about the bone marrow registry? What if they find out we're sisters?"

"I think you might want to leave that alone until after surgery. I honestly have no idea how they'd respond to it. But since it's all approved, best to keep them out of the sister drama at this point."

"I need to be able to let my family know details about Allison's health. I don't think Facebook is the way to go in case she can't get to her computer or phone."

"I can send her a message, but I think you're right. I don't know what kind of access to her devices she has right now."

They both sat quietly for a minute, thinking.

"I need to ask you something." Jake decided he might as well do it now.

"What?" Leah turned to face him.

"I've been searching my usual places to stay in New Orleans and not finding anything last minute. There's a big restaurant conference coming up apparently. So, how do you feel about staying with the Bergerons?"

A shadow crossed Leah's face. "I…guess that would be okay. Do they have rooms?"

"You know Mrs. B—she only rents to whom she chooses, so yes, she can accommodate us."

"It'll be nice to see them both. It's been a long time." He could tell she was thinking about their time together there.

Jake understood her hesitancy. It had been a lifetime ago. The Bergeron Bed and Breakfast had been a special place for the two of them. And going back together would bring back some important memories.

"It's fine. We've got to have a place to stay, right?"

"They'll be flexible both before and after your surgery. I don't want to send you down there alone."

Leah

"Jake, it's fine. I'd rather be with the Bergerons, where I'm comfortable, than a crowded hotel." I would suck it up. I would. Only, sitting here with Jake now made me want to curl up next to him for comfort. It seemed like I'd been alone and without him forever.

"Okay. I'm sorry it's worked out that we've got to go so quickly."

Suddenly there was an urgency that made all of this real. It made Allison real. "That's not under your control, but I hope we can find out more about Allison's condition."

"I'll check in with Charles, since he's struck up a friend-ship with her."

"Thank you." I put my hand on Jake's arm. The urge to touch him was undeniable.

He stilled, and those blue eyes questioned mine. Some-thing had changed since my conversation with Jenn. *Could I ever give Jake another chance?*

There were footsteps and rustling just above us in the grass. "I thought that was you two down here. Sorry, am I interrupting something?" Tanner called down to where we sat frozen with my hand on Jake's arm.

Jake snapped out of it first. "Oh, hey, man. Just finished lunch. We were discussing our trip down to New Orleans to get Leah ready for the transplant surgery."

Tanner made his way down the bank to where we were. "When do you leave?"

"Two or three days maybe. As soon as we can get loose." Jake covered well, I'd give it to him. The expression in his eyes had been unguarded and vulnerable.

Tanner had the *worst* timing.

Jake changed the subject completely. "Carson called, did I tell you?" He addressed his brother.

"About the mole?"

"That was the cover for the call. He's concerned that Leah and I are together again." Jake looked over at me then.

I snorted a little then, adding my voice to the conversa-tion. "I ran into him a couple days after I got into town. He wanted to know when I was going back to Paris."

"You two don't have to work with the old bastard every

day, so stop your whining."

We all laughed at that. "You win, for sure. So, when are you going to do something about that situation?" Jake had been on Tanner for several years about going into business for himself, but Carson had paid for Tanner's education, so Tanner agreed to work there for an undetermined amount of time. Tanner had wondered why his otherwise unhelpful father had suddenly become generous when it came to paying for law school.

"Soon enough, I hope. Maybe I can convince Carly to come to work for me when I open my own law office."

My ears perked up at the mention of my sister. "Should I tell her she has a job offer?"

Tanner laughed. "Not yet. But I'll keep her in mind for the future."

My phone vibrated, and I looked down at it. "Her ears must be on fire."

Carly: *Nana and Momma just got back. Need you here when you can get away. Bout to get loud in here.*

"Uh-oh. It's about to go down at Nana's. Momma just found out about Allison. I'm needed at home." I started to pick up the trash from our lunch.

"Hey. Leave it." Jake was instantly beside me. *Close* beside me, pulling the trash from my fingers. "I've got this. You go and do what you can to keep things from blowing sky-high over there. And, Leah, I'm here for you." He dropped the cardboard and squeezed my shoulders gently with his strong fingers but stopped at pulling me to him.

I barely squelched an impulse to throw myself at him

hard. "Thanks, Jake," I kind of mumbled, a little embarrassed to have Tanner spectating.

I dashed up the hill, already changing gears mentally.

"Bye, Leah. Good luck with the family stuff," Tanner called to my back.

"Thanks!" But I didn't turn around, just threw up a hand. My mind was already picturing what was likely going down at Plaisance House. I hadn't thought to suggest the hiding of sharp objects.

I tried to drive within the speed limit. I did. My hands were claws on the steering wheel. And I hoped nobody I knew noticed me flying through town like Cruella de Vil.

Poor Daddy. He had no idea. What would it do to him? He was a quiet man of solid character. Some might say a weak man, to submit himself to Momma's constant barrage of loud and forceful drama. But I'd say just the opposite. It took the strength of Thor to put up with that crap for a lifetime.

I was a mess by the time I drove up the hill, my car joining the other expected ones. Nana, Carly, Momma, and me. The four of us would sort this out.

I gulped a shaky breath just before grabbing the front doorknob. *God, grant me fortitude.*

The great tragedy was well in progress as I entered the sunroom. Momma was having vapors in a large wicker chair. Nana was pacing. Carly sat across from Momma in the matching wicker. Their eyes swiveled toward me as I entered, stage right. Momma sobbed when she saw me.

"Leah, I'm so embarrassed." Momma blew her nose with a horn sound, something I'd never mastered.

What an odd word. "Well, Momma, we've got to figure out how to go from here. Are we getting the story, or what?" I couldn't help but ask the question. I wondered if she'd be willing to spill all the beans about what and how it all went down.

Momma stiffened, as she did when under attack. "What do you mean?"

"I mean, are you going to start from the beginning and tell us the whole story? It would go a long way to help us understand how we've gone our whole lives not knowing we have a sister."

"A *half* sister," Momma corrected me. "She's your half sister."

Carly and I looked at each other. "Are you serious? After all this, *that's* your sticking point?" Carly stood and towered over our mother.

"Well, it's true. And you girls have no idea what I went through back then. What I suffered." Momma straightened in her chair and huffed in a prideful way that I recognized only too well. She wasn't going to be humbled.

"What about Daddy? You've lied to him your entire marriage. What about us? You've deprived us and your older daughter from getting to know her family." I could no longer be gentle.

"I'm not the first young woman this has happened to. And she wasn't the only adopted child in the world. We made sure she had a good home and a nice family who wanted her."

"Her name is Allison. And she's your daughter. Just like we are." Carly's voice was angry, so angry it shook. "And she's very, *very* sick. Enough that she's fighting for her life and needs a bone marrow transplant."

Momma hung her head. "I don't know her. I don't feel for her what I feel for you girls. Maybe I'm supposed to, but I don't."

Nana had been silent up to this point, letting us have our say. But she stepped forward now. "Karen, dear, nobody can tell you how to feel. This has been a big shock to us all. Totally unexpected. What the girls want from you now is the truth of how we came to be in the situation we now find ourselves."

"I suppose you're all wondering about it. I never would have spoken a word if this hadn't happened, you know. But here we are. Truth is, I met a boy when I was sixteen and he sweet-talked me into bed. The back of his IROC-Z, to be more accurate."

"What's an IROC-Z?" I couldn't help but ask.

"Sports car. It was *yellow*." Momma emphasized the *yellow* and stared at each of us if we should understand that significance.

"Anyway, when I told him I was pregnant, he laughed at me and said it wasn't his baby and he would deny it if I made any such accusation. Nobody had seen us together, as we'd not gone on any official dates. We'd sneaked around a little. His family was high society, way higher than mine, and I didn't dare make such claims. Momma and I decided I should take a trip and put the baby up for adoption. A closed adoption so nobody would ever find out."

Nana spoke up then. "This was not a nice boy, and his father was in politics. The family is still in Cypress Bayou and still in politics. We didn't have a lot of choices, you see. Unless your momma wanted to leave her home permanently or live in disgrace. I say that because this town has a long memory when it comes to women making mistakes they can't take back. We're still behind the rest of the country when it comes to small towns and small minds."

"Momma, I get why you gave Allison up for adoption, but why a closed adoption where she couldn't find you someday?" It was an important question for me.

"Nobody would've taken a second look at me for marriage if anyone found out. And if I'd found a husband, eighteen years later, my mistake might've caught up with me. I didn't dare share my shame. Your father married me under the impression that I was a virgin. That he was my only love. I didn't want to disappoint him like that. So, I never did anything to change the adoption status or open it. I was told I could do that later if I wanted to."

"I'm not sure how you passed yourself off as a virgin after giving birth, but wow, that's quite a story, even for thirty-five years ago. It's not like it was the fifties." It was hard to imagine that in the eighties this could've still been the prevailing way to think or behave.

I saw shame creep in then as Momma spoke. "We were at least a couple decades behind until the internet came in." There was an undeniable truth to her words.

"So, now, again, what about Daddy?" Carly wanted to know.

Momma hung her head and sobbed then. "I don't know how to tell him now."

"That's understandable, but you have to because we need to check on Allison. She's sick and all alone. And she's desperate to find her family, according to Jake."

Momma appeared wrecked. "Yes. I'll tell him. And someone should go to Allison. I don't want her to be alone."

Progress. Finally.

"I'll go to New Orleans, let her know we're in her corner, see how she's doing, and report back. That way, Leah can focus on getting ready for the bone marrow transplant without having any conflict with the donor registry."

Carly's suggestion made sense.

"Where will you stay?"

"I can crash on my friend Scott's couch in the French Quarter for a few nights."

"Are the two of you dating?" I had to ask.

Carly appeared shocked at the question. "Of course not. He's got a girlfriend."

"That sounds like a good strategy, dear. Your mother and I can deal with things here while you girls take care of things there." Nana hesitated on the word *things.*

"Things" meant Daddy. *Things* was a loaded word with so much hanging on it. "Things" meant telling him about a lifetime believing our momma was a weirdly religious woman who attended mass every day because she was righteous. Now she would rewrite his perspective by serving up a large heaping of truth.

That truth meant atonement and confession. Things Momma had been doing at church all those years. But she'd kept the confessing from her husband. Now she would atone to him.

I knew my daddy. And there's no way he would've stayed with Momma all these years if he wasn't committed to love her to the grave.

CHAPTER FIFTEEN

M Y SURPRISE SISTER was quickly becoming a real person even though I'd not yet met her. And my bone marrow donation surgery took on new meaning and a sense of urgency instead of the vague idea of saving someone's life. That someone now took form for us all.

With a plan in place, all seemed calmer by the time we'd broken up in Nana's sunroom, even Momma, though she still had the hardest work of all to do telling Daddy about Allison.

This story was evolving so fast and the processing of emotions had a lag time, I was beginning to understand. I'd been outrunning it so far, but I could feel it gaining on me. It was a lot. Plus, there was Jake. And he wasn't a small part of the whole here. I was terrified to just stop and let it all catch up.

"Leah? What are you thinking about?" Carly and I were in our pajamas, sitting in front of the television, about to watch some scary show about a haunted house. But we hadn't yet turned it on.

I'd been sitting and holding the remote and staring at nothing just a bit longer than usual, I realized. "I'm thinking that I'm afraid to sit still for fear of everything catching up with me." Honesty was always the best way to answer a direct question with Carly around.

She nodded. "I know what you mean. I'm worried about Momma and Daddy. Momma seems weirdly fine. I guess she's lived with her own secret all these years, so maybe it was a relief to let it out. But I'm wondering how Daddy will react. Then, there's our new sister. I'm concerned about how sick she is and if we'll get to meet her finally and then lose her."

"It all keeps swirling through my head. And what about Allison's dad? 'Not a nice man' who still lives in town, Nana said. You know this won't stay a secret. In fact, it would be wrong to try to keep it one. It would mean asking her to stay away from her birthright. The place she should be able to call home." I had another thought then. A dreadful one that had crawled into my consciousness while I wasn't looking.

"What if she hates us?" Carly spoke my ugly thoughts.

"I didn't want to say it, but I'm glad you did."

"I guess we have to be prepared for anything. Allison could be very, very angry that Momma gave her away and that we spent our lives here in Cypress Bayou, where she could have grown up."

"I only hope she's had a happy life with people who loved her." It was my most fervent hope for our new sister.

"I feel so guilty that we had each other and she was excluded from that."

Guilt. Yes, that's what I felt, too. "Me, too. Even though we didn't have anything to do with Momma's choices. Or Nana's. Don't you think Momma did what Nana told her?"

Carly frowned. "I hadn't really thought to lay it on Nana like that. But she was likely half of the decision."

"I don't blame Momma for getting pregnant, though. That would be too judgmental. I guess any blame is judgmental." All this was too close for my own comfort. The one thing I couldn't understand was giving up her newborn baby. When I'd lost mine, I would've given anything to have her with me alive and healthy.

Carly broke into my thoughts. "I see your mind working. Momma's situation wasn't anything like yours. Her back was against a wall of small town condemnation and looking into a dismal future."

Carly always saw me. "I just can't imagine giving my baby away."

She joined me on the sofa then, taking my hand. Her tone was imploring. "But people *do*. For so many reasons. And often, no matter how hard it is, it's the right decision for the baby. At least it is at the time. People can't always provide a good and loving home." Carly worked with women in impoverished situations, so she knew a bit about the subject, I guess.

But I had my own problem with Momma's giving up Allison. "Yes, but Momma didn't make her decision in Allison's best interest. She did it in her own best interest." And there, my friends, was the rub.

We both sat silent for a moment. Because it was indeed a truth that was hard to get around.

Carly spoke first. "It's up to Allison to make peace with it. Not us."

"I can live with that. That's between her and Momma. But it doesn't have anything to do with what kind of sisters we can be to her."

"Agreed."

I clicked on the TV then, and we were swept up into the terrible world of haunted mansions, terrified children, and ghosts with soulless eyes. What a relief from my real life.

Jake

JAKE WELCOMED BACK Dr. Lalonde, who'd been absent since Leah's arrival and who'd initially been assigned as the physician with whom she'd be working to facilitate her bone marrow transplant. At first, Jake had been annoyed at Lalonde for shoving cases at his team without any prior communication, but it had meant Jake had overseen Leah's case. Not that there had been much to do until now other than ordering lab tests.

But Leah had insisted he stay on her case, even after they'd realized the situation, so it was her decision. Once she'd signed off on his being her doctor, all was considered appropriate.

"Sorry about leaving you with my workload, Jake, but I knew you had backup with your team. Trips to Bora Bora don't come around all that often, you know." The man had returned tanned and in excellent spirits, so good for him.

"I'm glad you had a nice time. I've decided to keep Leah Bertrand's case, as she's having bone marrow transplant surgery in a few days down at Tulane."

Lalonde frowned as if he were trying to connect dots. "Oh, hey, weren't y'all—" He snapped his fingers when they obviously connected.

Jake interrupted him before he got it out. "Yes. We were. Not anymore, but I'm going down to make sure all goes well, so you're off the hook there."

"Oh, sure, man. No worries. Hope it all goes well. Glad she's a match."

They were in the conference room attached to Jake's office going over files of patients Jake had seen while Lalonde was gone.

"Mrs. Hardin passed away. Her family decided to place her in hospice care, but she died after two days at home."

"Oh, sorry to hear it. I'll contact the family. Nice lady. She's been a patient going on twenty years. I'm glad they took the hospice route. I hope it made things a little more peaceful."

On that they could agree. Jake had dealt with the end of life many times. It was never easy and always reminded him of losing his mother. "I think they were accepting."

Jake was clearing up notes and folders after Lalonde's departure from the conference room. He'd nearly finished when Elizabeth entered in a cloud of whatever perfume she wore. Though she was still in scrubs and a lab coat, she must have spritzed just before heading to his office because surgeons weren't allowed to wear heavy scents into the OR. "Well, hello there, stranger."

"Hi, Elizabeth. How's it going?" Best to keep it casual and friendly.

"Going better now." She flashed the thousand-kilowatt smile.

Uh-oh. "I'm heading down to Tulane to monitor Leah's

bone marrow donation surgery." In fact, he was heading home to pack up. They would leave in the morning.

Her smile disappeared immediately. "You mean you're going down to hold her pasty hand?"

"I'm going down because I choose to, Elizabeth."

"Are you taking all the minions with you?" She referred to his team, unkindly.

Jake tried not to lose his temper. *Why is she like this?* "My *team* is staying here to care for our patients."

She advanced into the room, like a warrior taking ground. "I ran into your daddy at the club on Sunday. Says he's not putting up with you getting involved with Leah again. Just a heads-up. Thought you'd want to know." Her smile now was smug.

She was throwing poisoned darts. No, shooting flaming arrows. One after the other to see if he would react.

The blood in his temples pounded. The woman was too much. "My father doesn't control who I date any more than you do, but thanks for that."

"Aw, somebody about to blow his stack?" Elizabeth continued to needle and to advance. Jake actually stepped back. "Well, *good!* I'm glad you're pissed because now you understand how I feel about your leading me on all these years while *she's* been gone."

Aware of Elizabeth's volume increasing, Jake moved around her and pulled the glass door shut. He couldn't avoid anyone passing by seeing their argument, with the entire wall made from glass, but he could at least decrease the loudness. "You wanted to be led on. I didn't ever lead you to believe I was interested in anything more than friendship."

As soon as he said it, he was hit by the guilt from that one night. The one he couldn't take back or deny.

"Are you brain damaged? Really? I specifically remember—"

Jake held up a hand. "Stop. One *incident* doesn't mean we were dating or were going to date. It was one drunken night. And I do take responsibility for it. But it never happened again. Did you notice that? Nothing *ever* became of it because there *is* nothing between us, Elizabeth."

Elizabeth smiled. Smug. She was staring over his shoulder now, past him through the glass windows and doors into the hallway.

Jake's back was to the hallway since closing the door. He turned to see who was there. His lungs whooshed out his breath. Leah stood just outside the glass door. *Where did she come from, and how long has she been there?*

Leah stared at him. She'd heard every word, based on her expression. Pissed. Hurt. But then her gaze moved to Elizabeth, who still wore a haughty and, unfortunately, hateful expression. Leah didn't retreat as he might have thought.

To his surprise, she stepped inside. "Looks like I've interrupted quite a discussion between the two of you. Do carry on." She motioned forward with her hands.

"Oh, I think we've quite finished here, don't you, Jake?" Elizabeth laughed as she spoke. "I'm guessing you've heard enough to know that Jake and I have a past." She nodded toward Leah as indication.

But Leah smiled instead and encouraged Elizabeth to continue. "Oh, come on. Surely you've got more to say.

Like, why you might have thought Jake thought you were his girlfriend. Or exactly how Jake led you on."

"Leah, we don't have to do this now." Jake very much didn't want to do this now. Right here in his place of employment. On display for anyone to see and hear.

Elizabeth was more than happy to oblige Leah. "Jake did lead me on. You've been gone a long time, girlfriend. Did you think he would sit around like a good boy for *years* waiting for you to come home?"

Leah didn't seem to have an answer to that.

Elizabeth continued. "Well, he did for a long time, you know. Then he got fed up and lonely. And men who get lonely find someone else for company. If that upsets you, you've got only yourself to blame."

Leah's lip trembled, but when she turned her eyes to Jake's, he recognized a deep anger. "I guess I don't blame you. But of all the people you could've reached out to, why did it have to be *her*?"

Elizabeth's brittle laughter rang out. "I think that means she thinks you could've done better, Dr. Hottie." But despite her attempt at humor in this bizarre situation, Jake could also see a similar glaze of anger in Elizabeth's glare.

Jake didn't have a clue how to fix this or to make it stop, but he did know it was his fault. "I'm sorry. To both of you. Leah, I didn't sleep with Elizabeth, but we did have a moment."

Elizabeth snorted. "Is that what you're calling it?"

He held up a hand. "I'm calling it what it is. Something that didn't happen. And I know you would like to hurt Leah by making her think it was more. We aren't dating, and we haven't had any other physical contact. Yes, we've gone to dinner as friends a few times when I've been in town. But let's face it, Elizabeth, we *have* been friends our whole lives. We work at the same hospital. I do turn to you for company from time to time."

That appeared to shut down Elizabeth's roll for a moment, at least.

"Leah, you and I can talk privately. I'm not going to discuss our relationship here and now. I'll just say I'm sorry."

Leah didn't react to that, but she and Jake both turned and stared at Elizabeth then.

She put up her hands. "Okay, fine. Clearly I'm not wanted. And you can think what you want, Leah. But your lover boy here remembers how it all went down." She pulled the door and *whooshed* through it in typical Elizabeth fashion. They could hear her heels clicking down the hallway, along with everyone else on the floor.

Leah spoke after a few seconds. "I think she's the only person I hate in this world."

Jake didn't know how to respond. "Leah—I—"

She held up a hand to stop his words, whatever they might be. "Don't."

But he wasn't going to let her cut him off again. She seemed to do that every time they had a conversation lately. "No. I admit that I've been an idiot at times and that I should have come to Paris, especially the last time, but things were pretty good between us before then. It felt like you blocked me after that. I've never stopped loving you, and I believe you know that. I wish you would at least communicate your feelings to me."

Leah stared at him. Her eyes teared up. "I—can't. Not now. There are too many other things happening. I'm terrified if I let something out, everything will burst into a million pieces and I won't be able to make sense of my life again. So, no. Not right now."

Jake frowned because he had no idea, specifically, what she was talking about, but he did know that she had some major stresses happening with her family and with the upcoming surgery. Obviously, she had way more going on under the surface than he understood. And today wasn't going to be the day to unravel the mystery. He wanted to help, but that wasn't allowed. "Okay. I'll pick you up at nine in the morning. Does that work?" He didn't want to sound uncaring, because he wasn't, but it was frustrating being left out of the loop.

Leah nodded. "Yes. Thanks for driving." She looked like she wanted to say more, but Jake wasn't about to ask. Somehow, when he asked, it didn't go well for him. Especially after the scene she'd just witnessed between him and Elizabeth.

He walked her to the door and thought to ask, "You stopped by. Did you need me for something?"

"The hospital lab called and suggested I stop by to sign some more paperwork. I thought I would check in about tomorrow."

"Ah. I spoke with Mrs. Bergeron. We're all set."

She had that look again. The one like she wanted to talk further. "It'll be nice to see them again. It's been a long time."

So long. And he dared not go into *that* conversation. The

one where they'd been together in the company of the Bergerons most recently. So, he didn't.

"Okay. I'll see you in the morning."

And tomorrow they would spend several hours together where neither could make an escape. Maybe it would make for good conversation. Maybe they could actually resolve some of the unspoken conflict. Or they would tear each other to shreds.

CHAPTER SIXTEEN

Leah

I PACKED PRETTY much everything I'd brought with me from Paris since my length of stay in New Orleans was a little uncertain. I mean, I'd been told what to expect, but no one really knew.

I'd gone over to Momma and Daddy's house last night to say goodbye to them both since they wouldn't be immediately traveling. Momma had told Daddy about her past the night before. The past he'd known absolutely nothing about before they'd met. His response had been to say nothing, according to Momma. To stare at her as if she were a stranger and head back out into the garden shed until midnight.

Momma had tried to follow, but he'd locked her out. Instead of hammering on the door half the night, she'd gone to bed. Daddy had slept in the guest bedroom farthest down the hall and been out in the garden before Momma woke up the next morning. He was avoiding the subject and his wife. I wasn't surprised by his reaction, honestly. He didn't do conflict well, and this betrayal of Momma's—as he might see it—was a lot to sift through emotionally.

Of course Momma wanted it done with. But she wasn't

having her way this time, and it was killing her.

When I'd stopped by the house, I'd had to seek out Daddy in the garden shed. It was dusk by then, and Momma handed me his plate of dinner as she pointed where he was. "Might as well bring him this so he doesn't starve to death out there since that's where he's living now."

"Momma, I'm sure he'll come around and be ready to talk at some point. This was a shock to us all. But mostly to Daddy." I put my hand on her shoulder.

"Thank you, Leah. I've regretted not telling you all but mostly him. I'm getting what I deserve, I guess." Momma went back to cleaning up the kitchen as I headed out to the shed.

I poked my head inside the shed. "Hi, Daddy. I brought your dinner. It's still hot."

He was at the potting bench, replanting something. "Thanks, Sugar. I'm not hungry, but I appreciate it." He hardly looked up.

"Daddy, I'm leaving in the morning for New Orleans. My surgery is in a few days."

His hands stilled. He wiped them on a damp cloth and turned to face me. The lines in his face were more prominent than I'd ever seen them. It was like he'd aged a decade. "My sweet girl. I wish I could be there with you."

"It's okay. Jake's going to be with me. I mean, we're not together or anything, but he'll make sure everything goes smoothly." I had to appreciate that about Jake, I guess.

Daddy sighed. "I haven't been myself the past few days. I guess you know all about it, don't you?"

I nodded. "I do, Daddy. And I'm so sorry you've had to

hear about this after all these years. I'm sorry Momma had this secret and she didn't tell you." I didn't know how else to approach the matter.

He motioned for me to sit beside him on a bench. "It makes sense now, you know? I've always felt like there was something I didn't know about your momma. Like there was some drama that happened to her before she met me and I had to pay for it."

I nodded again. "I can see how you could feel that way. She was always doing penance for something, wasn't she? I never understood how one woman felt she had to be in church so much."

"Exactly. Now I get it. But what I don't get is how she didn't trust me with it. How she could stay away from a daughter who might need her someday to keep the secret from *me*. So I wouldn't find out. To make things easier for herself. I know she's a selfish woman. Boy, do I know it, but this is too much."

"Yes. We've pretty much said the same thing to her. But being that Momma is, well, Momma, you have to expect that she would worry first about how the consequences of this would affect her. Not you, and not us. Not her first daughter. Her." I guessed most daughters didn't feel this way, nor husbands.

"That makes sense. And I've either got to forgive her for being who she is and who she's always been, or not." He hung his head. "I'm just so ashamed of her for the decisions she made."

"Yes. We all understand how you feel. But this is between the two of you, Daddy. The truth of it is going to come out, and we have to help Allison because she's our sister and she's sick." I hated that Daddy would feel the brunt of Momma's secret throughout the community. The petty gossip. The eye rolls and snickers. It wouldn't last long, but while it did, the discomfort for all of us wouldn't be fun. I likely wouldn't be around to feel it like Momma and Daddy and neither would Carly.

"Of course you should help your sister. And I hope your momma follows that course as well. As you all should. This young woman isn't to blame." The unspoken words were that Momma was to blame.

I gestured toward the plate covered in tin foil. "Please eat your dinner. I don't want you to waste away while you're brooding and trying to figure out your course. We all love you so much. Momma does, too. You know that, right?"

We rose, and he hugged me tight but didn't respond to my question. "Be safe on your travels down south, Leah. I'll be all right here. I've just got some thinking to do. Nothing wrong with making your momma stew a bit, is there?" He flashed a quick grin.

"No, there isn't. Not one bit." I wholeheartedly agreed with him there.

He hooked an arm over my shoulder as we walked together toward the door. "Keep me in the loop about the surgery. And about your sister's condition."

"Aw, Daddy, you're the best."

I found myself wiping a tear away as I moved toward the back door of the house. Daddy was worried about Allison and wanted us to keep him posted about her condition. He bore no ill will against her, as we should've known he wouldn't.

Momma met me just inside the house. "What did he say? Is he eating?"

"I think he needs a little space, but I do think he'll eventually come around. This isn't something you can rush." I had to figure out a way to give Daddy the breathing room he needed. "I think you should go to Nana's for a few days. Let Daddy think things through."

"Leave him?" Momma drew back in horror. "I wouldn't think of it. What will he eat?"

I suppressed a smile. It really did all come down to food. "Daddy won't starve if you're gone for a couple days. He might even appreciate you a little if you're not here taking care of him."

Momma frowned. "You might be right about that. The man hasn't gone without a clean pair of underwear his whole life. He went straight from his own momma to me taking care of everything for him. Our generation, you know?"

"It's just an idea. I do think he'll forgive you, but it might be easier for you both if he's not having to hide outside in the shed twenty-four seven."

"He's got a few leftovers in the fridge." Momma indicated the packed refrigerator with a side nod in that direction. "He certainly won't starve."

Jake

JAKE HAD FLASHES of Leah and his backstory as he drove the

short way to pick her up. It was a gloomy, rainy morning to drive several hours. Their trips together when they'd been younger and during college were such fun. They'd had adventures and romance and had truly been best friends. He missed her friendship as much as the romance. Well, maybe not quite as much.

His palms were a little sweaty, Jake had to admit as he pulled up to Plaisance House, a likely result of his teen-ish nerves. The first thing he noticed, besides the obvious grandeur of the place, was Leah's suitcase sitting on the covered front porch, along with a large canvas tote bag. She was clearly ready to go. Lateness hadn't ever been one of her qualities.

Jake didn't have to worry about his mail or closing things up while he was gone since he had Blake there at the apartment. But the idea of building a home on the family bayou land had really taken root, even more so since Leah had come home. Something about having her near him had such thoughts running rampant.

It wasn't raining hard enough to need an umbrella or rain jacket, but there was fine mist falling all around. Jake approached and raised a hand to knock, but the heavy mahogany door swung open. "Well, hello there, Jake."

"Hi, Nana Elise. I'm here to pick up Leah."

"Seems like old times, now doesn't it?" The older woman had an undeniable twinkle in her eye.

"I was thinking that on the way over."

"Well, come on in. I've made breakfast. No sense driving on an empty stomach." Nana made a sweeping gesture with her hands toward the kitchen. "Nasty morning."

Jake had already had a quick run, despite the wetness, and downed a smoothie around six a.m., but he wasn't one to turn down a breakfast spread when it was presented. "How kind. Thank you."

Leah called from upstairs, "I'll be down in a minute."

He looked upward and saw her dash from one room to another. Just a quick flash of honey-blond hair, a green top, and denim. "Take your time. I've been offered breakfast."

Nana set a plate in front of Jake piled high with bacon, scrambled eggs, and a fat cathead biscuit. "That's a lot of food. Thanks."

"There's butter and fig preserves on the table. And help yourself to orange juice." A carafe of fresh-squeezed OJ sat in the center of the table as well.

Leah breezed in, fresh and lovely, her hair still slightly damp and curling at her neck. "Good morning." Jake caught a whiff of her shampoo. Between that and the bacon, the combo was heavenly.

"Good morning." Jake tried not to talk with his mouth full, but it would've been rude not to reply.

Leah grabbed a biscuit and a couple slices of bacon, then sat down across the table. "Thanks for breakfast, Nana."

"Of course, darlin'. We all need to eat. Your mother and sister should be down shortly."

"Karen's here?" That surprised Jake.

"I suggested Momma give Daddy a little breathing room while he's considering his response to her bombshell."

"Probably not a bad idea." But it still surprised him.

"And it never hurts to leave a man alone in the house to let him see what that might feel like." Nana muttered the words as she pulled bacon from the griddle on the stove.

Jake controlled the urge to snicker. Nana was a slick one, he'd give her that. Mildly passive-aggressive and inarguably wise. "I guess he's never been alone?"

Leah grinned then. "Never."

"Remind me to never go against your collective wisdom. I wouldn't stand a chance." Jake shuddered at the idea of all the women here putting their thoughts together toward a common goal, especially if that common goal meant his defeat.

"You'd do best to keep it in mind." Carly spoke as she entered the kitchen, in answer to Jake's comment. "Y'all heading out?"

Leah nodded at her sister's question. "Shortly, yes."

"Momma still sleeping?" Carly looked around as if to find her.

The girls shared a glance. "I guess she is, though I don't know how she could be with all the noise happening down here."

Jake felt like an outsider in this house full of women. They had their own silent language filled with shrugs, shared looks, and very little explanation. It was more than a little intimidating.

"Let your momma be. She's lying low for now, I'm sure. I'm gonna bring her up a tray now and let her save face." Nana had indeed loaded up a lightweight tray with a plate of food, a glass of orange juice, and the newspaper. "Y'all don't leave before I get back."

Nana returned a couple minutes later as Jake and Leah were finishing up. "She said to tell y'all to be safe on the road and to keep her posted on what's happening once you arrive."

"I'll be heading down south tomorrow to check on Allison. Is there anything I should know?" Carly directed this question at Jake.

Since Leah was the marrow donor, they'd discussed it and decided it was best to keep space between her and Allison. "Only that Allison is going through some intense chemotherapy and radiation to prep for the bone marrow donation right now. She'll be in isolation from visitors so you'll be required to keep your distance and wear a mask, gown, and gloves if they do allow you to visit."

"Wow, I had no idea. Maybe your friend at the hospital could give her a heads-up that I'll be stopping by?"

Jake nodded. "I'll contact Charles on the way down, and he can tell her to expect you."

Leah

WE WERE FINALLY on the road. In the same car. Gloom all around with the weather. Headed toward the scariest scenario I'd faced in recent history. Besides my miscarriage two years ago. That had been terrifying.

Having Jake beside me was both comforting and discomforting in extremes. I could rely on him a hundred percent. Conversely, he was the one person who saw through me in a way that didn't allow me to rest.

"Are you comfortable?"

"Yes. I like your new truck."

"Thanks. I finally traded in the old yellow hound."

Jake's new truck was surprisingly comfortable, being that it was a four-wheel-drive model and sat pretty high off the road. The old yellow one he'd had in high school and college hadn't been such a smooth ride. But the adventures we'd had in that truck were so many.

"I miss that old truck." I hadn't meant to say it, but thinking about it made me smile.

"Me, too."

I stared out the window as Jake pulled onto I-49 headed south, glad I wasn't driving in the misting rain. "Feels like old times, huh?" His words held a wry remembrance.

We'd loved New Orleans together. The music, the food, exploring the city. We'd gone to Mardi Gras with friends every other year or so from the time we'd been old enough to head there on our own. My parents had been strict in some ways, but when it came to Jake, they'd trusted him. Just like I'd always trusted him.

"How do you feel about Pascal's Manale for dinner?" Jake suggested.

I'd just eaten breakfast less than an hour ago. Plenty. But the mention of Pascal's on Napoleon Avenue made my stomach growl in anticipation. Screw the romantic memories we'd had there; I'd never pass up the opportunity for their original barbequed shrimp just to avoid remembering happier times with Jake. "Are you kidding? I wouldn't miss it."

"God, I hoped you'd say that. I hope you don't mind that I made a reservation for us last night. I didn't want to take the chance of missing out, either."

"I do think that was a little high-handed of you, but you're forgiven this once."

"I kind of figured. I wonder if they'll remember us."

I shrugged. "Depends if we're as memorable as we think we are." Jake and I had spent several memorable (to us) dinners there in the past. We'd laughed and eaten and drunk for hours, interacting with the servers and staff.

"I guess you've got a point."

"Maybe you'll get a chance to hit a few galleries while we're in town."

I wanted to. Art was my business after all, and professionally, New Orleans had a strong international art scene. To pass up the opportunity of perusing the major galleries as well as the many smaller ones would be derelict of me. "I hope to. I've got clients who've requested paintings I might find here. It's worth looking. New Orleans is like a treasure trove when it comes to fine art." All art, really.

I squirmed a little in my seat. "What's our ETA?" I knew it would take us roughly another three and a half hours to get to New Orleans if we didn't hit the lousy traffic that so often plagued Baton Rouge. The road construction projects were endless on I-10 unless something had miraculously changed in the past couple of years.

The volume was turned down low, and the screen showed the music station instead of the GPS. Jake punched the map icon that showed the map of our trip. "Just after one o'clock if nothing changes between here and there."

"That's a big 'if,' isn't it?" I referred to the Baton Rouge traffic.

"We'll hope the best. My last few commutes between here and there weren't so bad."

I'd forgotten how much driving he did these days within the state. "Are you still traveling as much?"

He shook his head. "Didn't you hear? I've just replanted my team in Cypress Bayou. Signed a contract for two years for Cypress General as a home base. That's why I've got the sweet office and conference room. No more running all over creation. I've decided to take up golf."

I snorted at that. "Golf?"

"Why is that funny? Doctors play golf." He sounded mildly offended.

"I've never imagined you as a golfer is all."

"It's what's got me thinking about building a house on the bayou. I'm ready to put down roots, you know?"

That punched me right in the heart. *Our* house. *Our* future. I decided his question could remain rhetorical.

CHAPTER SEVENTEEN

Jake

LEAH CLAMMED UP suddenly, and Jake realized he'd stuck his foot in it by mentioning the house. "Leah, I'm sorry if my building a house bothers you. I can't put it on hold indefinitely."

"No. You shouldn't. It's your land, and you're free to do what you want when you want with it." As she said it, she continued to stare out her window.

"You know I wanted to build a house together." No time like the present to bring this up because she couldn't walk away from him now. He wanted her to know it wasn't off the table. That there was still hope for the two of them.

Leah turned to face him then. "So did I, Jake. More than anything."

"Then *why* won't you give us another chance?"

"I don't want to talk about this right now." Those words had become her mantra with him, it seemed. It was her go-to whenever he tried to have a meaningful conversation.

Not this time. "Leah, this is the perfect time to talk. We're stuck in a car together for the next few hours. There's nothing else to do. So, let's talk."

She glared at him. "Fine. But you asked for it. Keep that

in mind, Jake."

"Okay. Shoot." Something about her words caused a nasty sinking in the pit of his gut.

"You want to know what happened two years ago, when you didn't show up? Again?"

"Yes, I do." But did he?

She took a breath before she spoke. "I lost our baby. I needed you, and you weren't there for me."

Her words. They almost didn't register. Jake couldn't believe them. "Wait. You what?" He'd stopped breathing. Navigating the truck to the shoulder of the highway, he put the vehicle in Park. "Leah, you lost a baby? *Our* baby?"

She nodded but turned away from him, her shoulders rigid.

"How could you not tell me you were pregnant? Oh my God, Leah. *Why didn't you tell me?*" Jake could feel moisture gathering in his eyes. He felt a lot of things in that moment. Things that threatened to tear their way through his skin.

"Why? I was going to tell you in person when you arrived. I didn't realize I was pregnant for almost two months because my periods are so irregular. I was so hurt and mad at you for canceling your trip again that I decided to wait to tell you in person when you rescheduled. But you didn't reschedule, did you?"

Did you? Her words hung in the air between them like a guillotine.

Jake was light-headed with anger—and what? Frustration? Sadness? The urge to roar at Leah was strong. He'd never really yelled at her. Never. Instead of doing so now, he unlatched his seat belt and climbed out of the truck, careful of the passing vehicles throwing up road spit on his side. Gulping huge breaths, he walked around the back and tried to clear his head. *How could she not tell me about the baby? About losing the baby?*

Did she think he didn't deserve to know? That he didn't deserve to share the grief and pain? Did she think he wouldn't feel those things, too, because he was the father part of things?

All because he hadn't made the trip to Paris as scheduled. When he'd tried to reschedule, Leah had told him not to come. That she was too busy with work to spend time with him. Things had changed between them after that. He'd eventually stopped trying because she'd all but cut off communication.

It all made sense now. Not common sense, but at least he understood what he hadn't before. She blamed him for losing their baby. It had been two years, and she'd convinced herself he was to blame for their losing contact.

Leah'd had two years to process this. Jake had had none. This fresh hell hit him hard in the soft spots. The urge to blast Leah with hot, angry words hadn't yet subsided, so the idea of getting back into the truck and driving with her for the next few hours wasn't appealing.

Standing out on the interstate with cars whizzing by throwing up dirty mist from the rain wasn't exactly appealing, either, so he clenched his teeth and got back inside.

He had to know. "Were you ever planning to tell me?"

She stared out her side. "I don't know."

Jake put the truck in gear and pulled back onto the interstate. And said nothing.

Leah

THIS CONVERSATION HAD gone nothing like I'd pictured a million times in my head. In all those imagined scenarios, I'd not imagined the pain in Jake's eyes. The blame. The anger. I realized now that I'd been so wrapped up in my own grief that it truly hadn't occurred to me to consider how Jake might respond to this.

My lashing out at him for not showing up when *I* had needed him was purely a selfish and childish thing. Shame washed over me as a physical wave. I felt my skin burn. Being totally and completely wrong was a new sensation— and a bad one. I prided myself on being an empathetic person. A good person. I'd worked at that, knowing I wanted to be the anti-Karen since childhood. But I could now begin to see some of what had formed my mother. How she'd become what she was. In that one moment I'd looked into Jake's eyes, I *was* a version of Karen.

For two years, I'd deluded myself the same way Momma had. I'd told myself how righteous I was and how wrong Jake had been. No, he hadn't shown up for a visit, but it hadn't been a killing offense. I'd made it into a terrible betrayal because of what I was going through.

I glanced over at Jake. His jaw was set, blue eyes on the road. I didn't think I'd ever seen him this serious. I had to make this right. "Jake—"

He held up a hand as if to silence me, without turning

his gaze away from the road. "I can't talk to you right now, Leah."

"Okay-but-I-was-wrong." I said it double-time, before he could shush me again. Our starts and stops at conversations since I'd been back from Paris had been frustrating for both of us. Mostly Jake, I was certain. He was a person who liked knowing where we stood. I'd not given him that peace of mind in two years.

"How can you drop a bomb on me like that, then flip the conversation with an, *I was wrong* comment?" He shook his head as if to say I was the most inconsiderate person on the planet.

Because I was at the moment. "Because I am sorry. I've had a revelation of sorts, I guess. I've spent two years wrapped up tight in my self-pity. I mean, so tight. When I saw your expression back there, I understood."

"Understood what?"

"That it wasn't just me who'd suffered. I honestly believed at the time it was just me. That's how badly I took it."

"How would you know, since you didn't bother to tell me?"

"I wouldn't. I didn't. That's what I'm trying to say. I was selfish. As selfish as I've ever been about anything. I was completely overwhelmed with grief and emotion that I blamed you."

"I get it that you were soaked in misery, Leah. I'm feeling pretty rotten right now, being that I've just learned about this. But again, *how* could you not have told me?"

"I see now that I should have. I built a wall so high and made it where you weren't allowed in. Right after...it was rough—and ugly. And I believed you were the reason for my pain. I—I see it now. But just now. Like ten minutes ago. I'm so sorry, Jake." I knew my words weren't going to be enough to get us through this. But I'd just come to this new conclusion and still felt so exposed at my wrongness. Like I was one big vulnerable soft spot all over that could be pierced with the dullest of words. But I deserved it.

"I know you don't say things you don't mean, Leah, so I'm going to believe you. I can see where you might have gone down a bad path. But an apology doesn't make up for the fact that you kept this from me. At some point in the two years, I would've thought that might occur to you."

"You're right. I've been living so far away, it's made me believe I was insulated from that responsibility. I knew it was wrong not to tell you. I was punishing you."

I knew I was. I saw pictures of him living it up while I was suffering. And I'd made the conscious decision to make France my home as a further barrier to Jake and the pain of his desertion that was compounded by the loss of our baby. So, I'd dug into Paris like a drowning soul. Then, when Alaine had died and left me the gallery, I'd believed it was a kind of providence. I couldn't leave his life's work, now my life's work.

"For what? What did I do?"

"You seemed to be having a grand time without me while I was miserable."

His eyes narrowed, as if he tried to figure out what I meant. "Social media?"

I nodded. "I know that sounds stupid, but those pictures—all the smiling and hugging. It made me want to throw up when I was crying in my bed."

He ignored the part about the pictures. "How bad was it, Leah?"

"It was…bad. As in, hormonally postpartum bad. As in, I had to take antidepressants bad. My friend Alaine had to drag me away from the city for a solid month just to get me out of bed." I shuddered at the memory even now. Losing our baby was heartbreaking, but the dark depression that followed had been a truly desolate journey. I was beyond it now. And I could see that what I'd experienced wasn't "normal," if there was such a thing.

Jake's expression softened, as did his tone. "I wish I'd known, Leah. You know I'd have been on the next flight over."

"I know that now. I don't know if I believed it at the time because I couldn't even get out of bed, much less bathe or dress. The idea of anyone seeing me like that wasn't an option. It was the worst thing I've ever experienced." I hated admitting my weakness to anyone. Though I now realized what I'd gone through was chemical and hormonal, in addition to the grief, not a character flaw.

"At least I understand why you cut me out of your life two years ago. I had no idea what happened, besides the fact that I canceled my trip to see you."

"I wish that's all it had been. I mean, if you'd only done it once, maybe I wouldn't have felt like you weren't there for me. But the way you'd consistently put work ahead of me…" There wasn't any use trying to make Jake feel any worse than he did, but I needed him to understand. This grudge I'd been holding had to end. There were endless emotions flying around, but this part I had to let go.

I was exhausted now, as if I'd expelled my demons.

"You do realize those pictures were all posed for the moment and meant nothing, don't you?"

"I guess I hadn't thought about what they were or weren't. There were so many gorgeous women in them."

"I didn't post a single one of them. I was tagged in every one."

"But you weren't worried about un-tagging yourself, either, were you?" I had to get my dig in there. So, maybe I wasn't as over it as I said. But at least we both understood why I'd been so uncommunicative and that I'd been mostly wrong.

Jake rolled his eyes at me. "I never gave it a thought. I hardly log in to social media, and if you asked me to un-tag myself in a photo on Facebook, I'd probably end up breaking something."

That was true enough, I guess. But it still made me pissy. "Whatever."

"Sounds like we've spent the past two years not understanding anything about each other."

"Yes. I guess so."

"And we're gonna be spending a lot of time together in the next several days, so we should probably call some sort of truce for the time being."

"A truce?" I thought about that for a minute.

"Or something like it."

"As in, we don't talk about all this mess from our past like it never happened? Or we put it on hold for now and try to get along?" I was pretty game for either at this point.

"Neither. Maybe we could come to some kind of under-standing with each other. I'm not giving up on us, Leah. Now that I know what happened and you've had your realization that I'm not to blame for your miscarriage, maybe we can just relax a little and enjoy our time together." He paused but then continued. "And maybe we can suspend our old hurts while we're here and *try* to enjoy the time we have together."

"You mean besides the time I'm going to spend having surgery?" It was like he forgot why we were going to be in New Orleans. "We're not exactly on a vacation."

"Obviously. But we will have some time that won't be dedicated to your being in the hospital."

Could I relax around Jake? Could I truly stop the blam-ing and pushing him away? Because that would mean I would have to change. Change my thought pattern and my belief system where he was concerned. "I can try."

"That's all I ask, Leah. I know it won't be easy after all you've gone through. That great big wall isn't gonna come down in a day."

"No, I guess it won't." He was so right. I'd spent two years fortifying the wall around my heart against Jake. But he'd already made some progress in getting past some of the highest and thickest points since I'd been back.

"We'll start with dinner at Pascal's."

I nodded. "Agreed." I figured that was as good a place as any to start.

Jake

THEY WERE SILENT for the next two hours. Leah dozed against the passenger door while Jake paid attention to the road and the rain as his mind worked through the conversation he'd had with Leah. How could two people who'd shared their kind of history have such an obvious disconnect with each other?

As angry and hurt as he was in finding out she'd kept such a secret from him, he felt a great relief that she'd come to the realization that he wasn't to be blamed for any of it—besides the feeling that he wasn't available to her because he prized his work ahead of her. Which he'd never meant to happen. That was on him.

But now, the wall she'd built against him had just come crumbling down. The barrier between them was gone. Things wouldn't heal themselves, but maybe they could create a new path.

He felt a bit of hope for the first time in a long time where Leah was concerned. Jake glanced over at her where she slumped against the door. She was so beautiful. He'd missed their talks about life and the world, the important ideas they'd always shared. When Jake had worried about things, he'd always been able to go to Leah. Her reasonable and honest view of things had seemed to set him back on track. He had a strong urge to take her into his arms and comfort her. *How could she not have told me about losing our baby?*

That frustrated, angry feeling pulled at him again. This

was all so complicated. These conflicting emotions were going to take some time to resolve obviously.

The traffic was thankfully light as he drove across the Bonnet Carré Spillway bridge on I-10 into Jefferson Parish. It was a twelve-mile-long dicey expanse of trestle bridge that, once across, brought them into the suburbs of New Orleans. Kenner, Metairie, then over the next bridge into New Orleans proper.

Jake had driven this stretch so many times over the years that he knew every pothole in the road to try to avoid. And in Louisiana, there were so many. Road maintenance wasn't the state's top priority by any means.

Leah awoke just as they were crossing the bridge over City Park and the Greenwood Cemetery, whose historic monuments were situated above ground, due to the city's below-sea-level station. The traffic had slowed, and they were able to get a good look.

"I'm always amazed at these old cemeteries." Leah craned her neck, trying to get a better view of the site. "Being buried aboveground must make the haunting easier."

Jake laughed. "They say New Orleans is one of the most haunted cities around." The two of them had gone on ghost tours together years ago. Neither had a real belief in ghosts, but the tours had been fun. "Remember the Marie Laveau voodoo swamp tour we took?"

"The one where the woman spoke in tongues and her eyes rolled to the back of her head? Yeah, that was pretty freaky." She smiled at the memory. They'd had so many adventures together over the years, and he'd missed that.

"I think most of the attendees would've run away

screaming into the street if we hadn't been on a boat in the actual swamp. I've got to give it to them, they brought the creep factor."

"You almost had to do CPR on the one guy who hyperventilated so hard, he nearly passed out from fright."

"I guess we got our money's worth on that one." Jake and Leah had had to help calm several people down that night. "I was afraid those poor souls were gonna start jumping overboard into the swamp to get away from the voodoo witch."

Jake turned left onto Napoleon Avenue from Carrollton, one of the few left-hand turns allowed in the uptown area. "It still looks the same, doesn't it?"

Leah looked out the window and noticed where they were. "I love the city this time of year."

CHAPTER EIGHTEEN

Leah

WE WERE HERE. And just like when I'd arrived in Cypress Bayou from Paris, I'd forgotten what New Orleans was like all over again. It was a shock to the senses. A wonderful one. The homes in the uptown district were historic. All of them. Cypress Bayou had lots of old homes, but it was a small town. New Orleans had streets and streets of gorgeous old homes. Some of them weren't in great repair, but they still had such charm simply because of their age. It was like going through a portal in a time-travel movie.

Unless you'd visited New Orleans, or maybe Savannah or Charleston, I didn't think it was possible to describe the character of the place. The charm. The history. It was an immersion in a different culture within one's own country. There was simply no place like it anywhere.

Napoleon Avenue was separated by a grassy median and was one way on each side, with cut-through streets every block or two. The median was wide with enormous ancient oaks in the center. Just after we crossed St. Charles Avenue and the streetcar line, I saw the restaurant on the right. "Look, there's Pascal's." This meant the Bergerons' B&B was only a couple blocks farther.

A warmth spread through me as we neared the place where Jake and I had known such happiness together. My emotions were in such a jumble, but heading to the B&B was like a homecoming. I wasn't sure whether going there was a great idea, but for now, I planned to enjoy seeing the Bergerons and absorbing the sights and smells of New Orleans.

"Here we are." Jake put on his right turn signal and slowed way down. His truck was large, but the drive was two strips of concrete with grass growing in between that led to a packed-white-shell parking area behind the old gingerbread home.

I inhaled at the sight of the place. "It hasn't changed, has it?"

Jake smiled at me, which did funny things to my insides. "I've passed by several times when I've been in town over the last few years. I saw they were doing some work with a tarp on the roof last year after the hurricane passed through and stopped to make sure things were okay."

"Oh no. Were they okay?" I asked. The Bergerons were quite elderly, and it made me sad to think they might have had damage to their lovely home.

Jake nodded. "Nothing too bad. Some wind damage from an oak branch to the roof and a small leak is all. But the roofer came quickly and got things fixed up."

"So glad to hear it."

We parked and were climbing out of Jake's truck when Mr. and Mrs. Bergeron came shuffling from the back door.

"My darlings! Look at them, Mr. B. All grown up." Mrs. B held out her arms to Jake and me.

The tiny woman in the orthopedic shoes wrapped me in a tight hug. "Sweet Leah. We've missed the both of you, *cher*!" She hugged Jake just as enthusiastically.

"Mrs. B, you haven't changed at all. We're go grateful you agreed to put us up." The woman wore an ankle-length purple screen-printed caftan with fleur-de-lis in gold, which somehow didn't detract from her dyed red hair.

"I told Mr. B as soon as Jake called that we had to help the two of you because y'all are *our favorites*!"

Mr. Bergeron had been standing quietly waiting for his turn. "Young people, we've been waiting all day for your arrival."

"Hello, Mr. B. How nice to see you again." I hugged him as well. Jake and I had bonded with these kind souls when we'd stayed at their B&B during Mardi Gras years ago. It was serendipitous how each time we'd needed a place to stay in New Orleans, Bergerons' B&B had been open to us.

"Oh, my sweet. You look wonderful. It's so nice to have the two of you here together with us again." He grinned at me, his eyes still young, peering through a face surrounded by so much life lived. "Well, let's get you upstairs so you can get unpacked and settle, why don't we?"

I went to grab my small rolling suitcase out of the truck, but Mr. B laid a hand on my arm. "Oh, no you don't. This is still my job. How do you think I stay so fit?" He struck a hilarious Atlas pose that didn't quite ring true.

Jake had already pulled out the heavier bags and had them on his shoulders. Mrs. B clucked like a mother hen and herded us toward the house. "Come on, dearies. Let's get out of this misty mess. Lucky for you, the weather is supposed to clear up by tomorrow." It wasn't actively raining now, but the sky was heavy and gray, and the humidity was likely near a hundred percent. I hated to think how much my hair resembled a Silkie chicken.

Inside, Jake turned to Mrs. B and asked which floor our rooms were on. The house had three stories, which included the loft at the top.

I didn't like the sly look she gave us. Not one bit. "Well, my dears, since Jake called at the last minute and we'd had a fortuitous cancellation, the two of you will be on the top floor."

The honeymoon suite. "Wait, did Jake tell you we aren't together? He's just helping me with the bone marrow transplant at Tulane."

"Yes, he mentioned it, but I got the impression you were in a bit of a pickle. So, I figured since you were traveling together, one of you could sleep on the pullout sofa and not be fussy about that." Mrs. B didn't meet either of our eyes as she made her bogus explanation. She was matchmaking and wasn't trying hard to hide it.

What could we say about *that*? We *were* in a pickle, for sure. "Thanks, Mrs. B. I'll sleep on the pullout." Jake avoided my glare and started up the old staircase.

I was frustrated, both with the sweet but conniving woman and with Jake because I'd not yet determined if he was in on the deception. *Surely*, he wouldn't do something so obvious. So utterly transparent. It was like a made-for-TV movie in its plot predictability. The honeymoon suite? *Really?*

Jake

HE COULD TELL Leah was upset by this turn of events. And he didn't blame her. It was pretty obvious what the Bergerons were up to, and looking at it from their limited point of view, it was pretty sweet. In his defense, Jake had told Mrs. B they were no longer a couple, but he wasn't sure how convincing he'd been on the phone.

As they entered the roomy suite, he caught sight of the pullout sofa he was meant to sleep on. It was…small. And it was old. Old like the one at his grandma Jean's house, back when she'd been alive, old. As in, probably frozen-in-place old. The upholstery was a background of faded red with yellow cabbage roses. He knew what cabbage roses were from Grandma Jean.

Leah caught him staring at the old thing. Their eyes met, and they both burst out laughing. "Everything all right, dears?" Mrs. B's question was breathy from climbing up stairs to the third floor.

"Yes. Fine. Thanks." Jake didn't have the heart to complain.

He moved Leah's things into the bedroom, which had a four-poster bed big enough for more than two people. Way more. "This is nice."

Leah cut him a look. "Forget it."

"Y'all get comfortable, darlin', and let us know if you need anything. There's fresh towels and washcloths in the bathroom. The coffeemaker works, and there's Community Coffee there with all the fixings. A coffee bar is what they're calling it."

Once they were alone in the sizeable suite, despite the lack of beds, Leah and Jake busied themselves putting things away. There were a couple of antique dressers for clothing, including one in the shared bathroom for toiletries. It was a comfortable space, if a little intimate for those who weren't intimate.

Jake finally found the nerve to speak up. "I'm sorry about this." He entered the bedroom where Leah was transferring her clothing into the highboy dresser.

She turned to face him, her expression slightly amused. "I mean, unless you were in cahoots with Mrs. B, you aren't to blame."

He held up his hands in defense. "Definitely *not* in cahoots."

"I'm assuming you made it clear we aren't together." Leah's eyes squeezed a tiny bit. *Narrowed* might have been too strong a description.

"Perfectly clear. But I do think she only heard what she wanted. That we were coming here together and staying together, even though we aren't together."

"Hmm. I can see how she might have found a loophole there. As much as she wants us to be a couple again."

"She's a romantic. I mean, look at us. We're in her honeymoon suite."

"Yes, we are."

"Want to go out and get a coffee?" Since the rain had stopped for now and PJ's was just around the corner on

Magazine Street, he figured they might as well get out and breathe some fresh air. Plus, the honeymoon suite with Leah and that gigantic bed between them was causing some major discomfort for Jake.

"Café au lait sounds perfect."

Leah

MAGAZINE STREET WAS bustling as always during the lunchtime rush. Such an interesting mix of cultures, fashion, hairstyles, and every kind of people. Jake and I managed to snag a tiny café table on the sidewalk. We sipped our drinks as we immersed ourselves in the city. There were countless adorable dogs that passed on leashes and even a few cats. This cracked me up.

There was so much to see that we hardly spoke for watching the improbable parade of humanity file by. My café au lait, for some reason, tasted so much better here.

I caught myself grinning. "I always forget."

"Forget what?"

"What it's like here. How colorful and interesting the people are. How interesting it all is. The food, the art. Everything."

"Yes. I like to imagine how someone who's never been here might see it for the first time." Jake had a wistful smile on his lips.

What a shock to the senses it would be. I could hardly remember my first time. I'd been a little girl when Nana brought me here. "Yes. That would be fun to watch."

"Would you want to live here in New Orleans in your lifetime?" Jake asked.

I considered his question. "Not permanently. I think it would be fun to own a condo in the Quarter for visits maybe, if I could wish for things to be exactly perfect."

"I considered it for a little while when I was traveling back and forth regularly."

I nodded. That made sense, I guess. "The drive is too far to make here and back in a day."

"Yes, and I got tired of staying in hotels all the time. I'm glad to be back home in Cypress Bayou."

Home. I could feel myself digging back in. Thinking about my flat in Paris now since I'd been back in Louisiana a couple weeks felt a little lonely. I had friends there. A life. But I didn't have family. Alaine was gone. He'd been my family there. Having a business, however successful, somehow didn't seem like enough. I hadn't had thoughts like this in a long time.

"Would you ever move back?" The question coming from Jake was different than when Jenn had asked. It sounded light but with deeper roots.

I didn't respond right away. Because I honestly didn't know the answer in that moment. "I'm not sure." I took a sip of my cooling coffee. "It's complicated. I own a successful art gallery. It's different than working at one."

"I suppose it must be." Jake sipped his coffee, keeping his tone neutral.

"I mean, I do have a business partner who owns half of the business. He's running the place now."

"Is he capable of taking over permanently?" Still so neutral.

"Alaine left the business to both of us equally. I won't let my half go because I know that's not what he wanted, but I know Claude can manage running it." Every time I started to think about how I might get away from Paris, a smothered and trapped sensation threatened.

Thankfully, Jake segued. "You said you wanted to visit some galleries here in New Orleans?"

"Yes. I acquire paintings from all over the world to keep our offerings diverse. I've had good luck finding artists here in New Orleans. Plus, I also love New Orleans' street art. Sometimes I get lucky." I'd found several artists whose work I'd ordered long distance. It would thrill me to track down the artists in person while I was in town, if I had time.

Just thinking about pursuing art and discovering artists in New Orleans made my heart beat faster. The vibe here was rich and soulful and way less stuffy. But the art world, as much as I loved it, was pretty unyielding. Either you were in or you were out in Paris. My gallery was *in*. But it had to stay that way, so I had to continue producing talented artists and their work. I had less enthusiasm for modern contemporary paintings, but there was a big market for them, so I continued to search them out.

"We've got a couple hours to kill before dinner if you want to walk around and check out the galleries in the area." Jake likely noticed that I'd gone into my head for a minute, just imagining all the possibilities for my gallery here in the city.

"Ha. Thanks. I guess you've read my mind."

"Well, you glazed over there for a bit discussing art."

Magazine Street had several small galleries of all kinds, so I was thrilled to take a little time and have a look. When we'd been in college, it wasn't uncommon for the two of us to ramble around down here while I'd done this same thing. While Jake hadn't been an art connoisseur, he hadn't minded my spending time looking. He'd enjoyed the atmosphere and never seemed especially bored by it.

As we entered a small space with giant canvases on the wall, Jake got a call. "I'll be right outside."

Jake

THE CALL WAS from Tulane Medical Center. "Hi, Dr. Carmichael?"

"Yes, this is he."

"This is Clara Boudreaux from the immunotherapy team at Tulane calling regarding your bone marrow donor patient, Leah Bertrand. Yes, we'll need her here first thing tomorrow morning for pre-op. By eight o'clock. The recipient patient is being prepped for donation."

Jake frowned. This isn't how things were usually done. Not so urgent. "What's happened?"

"Can you have Ms. Bertrand here in the morning, Doctor?" Clara Boudreaux wanted to know.

"Yes, we just got into town this afternoon. Can you tell me why the urgency?" Jake wanted to understand what was happening.

"We aren't allowed to share the recipient's status, as you know, Dr. Carmichael, because of donor laws, but it's urgent that we get the donor marrow as soon as possible. Please make sure the donor patient doesn't eat or drink anything after midnight tonight."

"I'll make certain."

Jake wondered how bad Allison's blood counts were that they were calling in Leah so suddenly. And he wondered if Allison would sign a consent for one of the family to know what was happening on her end. He thought maybe Carly should go now. Tonight. That way, she might be able to communicate with Allison before the surgery.

Jake hated to cut short Leah's enjoyment of perusing the galleries and shops, but it was essential that they get things in place for her surgery. And it sounded like she would be going in tomorrow and not coming out until the donation was completed.

CHAPTER NINETEEN

Leah

JAKE ENTERED THE gallery just as I was admiring the layering of color on a canvas. His mouth was what caught my eye. It was set in such a frown. Not an angry frown, a worried one. "What's going on? Who was on the phone?"

"It was the hospital. They want you there first thing in the morning. For pre-op."

My stomach lurched. "Does that mean Allison is worse?"

"I don't know. I assume so, but they won't share anything about her condition with me."

"How can we find out?" I felt such a need to know. I'd not even met Allison, but I was worried sick. "I need to let Carly know what's happening. And Nana. And Momma."

We got out onto the street and wove our way back toward Napoleon Avenue and made a beeline to the B&B.

"We should start by contacting Carly to see if she can get down here tonight. Maybe she can see Allison and get a consent for the family to know about her condition."

I bit my lip, trying to keep up while fretting. "Okay. Let's do that."

We made the calls. To Carly, who would leave within the hour. To Nana, who would speak with Momma. I didn't think I could handle her right now. I planned to call her later, once she'd calmed down.

I packed my stuff back up to go to the hospital in the morning in case I didn't have the chance to leave after the pre-op. I paced, and I worried.

"Let's go to dinner. There's nothing else we can do in the meantime, Leah."

The rain had stopped, so Jake and I walked the two blocks to Pascal's Manale. During the slow stroll, we discussed what would happen tomorrow—or what would likely happen.

"I don't want you to worry about what's going on with Allison. You'll be busy with your own prep for surgery. All you can do is focus on what's in front of you. Carly will handle Allison. I'm sure your family will come down and will split time between the two of you once the donation is done."

I nodded. We were a little early, so not in a hurry to get to the restaurant. It was nice to meander a bit and have this time to discuss things. We sat down under the canopy of oaks on one of the benches that graced the stretch along the way. This was a peaceful area in the daylight, despite the crime statistics for home invasions. New Orleans wasn't without its issues.

The sidewalks were cracked and unlevel where the huge tree roots had pushed through. It was all so old and unlike some of the newer cities with carefully planned infrastructure. I wouldn't change anything about it. The same with Cypress Bayou, which had parts even older than New Orleans and such similar culture and character. The same, but nothing like it.

"I admit to being terrified of the surgery itself. I've read all the information about it and it doesn't seem that awful, but my irrational 'being poked' side is hiding in the closet and refusing to come out." I knew Jake wouldn't laugh at me or make fun.

"That's why those fears are called irrational. We can't explain why we feel how we do. You know I don't like chickens."

I laughed. "I'd forgotten about that. Roosters specifically, right?"

Jake shuddered.

"My phobia makes more sense than yours does."

"You didn't get attacked as a kid by yours."

"True."

The sun was setting as we entered the nondescript front door of Pascal's. "Oh my. The smell." The dreamy aroma of broiled garlic bread and barbequed shrimp filled the place. It's what people came here for. Huge shrimp swimming in Worcestershire sauce, butter, garlic, Creole seasoning, ready for dipping with chunks of crusty French bread.

"Welcome, folks. Let's get you seated." The host greeted us immediately and led us to a table for two.

"Would you like a cocktail or glass of wine?" Jake suggested.

"Can I have one? You know, surgery and all."

"I don't think one would hurt. Might settle the nerves."

We ordered a couple dirty martinis because they were so good here. "To good outcomes for all." Jake held up his glass.

"I wholeheartedly agree with that." We clinked.

"Hi there, folks, what'll it be tonight?"

We ordered two of the barbequed shrimp entrées with a stuffed eggplant appetizer.

"It feels like a last meal." I sipped my martini, enjoying the slight buzzy sensation in my body and brain.

"That's a dark thought. You're going to be just fine."

"Thanks for supporting me through this, Jake. I was secretly hoping I wouldn't see you at all when I first found out I'd be coming home."

His face fell. Damn. I'd hurt his feelings. "No, I mean I didn't know how I would face you after…you know. We haven't seen each other since then." Alcohol really did make me say the dumbest things.

"I get it. I told Tanner that every time I see you you break my heart all over again when you leave."

That sobered me up. "I—I'm sorry, Jake. I live in Paris. I can't not go back there. I can't stay when I'm done here."

"Forget I said anything. It was a conversation we had when I found out you were coming home."

Our food arrived then, and I didn't have to reply. I hoped he'd forget about it. The conversation had gone way too far into the weeds to simply laugh off.

We silently switched gears from our sad history to the incredible food in front of us.

We dug in. And it was so amazing, just like I'd remembered. But forgotten. "Oh. My. Goodness." I closed my eyes so I could focus on the flavor.

"Good, huh? Nothing like it anywhere else." Jake was equally enamored with his plate, as he closed his eyes in pure delight.

So, our conversation was over for now. And since there wasn't a way to fix the subject of my leaving when this was all over, there wasn't a reason to dig the topic back up once dinner was over. We'd been hitting highs and lows since climbing into Jake's truck this morning. It was hard to keep up.

Thankfully, we'd switched to water instead of ordering another round of cocktails. My mind would be clear once we returned to the B&B and faced bedtime in close proximity. Being too near to Jake was hard enough, but being too near to Jake with a fuzzy, tipsy head was just plain stupid.

He was so familiar, and I'd been without him for such a long time. Without anyone. I hadn't dated since my miscarriage. I was lonely and needy, both emotionally and physically. I wanted Jake badly. More with each minute we were together.

I hadn't admitted that to myself until today. Until I'd relaxed after my outburst in the truck. Until I'd finally forgiven him for the terrible thing that hadn't been his fault.

Now, I was having a hard time keeping my hands to myself, though I didn't think he'd caught on yet. Hopefully I hadn't put out those signals. Complicating our relationship further made no sense. Like he'd said, I would only break his heart again when I left. And mine.

We were vulnerable to each other. And staying together in the same room made things much harder.

"How about sampling chef's signature bread pudding?" the waiter suggested after clearing the table of our empty plates.

Jake and I had sopped up the last drop of butter with our bread, and I might've actually licked the bowl if not surrounded by waitstaff and other diners. But given the opportunity for bread pudding, we both nodded simultaneously at the server awaiting our reply. "Yes, please. But just one to share." I adjusted the quantity by holding up a single digit.

I turned to Jake. "I'm so full. But I can't in good conscience leave without a bite or two."

Jake agreed with me. "Yes, I'm stuffed, but I've had dreams about the bourbon sauce."

"You're gonna have to roll me home."

"Makes two of us."

CARLY CALLED AS soon as we got back to the B&B and were winding down.

"Hey there. Are you here?" I asked as soon as I connected.

"Yes. I want to stop by there and touch base before I head over to the hospital. Is that okay with y'all?"

"Sure. Do you have the address?"

"I just pulled in the parking lot, but I didn't want to barge in."

"Of course not. I'll come down."

Jake had turned on the TV and was sitting in one of the club chairs, flipping channels. "She's here?"

"Yes. Do you want to come down?"

"Sure. Maybe she's got some info."

We met Carly in the courtyard outside. It was a nice evening, and we sat together at a table surrounded by a high brick wall thick with flowering vines. The scent of gardenias and night-blooming jasmine filled the night air. "How was the drive?"

"Fine. Not too much traffic." Carly didn't sit for long, though. She stood and paced.

"What's wrong?" I hated seeing her so antsy. "Is there a problem?"

"I sent Allison a Facebook message to let her know I was coming to the hospital tonight."

"And?"

"No reply."

"I don't expect that she'll be checking her Facebook considering what's going on, do you?" I was trying to be reasonable, but it was a little concerning since Facebook Messenger had been our way of communicating with Allison, which sounded a little silly, but a cell phone number had seemed too personal initially.

"I need her to agree to see me. I doubt there will be much access to her besides family."

"I see your point." I thought for a minute. "Maybe her phone's not charged. Or she feels too lousy to check it."

Jake nodded. "Both of those things are possible. Let me see if I can contact Charles Thibodeaux and see if he's working at the hospital or has a cell phone contact for her." He stood and moved to the corner of the courtyard.

"Sit down, please. You're a wreck." I hated to see my sister this upset.

Carly sighed loudly and plopped down into one of the

wrought iron chairs. "Says you, who has to go into the hospital tomorrow. You look pretty cool, considering."

"I'm not going to think about it until I have to. And there's nothing we can do for Allison right now." I stated the obvious because that's all I had.

"Have you talked to Momma?" Carly asked.

"Not yet. I should've already called, but we just got back from dinner. What have you heard from them? Are they planning to travel?"

"I spoke with Nana on my way down. Momma is a bit of a basket case at hearing you're going to the hospital earlier than expected, which likely means Allison is not doing so well. She and Daddy are communicating now, but she's still staying at Nana's house. Not quite sure why, but I think she's making him appreciate her. I'm not sure when they're coming down."

"That seems kind of opposite, doesn't it? Isn't *he* supposed to be forgiving *her*?"

"I believe her thinking is that when he does, he's not only forgiven her but begging her to come back home to cook, clean, and do his laundry."

Momma was a ninja in the art of the deal. Manipulating it, that is. "He'll be begging her forgiveness and not even know why before this is over."

"No doubt." Carly laughed a little then. "I think they're gonna be fine. At least that's the impression I get. Momma seemed pretty calm until she found out about your surgery being moved up."

Jake approached. "Okay. Charles just finished his shift and will go and check on Allison. Carly, if you go now, you can meet him outside her room. Hopefully you can gain access that way. Last he heard, she was pretty much in isolation because of the heavy doses of chemo and radiation, so you may not actually get to see her, but maybe the two of you can talk about a consent form on the phone. She and Charles have become friendly, and he can make an introduction."

"Okay. I'm on the way. Please tell him not to leave until I get there."

"I'll forward his contact to your phone."

Carly nodded and grabbed her purse from the table. "I'll keep you posted."

I walked Carly to her car. "Please tell our sister I'm thinking of her. I know she must feel scared and alone right now. Thank you for coming so quickly, Carly. I know this will mean the world to her." We hugged tightly, and I could tell by her sniffle intake that she was trying as hard as me to keep from crying. "We'll help her get through this. It can't have been easy losing her mom earlier in the year and then getting sick." I couldn't put myself in Allison's place because it was just too sad.

"Good luck tomorrow, Leah. I'll be at the hospital and will check in. I've got a place to stay with a friend here in town, so I can come and go."

I hugged her tight one more time before she got in her car and drove away.

"You okay?" Jake put a hand on my shoulder as I stood staring at Carly's taillights as they disappeared down Napoleon Avenue.

I heaved a sigh. "Yes, I think so. There are so many moving parts to all of this. Me and my surgery. Allison and her illness. Mom and Dad. And what about Allison's father? We haven't spent a minute thinking about him. He's still there in Cypress Bayou. This will all come out, and what will happen then?" I turned to face Jake. "Then there's you and me. In the middle of all this chaos and stress, there's you and me."

He put one finger under my chin and lifted my face to be sure we were sharing a single gaze. "You and I are going to come to an understanding, you got it?"

I nodded because I believed him. I trusted Jake in that moment to do what was right for us all. He was willing to bear the burden of my stress, health, and our family's secret without even an eye roll. For me. And he'd pushed aside his very new anger and upset with me over finding out that I'd been pregnant with his baby, lost his baby, and blamed him for it for the past two years.

He'd already gotten on the road to forgiving me—or at least wasn't letting his emotions override spending time together while we started the slog through this mess.

"Thank you for not hating me. You have every right." I wanted him to know that I understood what this cost him right now.

His emotions were on his face. "I couldn't ever hate you, Leah. I'm not saying this hasn't been a tough day. And I have some strong feelings about all of it. But right now, I can see my way past them to help get us all through this."

"You're a good man."

He growled a little, like he was frustrated and torn between the angel and the devil in himself, then pulled me into his arms. It was a hug. He was big and warm and smelled so good. And familiar. And what was meant to be something comforting quickly turned into me nearly crawling up his body and melding into him like a spider monkey. When our lips latched on to one another, there might have been a shift in the most immediate atmosphere, something like a small atomic bomb detonation.

"Um…maybe…we…should…go…upstairs." He barely got the words out because his mouth didn't have enough time off to say them because mine was keeping his too busy.

We scrambled up the three flights upstairs. Neither of us even glanced at the ancient pullout sofa. I'm not even sure we locked the door.

The big bed beckoned like it bore neon lights with an arrow: *Put her down here.*

I had one final thought before we began stripping off clothes: *Did I shave my armpits?*

CHAPTER TWENTY

Jake

JAKE HADN'T INTENDED for that to happen. In fact, if someone had laid a bet on the top-ten things that might happen once he and Leah arrived in New Orleans, their making love like they were the only two remaining humans on Earth, hell-bent on continuing the species, wouldn't have been on that list.

Not complaining. But now that they were lying there naked, breath heaving, and sweating, things could get awkward. Maybe letting her speak first was a good plan.

Leah sat up, twisted in bedsheets, her hair a tangled mess, the moonlight streaming through the windows, and turned to face him. "I'm sorry. This was my fault."

Maybe he should have rethought the letting-her-speak-first idea. *How to respond?* "Um, you're forgiven?"

She laughed at that. "I mean, you were trying to be supportive, and I kind of...attacked you. So much for consent, huh?"

Jake held up his hands in surrender. "I consent. In fact, I'll sign something that says I consent from here on out. Never a question about it, so rest easy on that subject."

She punched him in the arm. "Such a guy, aren't you?"

There was enough light in the room for them to see each other.

"Do you regret...this?" He made a circle with his finger, as if to encompass what had happened, including their particular state of undress.

"No. No, I don't. It's kind of late now, isn't it? But I don't. It makes sense that with all the emotional stuff that went on between us that we might end up this way. We were full to bursting with frustrated feelings. And I mean, *this* wasn't ever our problem, you know?" She made a similar motion with her finger as he had.

"No, it wasn't. And I've missed it. I've missed you. All of you. You were my best friend, Leah." That came out a little awkward.

"Well, buddy, I missed you, too." She grinned at him.

"You know what I mean. We had a good relationship, even when it was long distance. For a while, we did."

"We did. I'm sorry, Jake. It's my fault. All of it." She snuggled up against his side, causing a physical response.

"No. I should have worked harder to visit more." He kissed the top of her head.

"Yes, you should have." She wiggled next to him. "Maybe you can make it up to me?"

He checked the clock next to the bed. Two a.m. "How many more hours until morning? Because I gave consent, if you remember?"

"Uh-huh. Well, I'm willing to meet in the middle for blame's sake."

"I've got lots to make up for. Better get started."

Leah

I COULDN'T BELIEVE it. Jake and I had spent the entire night making love. And *I* had started it. Not that I had regrets. I didn't. But we'd been apart for such a long time, and in my wildest dreams I wouldn't have imagined last night.

It also felt strange to go straight from Jake's arms to the hospital.

We'd gathered our things this morning from the B&B and said a fond goodbye to the Bergerons, with the understanding we'd be back after my donation surgery for me to recover for a few days before we drove back to Cypress Bayou. Jake assured me I would be sore after surgery, and the potholes between here and there—no matter how careful and slow he took them—would make for a rough trip home.

"Are you okay?"

I nodded. "A little nervous."

"Still no word from your sister?"

I looked down at my phone. "Not yet." We hadn't heard from Carly, and I wondered what was going on with Allison. "I'm gonna call her to let her know we're on the way. She can update me if there's anything. The waiting is killing me."

Just then my phone buzzed and showed Carly's name on the screen. "Hey there. I was about to call. What's happening?"

I put the call on speaker: "I finally was able to get in contact with Allison through Charles Thibodeaux a couple hours ago on her cell. She's in pretty rough shape, Leah. Her voice is extremely hoarse. She says it's from her lymph nodes being swollen against her trachea. She's coughing a lot, too."

"We're on the way to hospital now. Did you tell her that we're all in her corner?"

"I told her to try to hang tough. And yes, I told her we spoke with Momma. She seemed relieved and emotional to hear that news. I let her know she's got a strong support system she can't possibly imagine rooting for her. We're strange, but we're strong and loyal."

"Okay. Did you want to meet us at the registration desk in five minutes?"

"I'll see y'all there."

As we turned off Canal Street into the Saratoga Parking Garage, my heart sped up. "Okay, this is getting real now."

"Slow and steady breaths, Leah." Jake drew my hand into his after pulling into a parking space on the second level. "They'll have you do a bunch of paperwork first. Then you'll head back to have some baseline blood draws. You may or may not be admitted on the spot. In that case, you might go ahead and be escorted to a private room."

"I'll be in a room like a sick person?" That sounded pretty terrible, but it made me appreciate what Allison must be going through.

"They have to admit you before surgery because you'll need to stay in the hospital overnight after your surgery."

"I read about some places where they do it without having the donor stay overnight." I felt myself wanting to bargain because I hated hospitals so much.

"There are some situations where patients go in early

morning and leave in the evening, but Tulane has an over-night policy for liability reasons. Plus, the food's not too bad here."

THE NEXT TWO hours were a needle-hater's blur. I guess the only thing that made it somewhat bearable was the shiny new IV in my hand from which *all* the blood came. So, additional sticks weren't necessary. But getting there had been rough.

I was now firmly a patient at Tulane Cancer Center, aka Tulane Medical Center. I refused to remove my underwear when given a hospital gown (oh, the horror) to don for the duration of my stay. The choices for today's and tomorrow's lunch and dinner menus didn't sound terrible, but it *was* a hospital.

Jake had vacated the room to do some doctor stuff that involved me, I assumed. Carly was sitting beside my bed wrestling with the remote control. I had drawn the line at twenty-four seven cable news. She finally compromised. "Fine. We'll do HGTV."

"I'm not sure how you got to be Television Czar of my hospital room, sister."

"Oh, don't be so cranky. They'll bring your lunch soon. I'm just gonna stretch out on this chair/bed contraption and get a little nap in. I've got my phone with me in case I hear something from the family or from Allison."

"I guess you didn't get any sleep last night, huh?" I felt bad then for snapping at her over programming. After all, she had driven down and spent the night in the hospital's cancer waiting room near Allison trying to get in touch with her.

I yawned hugely then. "I'm sorry. I didn't mean to bite your head off."

"Wait, why didn't you sleep last night? Something to do with you and Jake?" She eyeballed me like only my sister could. "*No way!* Y'all got it on last night?"

"Of course not—" I tried hard to come up with a firm denial of the facts. But before I could, Carly had read my expression, which meant I was stone-cold busted.

"Don't even bother to deny it. It's about time the two of you stopped fighting it. I say good for you."

"It's not how you think. We're not back together."

Carly held up her hand to stop me. "It doesn't matter what I think. I'm just happy you've broken down the barrier between you."

I decided saying nothing else was better than trying to explain everything. Jake was likely to walk in at any moment and interrupt us anyway. "We can talk about it later. I'm going to take a nap to this renovation show until they bring my tray. Turn it down so I don't have to hear the hammers."

"Good idea."

Jake

JAKE GOT HOLD of Charles Thibodeaux as soon as he left Leah's room. Charles likely knew a lot more than he'd let on to Carly. It was important that Leah's family knew what was happening with Allison in case she needed anything.

Charles met Jake in the cafeteria since it was lunchtime and he was scheduled to work soon. "Hey, man, it's good to see you. I guess Leah's sister told you I spoke with her early this morning?"

"Yes. Thanks for sharing Allison's cell number. We appreciate your helping us out. It's a strange situation."

"Right now, I'm worried about Allison. She's struggling, man. Her oxygen sats are in the high eighties. They're worried about pneumonia. But her oncology team thinks if she gets the bone marrow in the next day or two, things will improve rapidly."

"Are you on her care team?" Jake wondered why Charles was so in the know and also so free with Allison's medical information.

"Not exactly. Allison and I have struck up a...friendship of sorts. Once she shared her story with me, I couldn't get her out of my mind. She seemed so alone and so sad. I've kind of become her person here at the hospital over the past week. I spend time with her when I'm not working and have been advocating for her with her care. I mean, someone has to." Charles had always been a nice guy, and his interest in Allison seemed to be genuine.

"Did she give you permission to share her information with Leah's family?" Jake had to know.

"Oh, yes. I'm sorry I didn't make that clear. She signed a HIPAA waiver and added me, you, and Carly to it. I told her it would be wise to leave Leah's name off. When she filled out the form, they hadn't gotten any information on her mom yet, so her name's not on it. But since she swears she doesn't have another soul in the world, she's taking a leap of faith that her birth family will have her best interests at heart. Of course, I vouched for all of you since we've known each other so many years."

"Wow, okay. That's great to know we can get updates on her condition. Do you think she should do a DNA screening? I mean, just in case?"

"The Bertrand family might want one, but all the information adds up. The birth certificate she tracked down in New Orleans. And, from what Carly quickly told me on the phone this morning, her mother and grandmother confirmed the details of her birthdate and adoption."

"I don't think there's any doubt of their relationship, especially with how strong the resemblance is."

Charles nodded. "I can confirm that it's like looking at Leah with slightly darker hair."

"Could you send a copy of the privacy document to my cell?"

"You got it. The hospital has a copy already on file, so there shouldn't be a hang-up if you request information on Allison's condition."

"The family will appreciate your help. Let us know when Allison starts to improve and is up for meeting them."

"As you know, there will be sterilization protocols for a while after the transplant." Allison's immune system was and would be as weak as a newborn's. Even a common cold could kill her. That's why they were so concerned right now. She'd have no defenses until she received Leah's healthy bone marrow that would help rebuild her immunity.

Jake nodded. "Sure. Of course. I was thinking more *mentally* ready."

"Ah. Gotcha. I vaguely remember meeting Leah's mom several years ago." Jake had to give it to Charles; he kept a poker face as he made that statement. No eye roll. No grimace.

Jake backed up the statement. "Exactly. If you've met Karen Bertrand, you aren't likely to forget her." He didn't want to come out and say Karen was a pain, but who knew how Karen would handle meeting Allison?

"I'll stay in touch. And Carly has her number and can contact her directly as well. Allison is very excited about finding them. She's hit so many dead ends in her search, and when she got sick, it seemed like it wouldn't happen. Finding Leah as her donor like this was nothing short of a miracle, and when Leah turned out to be her sister, well, you can imagine her joy."

"I'm thrilled to be a part of it. I just hope Allison's health stabilizes once she receives the transplant. Leah is anxious now that she's here."

"I don't blame her. Can you imagine what the family is going through? It's like a movie being played out in real life."

"Quite the drama, for sure." Jake didn't want to go into private family details about how much drama there actually was.

"Hey, do y'all know anything about Allison's birth dad?"

Jake shook his head. "I don't think it was a good situation. Someone in the community with a lot of political pull. Someone still there, I think, who wouldn't want to be outed at this point in his life for having a secret."

"Wow. Small town soap opera stuff." Charles was clearly fascinated by all of it. And Jake didn't blame him. It *was* fascinating stuff if one wasn't personally worried about how all of this might blow up the family of someone he cared deeply about. Charles cared, but he was a few steps back.

"Except it's real stuff, unfortunately. And I hope it doesn't cause a ruckus in Cypress Bayou when it all comes out." Jake thought about his dad and how nasty he could be when things didn't go well. What if Allison's dad was someone like that?

"I'm hoping once Allison gets through her medical crisis, she finds a place to settle that provides some peace for her. Maybe someplace near her family. But it sounds like that might be messy."

Jake hoped things for Allison and the Bertrand family would have a storybook ending. But Charles was right. This had *messy* written all over it. From Allison's cancer to Karen's keeping such an enormous secret from Bob all these years. And the gossip it was sure to stir up in town once they got home and the dust settled. "I think that will be a 'wait and see.' Who knows how all this will play out."

Charles seemed to let it go as he glanced down at his bowl. "Gumbo's good today."

Today's special was chicken and sausage gumbo, which they'd both ordered. They'd added a generous sprinkle of Tony Chachere's seasoning—a staple—from the container on the table. "Not bad," Jake agreed. But his mind was working on so many other things, the gumbo wasn't register-ing like it normally would. "Thanks for filling me in, Charles. I need to get back to Leah. They're getting her ready for surgery."

"When's she having it?"

"Early morning, if all goes as it should."

"Best of luck, man. I'll stay in touch."

"Thanks." They shook hands, and Jake cleared his tray, leaving Charles to finish up at the table.

CHAPTER TWENTY-ONE

Leah

CARLY AND I were arguing over who did a better job on *The Great British Baking Show* when Jake appeared in my hospital room. "What's the ruckus, ladies?" Then he looked up at the screen and nodded. "Ah."

"It's the biscuit episode. The judges got it wrong, in my opinion. I mean, who pairs chocolate with oranges like that?" Carly was highly offended.

"Sounds delicious." Jake was completely unfazed by our silliness.

"What's up?" I asked.

"I met with Charles in the cafeteria. Allison signed a privacy document allowing me, Carly, and Charles information about her condition. Obviously, your name is left off because of the legal stuff. Right now, she's struggling to fight off pneumonia. But her immune system should kick in to combat the bacteria almost immediately after she gets the bone marrow."

"That sounds serious." Carly said what I was about to.

"It is. We can only hope they're right about her immune system grabbing hold of the marrow and killing the infection."

"Should I call Momma and tell her what's happening?" Carly looked at me. "Or will that cause more drama and serve no purpose?"

I'd given this some thought. Normally, I'd have been the one keeping Momma from knowing anything that might set her off, but in this case, we were beyond that. She had to know. "I don't think that's our decision to make. Momma should have the information. Allison is her daughter, after all. And now that she's decided to embrace her, it's time to share everything."

Carly nodded. "I just didn't want to complicate things. But if something happened to Allison and they hadn't had the chance to reunite, well, that would be tragic."

Tragic didn't begin to describe the consequences of that. Momma wouldn't recover if we lost Allison before she'd had some kind of reunion and absolution from her. "Yes. It would. Let's do a FaceTime with Momma and Nana. We'll spin things as positive as possible but still tell the truth. I promised to call this evening anyway." I'd spoken with Momma earlier on our way to the hospital.

"Hopefully Nana has fed Momma a cocktail first." Carly sighed.

"Where are they staying in town?" Jake asked.

"Nana has a man friend who has a place in the French Quarter with a couple of extra bedrooms. He's been sweet on her for years. He's offered his home to her and my parents."

"Has Daddy agreed to stay with them?" I asked Carly because this was news to me. "When did this come up?"

"Just before y'all got here. He and Momma are hashing things out with regard to travel." Carly did a big eye roll when she said it. "Who knows how that will turn out."

"Has Momma been able to keep from saying anything about all this to anyone? I mean, I expect she's gone to the priest for counsel by now, but it would be easier if word didn't get out in Cypress Bayou until Allison is out of the woods and everyone is back home." I spoke my thoughts out loud.

Jake shrugged. "I said as much to Charles when he asked where Allison might stay after she got out of the hospital. And how, when this all comes out, it's likely to cause a scandal in Cypress Bayou."

"Here's hoping we control the narrative until we can't any longer." Carly crossed her fingers as if for luck. "I need to make a call."

Carly stepped out into the hall.

There were so many moving parts here. "We don't have control over the way any of this plays out, gossip-wise, I guess. It would be nice if we did." I had a thought then, an ugly one. "Jake, does your dad know anything about all of this?"

He frowned. "I haven't said anything about Allison. All he knows is that you're in Louisiana donating bone marrow anonymously."

"Has he questioned you about that?" I'd never hidden my feelings regarding Carson Carmichael. He'd always treated me with contempt, so there wasn't a reason to show him any respect. I knew he and Nana had some kind of grudge, but she refused to discuss it. Something about that made me think it was related to Momma and Allison.

"Not really. I guess he's made a comment or two about

how odd it was that you'd come all this way to donate bone marrow to a stranger. But almost everyone made that observation initially."

"Okay. I can't help but wonder if he's somehow connected to the mystery of Allison's father. All Momma and Nana will say is he's a powerful political figure who still lives in Cypress Bayou and he's not a nice man. That puts him in Carson's realm, doesn't it? And Carson and Nana hate each other." Cypress Bayou was a town with an army of lawyers and small-time politicians who were connected to other politicians and lawyers in the parish and throughout the state. That's how things got done. Mayors, sheriffs, judges in small and large towns linked to representatives and senators in state government were supported by this network. All connected.

"Could be anybody, I guess. The town has aldermen, city council members, judges, and on and on." Jake shrugged.

"And Carson makes it his business to know all the dirty secrets, doesn't he?" I hated the path my thoughts were taking.

Jake sat down beside me on the bed and took my hand that didn't have the hateful IV. "Leah, we know Allison's father is a resident in town. Even if Carson knows all about him, what good will all this speculation do? You should focus your energy on tomorrow. And on your family. Stop worrying about the things none of us can control."

My mind was so active with conspiracy theories about Allison's dad, I'd spun off on a crazy tangent. I took a deep breath. "You're right. Hopefully, he'll just keep to himself should he find out about her."

"Yes. This is known information. Nana and your momma are keeping it private for a reason. And that reason isn't to drive you mad." Jake grinned at me.

Carly reentered the room. "I'm going to head to my friend's place and grab a couple hours' sleep, but I'll see you both bright and early. Should we call Momma before I leave?"

I dialed Momma's cell number on my phone.

Momma didn't do FaceTime well. She kept putting the phone up to her ear.

"So, what you're telling me is Allison is sick but she'll get better as soon as she gets your bone marrow?"

"Yes, Momma. That's what her doctors believe. It might take a few days, though."

"What does Jake say?"

Jake chimed in because he was still in the room. "We're all on the same page. Hoping for the best after the transplant."

"We'll be traveling down tomorrow. Leaving early."

"Is Daddy coming with you?" Carly asked this question.

"He's coming with us. Says he'd rather drive than either of us. Typical man." Momma made a face.

"You don't like to drive, Momma, so that's a good thing. And you always say Nana drives too fast."

"Well, she does. So, I guess it's better he drives us." But the look on her face said the opposite. "But I'm not sleeping with him when we get there."

"I guess that's up to you. But why won't you sleep with him? I thought he was working to take *you* back." None of this made any sense to me.

"I'm using this situation to make some changes. Bargaining. Reshaping our marriage."

Reshaping—what?

"Momma, are you reading magazines? I saw that article in *Cosmo*," Carly piped up.

"Nothing wrong with using this opportunity to redefine our path." Stranger words had never been uttered from her mouth.

"Um—your path got redefined when he found out you'd been keeping a tremendously huge secret throughout your entire marriage." It didn't hurt to point out the obvious.

"Yes, but he's already forgiven me for that." She said it as though it was such a thing of the past.

I shook my head. I dared not try to understand. "Okay, Momma. I'll see you tomorrow after my surgery."

"I love you, Leah. I know I don't say that enough, but I do. I'll say my rosary for you tonight and see you all tomorrow."

Momma kept surprising me. "Love you, too, Momma. Don't worry about me. I'll be fine. See you then."

Carly and Jake added their goodbyes.

"Anybody else feel like aliens have taken over Karen Bertrand?" I marveled out loud.

Carly shook her head. "I can't believe she's reading *Cosmo*."

"I'm staying out of this one." Jake held his hands up as if he were out of his depth. Which he so was.

"I'll see y'all in the morning." Carly stood and grabbed her purse, then bent down to hug me.

"Thanks for all your help. See you tomorrow." We'd gotten word that my surgery was going to be at seven a.m.

When Carly left, Jake scooched me over so he could lie beside me on the bed. I had to say, I didn't mind it a bit. His warmth and nearness took the edge off my nerves.

"Are you staying here with me tonight?"

"If you don't mind sharing your bed." He kissed the top of my head.

"As long as you don't snore."

I COULDN'T SAY if either of us snored because the next thing I remembered was waking up to bright lights and what seemed like organized chaos. I had time enough to make a quick trip to the bathroom before being whisked away to pre-op where I stripped out of my current gown into another, sans panties. I was hooked to a blood pressure monitor, an IV bag filled with some kind of fluids, fitted with a pulse oximeter on my finger, and made to sign more documents. The anesthesiologist stopped by and told me I could die from anesthesia though I probably wouldn't.

Next, the surgeon popped in and introduced herself and then explained the procedure. She was a tiny black woman with kind golden eyes. Before she left, she said, "I'd like to thank you for donating bone marrow to a stranger. It's not something everyone is willing to do."

I had to bite my tongue not to spew all the whys I was doing this. To confess how personal this was, and had become, for me. "I'm honored to do it."

"Well, we're going to make this experience as painless as

possible for you."

Jake appeared from the other side of the curtain that had been pulled around me for privacy. The area was a collection of small cubicles with all the required equipment rolled into them. There were heart monitors, computer stations, and lots of sets of drawers that held all the things, all shrink-wrapped and ready to deploy.

"Hi there. Don't you look cozy?" He sat down in the chair next to my bed.

I smiled at him from under the warm silver blanket that looked like something from outer space, provided by my very own nurse. "I think maybe they're buttering me up with something in my IV."

Jake laughed and glanced up at the IV bag. "That's probably true."

"The surgeon just left."

"Yes. I saw that you have Dr. Boutte. She's an amazing surgeon. I've known her for several years. You're in great hands."

"Have you checked on Allison?"

Jake nodded. "She's holding steady. Nothing has changed since yesterday."

"I'm assuming that's good. We couldn't expect her to get any better until the transplant, right?"

Jake shook his head. "She doesn't have an immune system to fight and get better yet, so no worse is good."

"Hello?" Carly came through the curtain, making the area much smaller. "They said I could come back and say hi before you went into surgery."

"I'll go out while the two of you talk." Jake excused himself. "Be right outside."

"I couldn't let you go under without putting my face in front of yours to tell you that I love you." Carly leaned down and smacked a wet kiss on my forehead.

"I'm so glad you did. I know the rest of the family will be here at some point, so keep them in line, would you?"

Carly laughed. "Don't worry about a thing. I'll make sure the entire Tulane cancer wing doesn't think we belong on *The Jerry Springer Show*. Wasn't that what Momma used to watch when we were kids? I used to think we'd fit right in."

"You know that show was canceled a couple years ago, right?" I pointed out.

"You get my meaning. I'll see you on the other side of surgery." She waved as she disappeared behind the curtain.

My phone rang inside my purse, which was inside a bag with my clothes provided by the hospital. Jake came in just in time to fish out the phone and hand it to me before I missed the call. "Hello?"

"Are you avoiding me?" It was Jenn.

I grimaced because I hadn't spoken with her since we'd found out about Allison. I should say I'd spoken with her, but I hadn't filled her in because we'd all sworn not to tell anyone outside the family. "Of course not. I'm so glad you called because I'm about to go into surgery."

"You're *what*? I called early to wake your butt up and drag you to Pilates again. Holy cannoli, where the heck are you?"

"We're down in New Orleans. Things have gone a bit haywire in the past couple days, and we left town after we got a call that my bone marrow recipient's condition had deteriorated and required pushing up the donation."

"I can't believe I'm just hearing about this." Jenn sounded distraught. "We're just reconnecting and now you're having surgery."

"I'm gonna be fine. A day in the hospital, two at most. I'll call you or have someone call you just as soon as it's done. We do have a lot to talk about, though. So, hold that thought, and we'll catch up as soon as I get out of surgery."

"Okay. Now I'm curious. But I'm more worried about you."

"Jake's here and says he'll call you when I'm out." Jake nodded that he would as I said the words.

"Jake's with you? Are you two—" I could hear the burning curiosity in Jenn's voice.

"They're about to take me back. Talk soon." I hung up then because I didn't want to stay on the phone as Jenn demanded the truth. I wasn't ready to tell that truth because I didn't know it yet. It was far too complicated beyond the moment to think about now.

CHAPTER TWENTY-TWO

Jake

THE PROCEDURE ITSELF only took an hour and a half once a patient was under sedation. It was the longest ninety minutes of Jake's life. He paced. He stared out the window. He checked his watch. *What's taking so long?*

He stayed out of range and had had to walk away from Leah's family due to her mother's compulsive need to ask *him* what was taking so long. With his own nerves stretched like guitar strings, it didn't bode well having her on his last one.

Normally, he was a pretty amiable guy. But not today. The waiting was maddening. The realization hit Jake that if anything happened to Leah while she was under anesthesia, he wouldn't be able to go on. It nearly brought him to his knees.

He'd always loved her. Since they'd been kids. But somehow, since she'd been home and they'd crashed through their wall of truth, as brutal and terrible as the truths were, their souls had found home with one another. And Jake couldn't survive with a homeless soul again. Leah was his home. He wasn't at all certain how they would work out the separate continent thing, but somehow they would.

Jake was a physician, and he understood that this was a minor procedure. He knew Leah was healthy and the likelihood of anything tragic happening to her now was almost nonexistent. He was just having a moment.

"Dude, you look like shit. Has something happened?"

"What?" Jake looked up to see real concern in Tanner's expression. "No, it's all fine."

"What's wrong with you, then? You look like somebody died."

"I don't know what I'd do if anything happened to her, man." Jake and Tanner sat down in chairs that lined the corridor.

"Get a grip, Jake. Nothing's going to happen." Tanner was his voice of reason, and clearly Jake needed one right now.

"I know. But it hit me while I've been waiting for her to come out of surgery that she's my whole world." Even Jake could hear how pathetic he sounded. Thank God his brother had arrived.

Tanner put an arm around him. "I thought this was something you already knew."

"Yeah. We had a long...talk. Things are better between us now."

"So, you need to splash some cold water on your face and pull it together. She's gonna be just fine, and you know it."

Jake stared at Tanner a second then asked, "What are you doing here?"

"Drove down to give a little moral support, man. Heard the secret sister isn't doing so well."

"Thanks for coming." Jake was glad for something else to

focus his thoughts on. "No, she isn't. Hopefully getting the marrow in her quickly will get her back on track."

"How soon until you know?"

"Soon. A day or two after donation should give us some indication."

"*Tan-nuh Cah-michael*, as I live and breathe," Carly affected her best Scarlett O'Hara when she came around the corner and spotted Tanner.

"Hey, squirt. Did they take off your braces already?"

"Bite me. What are you in town for?" she asked him.

"Came to check on y'all. How's your momma holding up?" Tanner and Carly really did like each other. They just had to get the insults out of the way before behaving like adults.

"She's our momma. You know. Lots happening there. At least she and Daddy seem to be able to sit in the same room without drawing blood at the moment."

"I'm guessing that's an improvement." Tanner shrugged.

Carly smiled then. "We'll withhold judgment until we're sure it's safe."

"Guess I'd better go say hello." He stood and walked toward the waiting area, leaving Carly and Jake alone. The two families had known each other forever. As in, their whole lives. So had most everyone else in Cypress Bayou.

"Seriously, everybody okay?" Jake asked her.

"They're okay. Nana's keeping them in line." Carly paced and sighed. "How much longer?"

He checked his watch again. "Should be anytime now."

❧

Leah

I HEARD MYSELF moan before I realized I was awake. Because it hurt.

"Hey there, Leah. Can you open your eyes for me? As soon as I see your pupils, I'll give you something in your IV for pain." A man's voice permeated my brain.

I opened my eyes for the promise of pain meds, but the bright light made me snap them shut. "Ooh."

"Sorry about that. They make me do it. Light's off now. You can open." I trusted that to be true, so I tried again.

"My back hurts." And my throat was dry, so my voice was super croaky.

"Here, let's sit you up a little and you can try a sip of water. Just a sip at first so we can see if you're nauseous."

The movement of the bed hurt my back. "Ow."

"I know it hurts. We're working on both problems right now. Water, then meds."

I sipped through the straw tentatively though I wanted to gulp.

"How's that?" the hot scrub-wearing dude asked.

I nodded.

"Wonderful. Now, let's reward you with a shot of the good stuff." He uncapped a syringe and slowly fed it into my IV port. Almost immediately, I levitated off the bed. Or that's what it felt like. I wasn't sure if my back still hurt.

"Yes, it works like a dream, doesn't it? By tonight, we'll begin pain meds by mouth. But for now, you get this. I'm gonna go get Dr. Jake, who I hear has been wearing out our tile out in the waiting room. Is that all right with you? Then, we'll let your poor momma come and lay eyes on you."

I nodded and smiled at the lovely man. Was he the duke on that Netflix show Carly and I'd just watched? *Bridgerton*? Why was Simon at my bedside? As he walked away, I wanted to call to his back not to leave. Oh yeah, Jake. He was cute, too. I liked the magic pain meds.

"Hey, you." Jake appeared beside my bed after what seemed like a second.

"You're almost as cute as Simon, don't worry."

His expression was mildly curious. "Who's Simon? Should I be jealous?"

Simon stood beside Jake, so I pointed. "Him. He's Simon."

"I think her meds are working nicely now. She was feeling pretty rough once the anesthesia wore off."

"Ah. Got it. So, how are you feeling?" Jake sat down beside me and held my hand.

"Great. Whatever was in that shot worked. But I feel like I'm floating off the bed."

Simon spoke to Jake. "Family can come back two at a time until we get her in a room for the night. I'll be at the nurse's station if you need me, or she can use the call button."

I gave Simon a thumbs-up and a gracious smile.

I WASN'T FLOATING nearly as high a few hours later when the pain returned and I was back in my room. "I'm sore."

"I know. They want you to take painkillers by mouth so they can take out your IV, which means they'll wear off every four to six hours." Jake was there, beside my bed, seeing to my needs. I'd seen my parents and Nana briefly when I hadn't been feeling any pain in recovery. Carly had promised to keep them occupied until this evening so I could get some rest.

"But it hasn't been four hours yet, has it?" I asked. It was a bone-deep ache I felt, unlike anything I'd experienced before.

"Not quite, but let's see what else they can do for you in the meantime. There are other meds they might be able to bridge between doses that'll help you get comfortable." He pressed my nurse's call button.

As my doctor, I'd thought Jake would have more say in how all of this went. But once we'd gotten me admitted, the Tulane oncology crew took over and Jake was relegated to sitting it out. This handoff had surprised him, too, he'd admitted. But this specialty wing of the hospital utilized only their doctors and staff.

There was a knock on the door as I turned on my side with Jake's help, and he gently wedged a pillow beneath my hip. "Hello? Can we come in?" Momma, Daddy, and Nana chose that moment to visit. Of course they didn't wait for permission.

"You're a little pale, Leah." Momma frowned as she approached my bed, then she turned to Jake. "Isn't she a little pale?"

"She's in some pain right now. I was just about to call her nurse about it."

Nana patted my hand. "Should we come back later?"

Momma wasn't having it. "What's the difference? She'll still be in pain whether we're here or not."

Daddy looked like he wanted to object to Momma's comment but instead addressed me. "Can they do something to make you more comfortable, Sugar?"

I smiled, despite the jackhammer inside my pelvic bone. "Maybe. Jake's checking."

"I'll just go ask at the nurse's station." Jake slid out the door. The place had gotten crowded.

"They won't let us anywhere near Allison. Carly has to call her nurse to check on her status. You would think that her own family wouldn't get the runaround." Momma was apparently already behaving high-handedly where Allison was concerned. "And apparently, *I'm* not on the approved list to ask questions about her condition."

"She's in an isolation room because she is susceptible to infection, Karen. Remember? That's why we can't see her. Everyone here has been very kind." Nana's patience with our mother was so impressive. "And you aren't on the list because she didn't have your name to put on it at the time."

Momma frowned. "That's because y'all were working behind my back at the time."

I wondered how Daddy was faring during all this chaos. He was standing in the back corner of my hospital room, allowing the women to do what they did. My heart ached for him. I knew how worried he was about me even though I wasn't in any danger and the surgery was over. He hated to see me in pain. Always had. When I'd been a little girl and had the flu, he'd paced and fretted until my fever had broken.

"They're supposed to call with any change in her condition, so we should trust that." Nana gave Momma a meaningful look. Not sure if Momma caught it.

My shift nurse came in then, her eyebrows going up at seeing the number of folks in the room. "Looks like y'all are having a party in here."

Momma piped up—of course. "We're her family. Can you make her feel better?"

Mona, my nurse, a consummate pro, was likely used to dealing with the Karen Bertrands of the world every other day. She held up a tiny white cup with what I assumed had a pill to give me some relief. Too bad it wouldn't shut Momma up. "I've got just the thing."

"Thanks, Mona."

"You get some rest if you can. They'll let you out of here tomorrow sometime if your bloodwork checks out. We're going to get you up and walking the halls after your pain is better. It will help with the stiffness."

I nodded. I knew that after so many kinds of surgeries, ones far more serious than I'd had, they had patients up and walking within hours. Staying in a bed made one want to stay in a bed, I guessed.

"Okay, we've laid eyes on her. You heard the nurse, let's clear out of here and let Leah get some rest." Daddy made the declaration, and when he did, he began ushering Momma forward.

It was surprising, his *handling* of the situation. Momma spun around as if she were going to argue, but Daddy had a no-nonsense look about him, both on his face and in his bearing that booked no argument.

There was a tense moment in the room where it could've gone either way. But surprisingly, Momma leaned down and kissed my cheek. "Your father has decided it's best for us to leave you in peace now. Call if you need anything. And let us know when they release you tomorrow. Maybe we can meet for brunch." Momma said this in a cheerful tone. She loved a good brunch.

"It's not likely that Leah will be up for brunch tomorrow. I'm planning to bring her back to the bed-and-breakfast so she can recover for a day or two." Jake slid back into the room during this exchange and stepped up to respond to Momma's suggestion.

She nodded. "Oh, okay. I guess you shouldn't push yourself, then. Still, let us know when you get released. We're hoping to stay in town to meet Allison."

"It might be weeks before she's strong enough to have visitors, so you need to prepare yourself to be patient." Jake spoke as a doctor, but also as my advocate. Momma's strong suit was anything but patience.

Her shoulders slumped a little. "Well, we can't stay here for weeks. We'll have to leave and come back, I guess."

"Maybe we can make her a video from our family in a day or two and all introduce ourselves and give her some encouragement." It was a suggestion that might work.

"That's a great idea. Let's talk about it some more with Carly." Nana agreed with me, so that helped my cause.

My dinner tray arrived just as the crowd dispersed. We'd ordered an extra for Jake since he planned to be here. We ate our blackened catfish, green beans, and dirty rice with the

TV turned down low.

"Tanner's in town. Said to tell you hello."

I nodded instead of answering because my mouth was full. I wasn't exactly surprised by this fact. Tanner often did business in New Orleans with clients.

"He came down to hang out with me during your surgery. And he has a couple clients to meet with while he's in town."

"That was nice of him." My entire family had done the same. "Did he think you needed him there?"

Jake set his tray on the side table. "Leah, I was a nervous wreck. You'd have thought I'd never seen the inside of a hospital waiting room. I nearly embarrassed myself in front of your family. I had to stay away from them so they wouldn't see how worried I was."

"Why were you so worried?" His confession surprised me. Usually he was so composed involving anything medical.

Jake shrugged. "Because it occurred to me while you were under anesthesia how vital you are to me. And that if anything happened to you, no matter how unlikely, I wouldn't know how to go on." His expression was so vulnerable. So sincere. "That's why Tanner was there. He knows how much I've always loved you and still do."

My heart stopped beating for a second. *How could I have doubted him?* Or thought for a moment he had feelings for anyone else? "I love you, too, Jake." A warm tear slipped down my cheek.

"So, what do we do about it?"

I shook my head sadly. "I don't know."

NANA ALWAYS SAID that there were no unsolvable problems in this world besides death. I questioned that as I left the hospital with Jake. How could I spend my life with him when I lived in Paris, France? His career was firmly built in Cypress Bayou, Louisiana, complete with family, land on which to build our dream home, and a newly signed contract for the next two years at the hospital.

That left me to figure out how to own and run half of a successful Parisian art gallery an ocean away. I had a flat in a nice section of the city, not far from the gallery. I had friends. What I didn't have was the love of my life there with me. And I'd made a death vow to Alaine to guard his life's work. Well, I'd made it after he'd already died, but it felt very much like something I couldn't break.

I didn't want to leave Paris. I loved it there. But I wanted Jake.

At the moment, though, the pain in my lower back was pretty bad, so I went from fretting about my impossible situation to wishing I would stop hurting.

"Are you okay?" Jake could see on my face that I wasn't myself.

I frowned. "I wish I could get comfortable."

"The medicine should be kicking in soon. I'm sorry." He kissed the top of my head. I knew he felt helpless. We were upstairs in the bedroom of the B&B. Jake had picked up some coffee and beignets as a treat, hoping it would improve my spirits.

My phone buzzed, and I saw Carly's number appear on

screen.

I tried to sound cheerful. "Hey there. What's up?"

"I called to check on you. That's what."

"I'm hurting some, but these beignets aren't hurting my feelings."

"Well, I have some news. Allison is showing signs of responding to the bone marrow. I just heard from Charles, who just got the first word from her care team. They are 'guardedly optimistic,' I believe is the term he used."

"That's fantastic." A tightness in my chest that I didn't realize had been there loosened a little. I breathed out a big sigh. I covered the mic and repeated what she'd said to Jake. He gave two thumbs up.

"Have you let Momma know yet?"

"I'm about to meet them for an early dinner at Brennan's. Nana's friend got us in for a last-minute reservation. That's why we're going so early." Brennan's stayed booked up year-round, so Nana's friend must've had some clout, even for an early reservation.

"Sounds amazing. I wish we could join y'all." I had no intention of going out anywhere tonight. Maybe tomorrow I would be up for it.

"Me, too. You'll be missed. You know how much Momma loves Brennan's."

I laughed. Brennan's had always been her favorite restaurant in the city. "Have some bananas Foster for me."

"You know it. We'll be celebrating good news tonight."

I felt slightly left out. It was the same sensation I frequently got when I spoke to someone in the family while I'd been in Paris, as they gathered together at home and I couldn't. I'd told myself I hadn't missed it. But now, being here, I knew that was a lie. I was a part of this messed-up, mixed-up family.

As I hung up with Carly, Jake asked, "What's wrong? Are you hurting?"

"No. The medicine is working. I guess it's that I wish I was with them. You know, having dinner, arguing with Momma. Just being with my family like we used to."

"I'm not enough, huh?" Jake nuzzled my ear.

"Oh, you're too much." I laughed. "But you know what I mean. I've been away from them—and you—for so long."

"I know they're glad to have you back here. And you know how I feel about it."

"I don't know how to leave again." It hit me that leaving meant leaving all of them. I had a new sister now I hadn't even met. *How could I leave now?* Not this minute, but very soon.

CHAPTER TWENTY-THREE

J AKE SPENT THE night in the bed with me, holding me gently. I tried not to think about my impending departure within the next week or so and just focus on enjoying his body next to mine.

By morning, I was still sore, but the pain wasn't so overwhelming. I was relieved that this recovery wasn't going to be a long-lasting thing because there were too many things I wanted to do in the coming days.

"How about we do some walking around today? Not too much, but it would help to get out and move around."

The idea came to me in a flash. "Can we go out to the Bywater area? I hear there are some new galleries and restaurants out there." It was an up-and-coming area of the city where they'd begun revitalizing old unused warehouses. It was a Mississippi riverside mix of arts, industry, and residential life. I'd been out of the country but through friends and contacts had heard great things, though I'd not yet had the pleasure of seeing it for myself.

"Sure. Sounds good to me. I've only been there once for dinner. It's a cool area. We should take my truck, though. You'll be more comfortable."

I nodded in agreement. "Makes sense." We'd always loved taking the streetcars through the city, but Bywater was pretty far and would require a series of stops and even getting on a bus or two.

I was slow moving getting ready, but we were out the door within an hour. Once my over-the-counter meds kicked in, I felt pretty good. I might regret it later, but getting out and exploring gave me something to look forward to.

Jake put a call in to check on Allison. She was holding steady and her numbers were still slightly better than before the transplant, so the doctors were guarded in their optimism. I didn't think I could have gone out and enjoyed my day unless I knew she was doing okay.

We arrived about forty-five minutes later. Bywater was lodged between the far eastern edge of the French Quarter and the western section of the Ninth Ward, so we had to drive through lots of traffic lights. There was no getting anywhere quickly in New Orleans. It took as long as it took. The smell of salt and fish hung in the air. Bywater sat along a series of railroad tracks near the natural levee on the Mississippi. We'd passed rows and rows of colorful shotgun houses and old Greek Revival homes.

I could feel a tingle of excitement. "What an amazing place. It's like stepping back in time while stepping forward." I was in awe over the repurposing of the old warehouses for art lofts and galleries and recording studios. I'd read about it, but to see it in person was pretty awesome. There were cafés and restaurants alongside other retails spaces.

Jake nodded. "It's so vibrant."

I also noticed several spaces for sale or lease. It got me thinking. As we made our way around, holding hands and appreciating the progress and non-progress of the area, my brain worked in the background. There were people all around. Chatting at cafés, strolling along the riverbank. Locals and obvious tourists. Not like in the French Quarter where it was a frenetic rush of selfies and noise. This was busy but not chaotic.

I could recognize artists when I spotted them. With paint on their hands and clothes even when they weren't painting. They stared at the sky and out at the water, imagining the next canvas. Many of these people were artists and dreamers. I'd heard of the working spaces offered to art students and those who simply loved to create.

My brain worked.

Sitting here made me think about Alaine and the gallery in Paris. And how much I loved it there. And how much I loved it here and in Cypress Bayou. I was so at odds with my life right now. Coming to understand that I had one life to live and that it was passing by so quickly made my heart speed up. Made me want to *do* something. But I couldn't do anything right now. *Could I?*

I said nothing to Jake, who kept placing a hand on my back or shoulder from time to time and raising an eyebrow or asking if I was okay.

We sat and took a break from exploring at a small café on the riverfront. The mighty Mississippi's water was so dark and so deep. I didn't like to look down into the river because of the way it churned and swirled. As a child, I'd heard of people falling off ships or barges and never resurfacing.

I shuddered thinking of it.

"You good?"

"Yes. The river intimidates me."

"Me, too. It's a force of nature. Bigger than any of us."

But something about it was primal and exciting, too. Sitting here beside it had me getting worked up about something in a good way. I wasn't quite sure what that was—yet.

We wandered through a couple of galleries and then through the open-air covered space where artists had set up their paints and canvases. A model wearing almost nothing posed for artists. Others worked from photographs. Some painted outside since the day was nice, though slightly overcast, painting street scenes. And my brain worked still.

"Are you getting tired?"

I nodded. "A little. Maybe a nap at the B&B, then dinner with my family? Carly mentioned heading out to the lakefront for shrimp po'boys at R&O's around six." R&O's was a bit of a dive, but the po'boys were our favorites anywhere in the city.

"That sounds like a great plan." Jake hadn't ever turned down a shrimp po'boy that I was aware.

Jake

WHEN THEY RETURNED to the Bergerons' place, Leah took a dose of pain relievers and instantly fell asleep. Jake wasn't tired, so he decided to have a run while she napped.

Their morning had been nice and relaxing, but he could tell Leah had a lot on her mind. Jake did, too, and likely those things were similar.

Tanner called as Jake neared mile two. He put his brother on headphones. "Hey, man. What's up?"

"Are you winded?"

"Running."

"Ah. Wanna meet for a beer? I just got out of a meeting uptown not far from where you're staying." Jake knew Tanner would be in town for a couple days on business.

"Sure. I'm just out while Leah's napping. I've got time for a quick one. Better make it an outdoor dive. I'm pretty sweaty." The bars were casual and numerous all over New Orleans, just like the cafés.

"Ms. Mae's, corner of Napoleon and Magazine. I'll grab the beers and meet you outside."

"I know where it is." There were a couple two-tops outside amid the foot traffic that rustled by, if Jake remembered correctly. Medical school here had been a series of places to study and places to eat and drink. Jake had worked hard but hadn't refrained from enjoying what New Orleans provided in the way of fun, food, and bars. That would have been a waste.

"I'm about a block away. See you in a few." He'd been running along a less populated area along the river close to where they would meet, not wanting to stray far from the B&B in case Leah needed him for anything. She was obviously fine, but it was a weird time and he hated to be out of pocket should there be an emergency with anyone in her family.

"Wow. You are a mess. Glad we're here in New Orleans because nobody cares how you look or smell." Tanner was dressed in a sport coat and slacks straight from a meeting, so the contrast between them was pretty stark. "You'll forgive me if we don't hug."

"You sure? I'm feeling the love now." Jake pretended to go in for a big sweaty bear hug.

Tanner stepped back to avoid him. "Hey, watch the jacket, dude. I only brought one. Don't drip on it."

Jake had worked up quite a sweat, and the cold Abita was perfect timing. "Now, if I only had a towel."

His brother handed him a stack of napkins.

"Good enough." He wiped off his face. Tanner handed him a beer, and they clinked the bottles, something they'd always done. "Something on your mind?" Jake could tell there was by Tanner's manner.

"I heard from Carson last night. He's pushing hard on this Allison thing. Asking lots of questions. I don't know who her father is, but I think he must. I know Karen Bertrand's having a surprise daughter isn't gonna stay secret for long, but the speculation about who the father is will begin as soon as the news breaks around town."

"True enough. What else did he say?"

"Just something about not letting the cat out of the bag regarding who 'the girl's' father is or people would get hurt."

"What the hell did he mean by that cryptic bullshit?" Jake could always find new levels of disgust for his sperm donor.

"How long have you known our father? He tosses that out and then refuses to explain. Just says to warn Leah's family to keep their mouths shut. Especially Karen and Nana."

As connected in town as Carson was, it shouldn't have surprised either of them that he had inside information regarding Allison's dad. Plus, he'd been around Cypress Bayou around the time Karen would've gotten pregnant. The secret of her pregnancy had stayed buried this long, which was no small miracle in a place that thrived on rooting out every tiny hint of scandal and embarrassing information. That meant whomever Allison's dad was, he'd never told anyone—or anyone besides someone infinitely trustworthy. Which meant Carson was possibly one or the other.

"Do you think *he* could be Allison's dad?" Tanner spoke the words out loud that both of them had likely been thinking. "It would explain some things. Like why he and Nana despise each other."

Jake frowned even harder than he already was. "Of course I've thought of it. But I just can't imagine it. Carson would've found a way to use the information already to his benefit somehow. Don't you think?"

"I don't know how he would do that, but it's almost adding up. I guess you can never tell with him. He's always got an agenda, so you're right about that." Tanner took a swig of his beer. They sat for a moment, not speaking. "Why do you think Karen or Nana refuse to tell the family? Surely they trust their own girls."

Jake had wondered this but hadn't asked Leah yet.

"Maybe you should start that conversation when you get back to Leah, seeing how Carson is on a mission to stir shit up."

Jake nodded. "I'll do it. Nobody wants trouble on their doorstep in the form of Carson. And we both know he won't stop until he gets what he wants."

"Whatever that is." Tanner raised a hand then as if something just occurred to him. "You know, it could be he just thinks he knows something and can't stand that he isn't in on things."

"That *could* be."

Leah

I WOKE UP with a not-yet-fully-formed idea. *The* idea. The one that might work if I could figure it out. My brain had been operating while I slept. But there were so many details that would have to be seen about. I couldn't say it out loud yet because I didn't dare to hope or give hope to anyone else. Because it would be unfair to do so. This was going to be hard to keep to myself. Maybe I could run it by Carly. But when?

I could make calls and inquire about some things. That would help me to know if this might become a reality. I'd surreptitiously taken a couple photos that included the real estate signs when we'd been in Bywater. I'd had a tingle even then. I looked into the other room. Jake didn't appear to be around.

Just as I began to dial the number, I heard Jake's key in the door. These old doors didn't have electronic keys, just the old-fashioned metal locks. In this instance I was glad because I didn't have to explain who I was talking to as I quickly stopped what I was doing.

"Hey there. You're all sweaty." And gorgeous. Which made me smile and more resolved than ever to make this work. If not Bywater, then someplace else in the city. I would make this work. It was a solid idea. I had plenty of Alaine's inherited money, and he would've loved this idea.

"How are you feeling? Any pain?"

I shook my head. "Not much. But that nap was illuminating."

Jake gave me a strange look. "I've not heard a nap referred to quite like that before."

I smiled at him, still not ready to reveal my possible plan. "Let's just say I'm feeling more positive than I have in a while."

"A bit cryptic, but I like the sound of it."

I didn't add to it. "How was your run? Looks like you got your sweat on."

He looked down at his soaked shirt. "Wanna join me in the shower?" His eyebrows did a dance.

"Mmm, so tempting, but I'll let you take care of that yourself." I gave him a little shove toward the bathroom. He turned back and gave a hurt look.

I could make a phone call or two while he showered, though *not* joining him was a sacrifice. "Sorry, I need to call Carly." Since I'd just had surgery, that was an obvious excuse.

"Yeah. Okay. We should talk when I get out of the shower. I met Tanner for a beer around the corner after my run. Carson is asking questions."

I did *not* like the sound of that. At all. "Yikes. Okay. Get clean, and we'll talk."

The second he turned on the water and I heard him step into the shower, I pressed Send on the number I'd entered into my phone.

"Hi, this is Josie with Latter and Blum Realtors. How can I help you?"

"Hi, Josie, I'm calling to ask about an art warehouse space in Bywater—"

I didn't finish because Josie grabbed hold of the conversation like a farmer's wife grabbed a Christmas goose. By the neck. "Dahlin', that's the *best* property, isn't it? And it's a steal if it's what you're lookin' for. Just listed it last week. Right by the river, ya know."

"Yes, I was out there earlier today. Is the zoning compatible for a gallery? Is there living space above?"

"That's the thing about the area. It's total mixed use. The zoning allows the owner to decide how the space is used. Retail, yes, but there's a loft overhead with a darlin' apartment. It's big, with brick walls and so much light, ya know?"

I could feel my heart beating faster. My breath was coming out like a panting puppy. "What are they asking?"

"A million five, but all is negotiable, dahlin'."

I'd figured it would be at least a million. "Can you find out *how* negotiable from the seller? I haven't hired a Realtor yet, but I'm just beginning my search."

"Sure thing, plum. I'll give you a call as soon as I find out."

"Can you text me?" I didn't want to get the Realtor's call at an awkward moment and have to answer questions if I wasn't prepared to do so.

"Well, of course." We exchanged information.

CHAPTER TWENTY-FOUR

Since R&O's was out in Old Metairie on Lake Pontchartrain, we had to drive there in Jake's truck. It wasn't far, but it required getting on the interstate and out of the city proper.

"So, what did Tanner have to say?" I was dying to know.

"He said that Carson is overly curious about your bone marrow recipient. We haven't given him any information, but he's insinuating that he knows something and insisting we tell him about her."

"As in, you think he might be Allison's dad?" This was almost too much.

"Tanner and I think it's possible because the age is right, but if he knew he'd fathered a child with your mother, don't you think he'd have come out and said something about it by now? Or your mother would have?"

"After all these years, I would guess that secret might have come to light. And I think Momma would have forbid you and me dating when we were younger. But she never seemed to have an issue with it, other than that you were a boy and bound to bring me to ruin."

"She was right about that, wasn't she?" Jake snickered but then asked, his tone becoming more serious, "So, why do you think she and Nana are keeping who Allison's father is locked up so tight, even with you girls?"

I had to think about that for a minute. "The reason the women said it was essential to keep quiet was because they were threatened by the father, or maybe the political influence of the family. But honestly, I can't imagine they wouldn't trust us with the name."

Jake flipped on his right blinker at the Old Metairie/Lakefront exit. "Tanner and I were wondering about it, and with Carson dogging him with questions about who the bone marrow recipient is, it made us think there's some connection."

"Besides the obvious that's probably not the obvious, what do you think that could be?"

"Maybe it's a friend of his or a client with a stake in the information *not* getting out."

"Or it's him."

"Yes, the obvious."

I thought for a minute how tough all this might be for Daddy. Learning about Allison was one thing, but finding out who the mystery man was who'd fathered her might've been more than he could handle.

I shared this with Jake. "Maybe the reason they aren't talking about Allison's dad is so Daddy won't find out or so he won't get upset. What if it's somebody he knows really well? How awkward would that be?"

"I hate to say I hadn't thought of that, but I honestly hadn't."

We pulled into the parking lot. It was an unpretentious diner-ish place. New Orleans was like that. Some of the best restaurants in the city boasted a meager façade. We were a

few minutes early but never earlier than Momma and
Daddy. If you weren't forty-five minutes ahead of schedule,
you were late. We would need to remember to tell Allison
that.

"So, unless they bring it up at dinner, no talk of Allison's
father, okay?"

"Deal."

THE RESTAURANT WAS loud. The floors were tile, the
tablecloths were red-checkered vinyl, and the napkins were
paper. The sounds of voices, the clinking of ice in glasses and
silverware, and chairs scraping across the floor added to the
volume. It was a large open diner that served mostly fried
seafood and po'boys.

Momma, Nana, Carly, and Daddy were seated near the
back. The place was nearly full already even though it wasn't
even six o'clock. I locked eyes with Carly and raised my
eyebrows in question to get the dynamic for how things were
going with the women and between Momma and Daddy.
She gave an infinitesimal eye roll in return, which I translated to be, *Not spectacular.*

"Hi, darlin', how are you feeling?" Nana looked me up
and down to take stock.

"Pretty good. I'm still a little stiff and sore, but as long as
I keep a dose of anti-inflammatory in me, I seem to do pretty
well."

"Well, you look right as spring rain, dear." Daddy stood
as we approached and kissed me on the cheek.

Momma appeared slightly miffed, but since it was her usual state of being, I wasn't especially concerned about it. "Hi, Momma. How's it going?" I braced to hear my answer.

"Well, the water pressure here is the absolute worst, you know. I can't do a darn thing with my hair. And Mother and I are sleeping on a queen mattress that I swear *has* to be thirty years old. Your father offered to take the pullout sofa in the office. It's probably more comfortable than what we were given." She sniffed and shot Daddy a resentful look like it was all his fault.

I could imagine why he took the pullout and left the women together. He'd traveled with Momma enough to know she didn't do it well or gracefully. "I'm sleeping just fine. You ladies are welcome to switch beds with me if you'd like." He said this without a detectable hint of sarcasm or nastiness.

The waiter fortuitously stopped by and dispersed a tray filled with short clear glasses of iced water beaded with moisture that had obviously been sitting for a while. "Hey there, folks. What can we get y'all tonight?"

We all ordered shrimp po'boys, so that made it easy. Momma liked hers with cocktail sauce on the side and no pickles. Half of us ordered a beer, and the other half ordered root beer. "Coming right up."

Carly spoke as soon as the waiter turned to go. "I talked with Charles just before I left to come here, and he said that Allison is in good spirits today, according to someone on her medical team he spoke with, though she's hoarse and her voice is pretty much shot."

There was a collective sigh around the table. They were

all still here because of Allison. Well, me and Allison, but since I'd had the surgery and now was doing well, I think my family was hanging around the city waiting to hear some definitive news on her condition.

I spoke up. "That's a relief. I'm glad to know she's hanging in there mentally. It's loud in here, but maybe we can do a quick video by the lakefront after we eat." I suggested it because there wasn't much else to do for Allison at the moment.

Nana followed up with support for the plan. "Yes. That's a great idea since we're all here together. I believe she would like to see our faces and hear our voices. What a fine way for her to know who we are."

"I don't know if this is how I want to meet my daughter for the first time. It seems so impersonal." Momma was skeptical about the idea.

"You can write down what you want to say if it helps. If that will make it easier for you. This is something to encourage Allison and brighten her spirits. Remember, she recently lost her mother, so she's likely feeling very alone while going through this extremely challenging fight." Carly, as usual, gave a good suggestion and pointed out that this was to help someone else.

"Well, maybe I could make a few notes on my grocery list." Momma picked up her purse, stuffed full of breath mints to nails files to Lord knew what else. It weighed upward of twenty pounds.

Daddy cleared his throat. "I hope I'm not being too presumptuous, but I'd like to introduce myself in the video, if you think that's all right. If I understand correctly, this young woman is alone with no family in the world. I've done a decent job of being a dad to you girls, so maybe your sister will allow me to step into that role for her. If you think that's all right."

Tears clogged my throat and threatened to freefall. I dared not look at anyone else, or I would bawl there in the middle of R&O's.

I was shocked when Momma responded. "Bob, I can't think of anyone better to welcome Allison into our family. I failed her as a newborn and even later when I didn't open up her adoption out of fear. You're her hero, willing to take on a new daughter at this stage in our lives. She couldn't do any better."

I grabbed the napkin from beside my silverware, glad it was a paper one. I think everyone at the table did the same.

That was my family in a nutshell. Lots of nuts and nut-shells all mixed together. One minute we were hugging and kissing, the next we were having an intervention. Now that we'd discovered a new member, well, the poor dear would need a crash course in all the many and varied nutshells we were.

Once we'd moaned and groaned our way delightfully through overstuffed fried shrimp po'boys with french fries and hush puppies, we waddled across the road on foot to the seawall where the lake was whitecapping against its banks.

The wind was blowing our hair around, but it was nice to be outside in the fresh air against the backdrop of the Harbor Marina.

We set up Carly's phone to record, since it was the new-est model with the best camera. None of us was especially shy about speaking on camera, but this was a very personal and emotional thing, so we each said a few words to Allison in private. She had Allison's number and would send the recordings to her.

We then took a group selfie to send so she could see us all together. Our family. Her family. Her support system who would be there for her because when you get one of us, you get us all. I hoped we didn't overwhelm her with *us*.

But I would be going back to Paris. Or would I?

One Week Later

I'D BEEN CLEARED to travel back to Paris. My blood levels were close to normal again, and I was nearly pain free besides an occasional twinge in my lower back. I knew there was no avoiding it. I still hadn't discussed my bright idea with Jake that might get me back here permanently. I was afraid to raise his hopes and mine. This was something that required all the moving parts to fall into place on two continents.

It also meant buying and selling property internationally, taking into consideration currency exchange. I would need to move money from Europe to the US, which meant I would lose a great deal by doing so. There were a lot of things to consider.

Allison was slowly improving and would hopefully continue to do so in the coming weeks. This was a marathon for her, and we knew to expect setbacks along her journey.

I'd discussed the situation with Jake and decided to meet with Georgia Jones from the bone marrow registry. Deception wasn't a strong suit for me, and I had a true desire to set things straight. It was a tense two hours while I'd explained the extenuating circumstances regarding learning of our kinship. The legal team was there to help figure out if everything was still aboveboard. I'd brought Tanner along as my representative counsel.

In the end, the registry's attorneys decided there was no ill intent on any of our parts. They'd never had a case where during the donation process, a sibling was discovered to be the donor, so there wasn't precedence. They waived the one-year communication restriction since Allison wanted and needed the support we offered.

Jake hadn't attended the meeting because he'd had to be back at Cypress General for an urgent case. I'd never seen Tanner in a professional situation, and I had to say I was impressed. He was intimidating. No wonder he was such a successful attorney.

We walked outside the law office Tanner shared with Carson on Front Street. It was a sunny, warm day. Tanner and I crossed the brick street and sat on a bench overlooking the bayou. We'd both parked in the overflow lot nearby.

Outside in the sunshine, relief washed over me. "Thanks for having my back in there. You were awesome."

Tanner grinned. "Of course. Jake would've had my hide if I hadn't worked this out."

"I'm so relieved it's over and there won't be any repercussions. I felt like it was hanging over our heads and we were sneaking around trying to communicate with Allison."

"We've got signed forms that state you're all in the clear." He held up a folder with the paperwork inside. Of course we'd signed electronically as well. "How is Allison doing?"

"She's hanging tough. It's going to be a long road to recovery, so she needs to be near a hospital for a few months. I don't think they plan to release her for at least another three weeks. She still can't have in-person visitors for another week or so."

"Where will she live after she leaves the hospital?"

It was something that had been bothering me. "I don't know. We haven't had the chance to find out much about her or her situation. I don't know if she owns a home in Illinois or what."

"I see what you mean. I'm sure Jake will keep me in the loop, and I'll do what I can to help legally."

"Our family appreciates your support, Tanner. Jake tells me you're trying to get things in order to start your own practice." Tanner had gone into practice with Carson right out of law school as a way to pay off tuition debt instead of having loans.

He shrugged. "I don't know when that will happen, but I'm not making any announcements. Carson is against anything that would allow me any happiness or independence from him professionally. I'd rather be up to my eyeballs in student debt and be away from him."

I felt awful for him, knowing how he and Jake considered Carson a giant narcissistic boil on the butt of humanity. I believed that was the description they used regularly.

"I hope you figure a way out soon. I'm sorry it's taken so long." I didn't know what else to say.

"Carson is still very edgy about Allison. He's determined

to find out details. It wouldn't surprise me if he hasn't already hired a private investigator."

"What's he trying to find out?"

"Who she is, and if she's who he thinks she is. He hasn't gotten what he wants from any of us, and it's driving him mad."

"Maybe he's been hired to find out. Everyone in town knows I came back to donate bone marrow to someone anonymous, but the gossip swirls that it must be someone related."

"It could be that he's just frustrated because he doesn't know. Or it could be he's involved somehow. Tell Allison not to answer any calls unless she knows the caller. They will leave a message if it's someone who is legit."

"That's a good idea. I guess getting hospital or phone records isn't that hard for an investigator or a hacker, huh?"

"Not that hard for a good one."

We sat quietly for a minute or two.

"When are you leaving to go back to Paris?"

I felt a little squirmy under Tanner's unwavering stare. "Tomorrow."

He nodded, turning his gaze toward the water. "I thought you and Jake had made some kind of break-through."

"We have. But I need to figure out how to make this work for both of us." I didn't go into details because Jake still didn't know about my plan.

"Your leaving will break his heart, you know?"

"He knows it isn't forever. And he knows I love him."

"Well, that's something."

CHAPTER TWENTY-FIVE

Jake

S HE WAS GONE. Again. Back to Paris. Jake was ready to break his latest work contract with Cypress General and get on a plane. There were a few problems with that besides that he didn't speak French or have a job in Paris.

Leah had asked him to be patient. She'd asked him to be patient four years ago, and that hadn't worked out. But they were in a good place with each other, and he trusted her to follow her heart. He didn't know where that might lead, but Jake was willing to do whatever it took with her as priority. Before, he'd not put her first, and it had taken him until now to realize it. He'd expected her to make all the sacrifices.

The last thing she'd said before getting on the plane in Shreveport was that he should consider breaking ground on their house on the bayou.

Jake was finishing up with a new patient who'd been admitted with a full-body rash and a high fever. Of course, he was in isolation and the staff caring for him had to suit up in full protective gear in case he was highly contagious.

Just as he completed the decontamination process, Jake got a call from Nana asking him if he could come to her house. "Hon, we've got a situation brewing over here. And if

Tanner's available, we could use him, too."

He wanted to ask a million questions, but she hung up before he could ask even one. Good thing Jake was done for the day and could head over. He called Tanner on the way.

"What's going on?"

"Nothing good, from the sound of it. Nana pretty much said for us both to come immediately and then hung up." He wondered if someone needed medical help. But then why would Nana ask for Tanner? The need for legal and medical help at the same time at someone's home didn't seem likely. Unless this was a family situation. His family. Carson? Maybe. He'd been terrible to the Bertrand family in the past.

When Jake drove up, he recognized Elizabeth's red Porsche and Judge Keller's black Range Rover. Was that Tootie Keller's sedan? And Carson's car alongside Karen Bertrand's. Thankfully, Tanner arrived as Jake was climbing out of his truck.

He looked around at the ensemble of vehicles and whistled low. "This cannot be good."

Jake didn't bother to knock as he took the raised voices inside as his invitation to enter. The scene was as follows: Nana stood beside Karen, as if in protection of her. An ally. Carson appeared ready to pounce on both, as did they all. Elizabeth stopped screeching when she saw Jake and Tanner, though her eyes were fixed on Jake. Not a one of them appeared happy.

"What's happening?" Jake addressed the group.

They all spoke at once. Loudly. Gesturing and pointing.

"*Enough!*" Tanner barked over the din.

"Nana, since this is your home and you called us over,

can you tell us what's going on?"

"Certainly, dear. Tootie arrived first. She apparently overheard a conversation between the esteemed judge and Carson regarding our dear Allison's paternity. The cat is now out of the bag. Judge Keller is Allison's father."

Jake stared, trying not to let his jaw drop. Then he and Tanner exchanged a look of understanding. "So, y'all decided to come over here and terrorize Karen and Nana?" Jake spoke up.

"This *cannot* get out. Imagine the *scandal.*" Tootie's voice shook with horror. "I can't believe you did this"—she pointed a finger at Karen—"with my husband."

This was almost laughable. Almost. Jake managed to keep a straight face. Karen narrowed her eyes at Tootie. "Thank God he's your husband and not mine."

"I have a half sister, which means I'm connected to Leah Bertrand by *her.* This is the *worst* day of my life." Elizabeth looked to Jake for support.

He pushed her away. "Are you serious? Do you even hear yourself?"

"Do any of you even hear yourselves?" Tanner nearly yelled them down. "This all went down when y'all were sixteen, if I'm to understand this correctly. *Sixteen.* We all remember what it was like to be sixteen."

A cringy look went through the assembled group. Yes, they all remembered.

Carson spoke up then and pointed to the judge. "What we're trying to avoid is damage to our reputations. He's up for reelection this year. And we won't have this come out, or there will be consequences."

"Consequences for the truth?" Karen spoke then. "This isn't gossip. This happened. We have a daughter who is gravely ill and in the hospital. What kind of people are you to threaten *consequences* because the truth comes out instead of reaching out to this young woman? Hasn't she suffered enough on our accounts?"

Judge Arthur Keller appeared ashamed for the first time. "I'll not deny the paternity, Tootie. I can't. I've already admitted to it. And with DNA, eventually it would bear out. The best thing might be to bring her into the fold publicly. It might show well to our constituents."

"Are you serious? A minute ago you were threatening consequences. Now you want to be all phony and pretend you're welcoming her into your *fold*?" Karen nearly yelled at them.

"This is preposterous." Tootie stalked off and slammed the front door.

Nana stepped forward. "I believe Allison's been through enough for now. If she wants to know who you are, we'll address it when it happens. Leave it be for now. Fighting cancer is a tough enough battle."

Elizabeth glared at Jake as if all of this was his fault. "I can't believe you didn't tell me about this."

"I don't have to justify anything to you, Elizabeth. And no, I wouldn't have told you even if I had known because it wasn't my story to tell."

She stalked out through the front door, a replica of her mother, only a foot taller and in higher heels.

"So, we say nothing? And let it come out on its own?" Arthur's eyes darted around the room for confirmation.

"Looks that way, Arthur," Tanner answered him. "But there'll be no legal libel attached to this. You've admitted paternity, and nobody is agreeing to anything as far as keeping quiet. Got it? You deal with however it comes out. If it comes out."

Carson glared at his two sons. "I tried to get ahead of all this, but neither of you were willing to help us out."

"Too bad. This isn't your business anyway," Jake reminded him.

"I've known about this since we were sixteen-year-old boys. Arthur came to me when Karen told him she was pregnant. So, yes, it's still my business since Arthur is my client and my friend."

The judge placed a hand on Carson's shoulder. "It's done, Carson. The secret isn't a secret anymore. In a way, I'm relieved. It had to be worse for Karen to give up her baby because we insisted she keep it quiet."

Jake thought Karen might physically attack the man who was so incredibly clueless as to the angst she'd experienced due to his threats.

But Nana spoke up. "*Can* you imagine how this affected Karen's life? The lifetime of worry and the pain she endured because you threatened to deny having a relationship with her? Because you wouldn't claim the child? Bob didn't know Allison existed until a few weeks ago. She had to keep a secret like that from her *husband* because of you and what women in this world go through to keep a good reputation."

"I'm truly sorry for causing you such pain, Karen. I hope Tootie will come around and realize the fault was mine entirely."

The two men exited, leaving Karen, Nana, Tanner, and Jake in the silence that remained.

Leah

Two Weeks Later

I'D DONE IT. I'd sold my half of the gallery to Claude, who was so thrilled to have it and be rid of me, he'd paid more than what I'd believed possible. We'd had an appraiser go through all the works, the building, and the intangible business worth itself. I'd sold my flat to the next-door neighbor, fully furnished, for twice what I'd paid for it, as the value in the area had increased drastically since I'd moved in. Plus, I'd made some improvements that had increased its value. I'd donated clothing that was too much for small-town Louisiana.

I'd told no one of my plans. Not even Carly.

Of course, they'd told me about Allison's paternity. I'd had to let that settle in for a few days. The very idea that my new sister was as related to Elizabeth Keller as she was to me, well, it blew my mind. Not in a good way. I'd heard Elizabeth had had a similar reaction.

Now, I was right back where I'd started six weeks before, driving to Cypress Bayou from Shreveport. But I'd bought a car in Shreveport instead of renting one. I loved the smell of a new car. I hadn't ever had one of my own, so that was exciting.

The crawfish boil was in four weeks, and it sounded like everything was right on schedule. After the initial upset with my leaving and the confrontation with the Kellers, Momma and Nana had buckled down and gotten busy with finishing the decorations.

I'd spoken with Jake nearly every day and texted on the days we didn't talk. I thought he knew I was planning something big. But I refused to tell him what it was because I didn't want to jinx my homecoming. I hoped he'd made some progress on plans for the house. Like finding a builder.

When I took the exit from the airport toward home, I called Carly. "Hey there. I've got some news."

"What's happened?" Her tone was cautious, and I couldn't blame her with all the things we'd gone through lately.

"I'm on the way home. As in, I just got on I-49 headed toward Cypress Bayou."

"No way! I can't believe you're coming back for another visit so soon." Of course she would be happy about my return.

I laughed. "It's not a visit. I sold the gallery to Claude and sold my flat. I'm moving home." I could hardly keep the giggle from my voice.

"What? Get. Out. I assume Jake knows."

"No, he doesn't. I haven't told anybody. You're the first to hear it because you won't be in town when I arrive. I can surprise them in person."

"Um, yes you can. I'm home, too. I drove in this afternoon. I'm done with my internship. I'm moving home, too."

"*What?*" Her words thrilled me. "That's the best news,

Carly. I'm so excited." And I was so excited. It seemed as if there was a cosmic slide toward our family center.

"I can't believe we'll both be back in Cypress Bayou."

As I turned into my parents' driveway, more emotion hit me. I was home. In so many ways. Carly's car was already in the drive, along with Nana's. But not Jake's because Jake didn't know yet. After I surprised the family, I had to find Jake.

I FOUND JAKE sitting on the dock in one of two Adirondack chairs with a small cooler beside him, a beer in his hand, staring out at the dark water of the bayou. Brooding? That wasn't like him.

He noticed my approach once I stepped onto the dock from the land. "Leah?" He stood and stared a second as if he wasn't sure if I was real.

"Hey. Yeah, it's me."

We reached each other about midway across the weathered wood planks. "You're back." He put his arms around me and kissed me like it had been years since we'd last seen each other.

"What—Why—"

I laughed. "I've got a story for you, so how about we share whatever's in that cooler and have a seat in those lovely new chairs, and I'll share it with you."

"I'd like to hear this story." He took my hand and led me to the platform where the chairs sat waiting for us.

I'd gotten a text back from Josie, the Realtor from Latter

and Blum, regarding the property in Bywater. It had been several days so I hadn't been sure if I'd hear from her. But the news was promising. The seller was in a bit of a pinch, it seemed, and was willing to take a low offer on the property to unload it as fast as possible. It was a new listing, but this seller was motivated with a capital *M*, according to Josie.

As we settled under the stars, peace settled within me. This was right. And now was the time to do it. I started my story the same way as with Carly. "I have some news."

Jake sat beside me. Close enough to hold my hand, which he did. "Oh? That sounds speculative."

"I've decided to move home."

Jake tensed. "Home? As in, home to Cypress Bayou?"

"Yes. Sort of. It came to me in a moment of clarity that I didn't need to live in Paris and run Alaine's gallery to honor his memory. He left me a lot of money and half of a thriving business. But he didn't mean for me to sacrifice my life for it if that's not where my life was headed."

"So, how can you reconcile that?" Jake knew me and understood I had to do that.

"I want to start a gallery in New Orleans and maybe a small satellite one here. I have so many connections everywhere, and my favorite thing to do is find new artists. New Orleans is a gold mine of opportunity. I don't just want to sell paintings; I want to support artists and discover talent with scholarships and community."

"I'm impressed with your idea." Jake squeezed my hand. "I'm mostly excited at the thought of you coming home, though."

"I wouldn't want to live in New Orleans. I mean, I

would have to part of the time. The space I saw when we were in Bywater has a loft apartment. I could go back and forth." I could hear the excitement in my voice.

"Hmm. That's a lot of travel. But I've been doing it for years, so I know it can be done."

"It's four hours in a car. If I broke it up with a few days between, that's not a big deal. Plus, once I got things running, I would hire a manager." So much of what I did was done online these days, but it would require a good manager. "This would be a fantastic way to move what I do in Paris here."

"What about the gallery in Paris?"

"Claude bought me out. He's been asking to from the moment we found out we were joint owners. I can purchase the Bywater property with the sale of my part of La Toile."

"It just took your deciding it was okay to do it, huh?"

I nodded in the dark. "I couldn't see any way beyond where I was before. I guess I wasn't properly motivated. But I want you to know that you weren't my main motivator in this decision. It's important that I tell you this because if for any reason things don't work out between us, you need to know that Louisiana is my home. It's where my roots and my family are. I refuse to do anything only for a man. Even if that man is the love of my freakin' life."

He leaned toward me a little. Enough so that I could feel the heat transfer from his body to mine. His words weren't a whisper, but they were said quietly with conviction. "That stings just a little, but I deserve it. I didn't put you first, Leah, and just so you know, if you'd refused to come home, I was planning to break my contract at the hospital and move to Paris. Immediately."

I turned my head and stared at him, our faces only inches apart. "Are you serious?"

"I guess you'll have to call my bluff to find out."

"Nope. I'm all in."

"How do you feel about a house with a dock on Cypress Bayou?"

"All. In."

EPILOGUE

One Month Later

THE RAIN HELD off on the evening of the annual crawfish boil. Plaisance House was filled with warmth, family, and laughter. Fortunately, all the people from in and out of town who'd toured the house as part of the celebration had done so the week before, so this weekend was family and close friends only.

But outside, the entire town and surrounding areas had arrived. The tents were up, the lights were strung through the trees, the picnic tables were all around—not in rows but spread about so it felt intimate. There were candles on each table scented with gardenia and magnolia, not to compete with the actual night-blooming jasmine all around them.

Dusk was settling in, and the band had managed to entice the crowd to sing along with their lyrics. *Jambalaya, crawfish pie, filé gumbo. Son of a gun, we'll have big fun on the bay-o... me, oh my-oh.* Of course, the lyrics were never exact, just a broken up version of the chorus that was so catchy.

The Preservation Society had outdone themselves as always. The event was filled with music, fellowship, and laughter. And food. So much food. Boiled crawfish, smoked sausage, ears of corn, onions, and potatoes. And the weather was warm, though slightly humid. This was a night of celebration. More so for our family, as we were all together and had each other and so much to celebrate.

If ever there was a complicated family dynamic, it would have to be ours. We'd finally gotten Allison out of the hospital and home to Cypress Bayou temporarily. Temporarily because she still required medical care until her white and red blood counts were consistently back to normal, which they weren't quite yet.

We were getting to know Allison via FaceTime calls, though she was still in the hospital. She was a delight to us all and had had a surprisingly interesting life before she'd met us. Raised by a military dad and very fun and colorful mom, she'd traveled extensively and was an accomplished knitter and cook. And much to our surprise, she wasn't the least bit intimidated by our mother. I'll just say, Allison was no shrinking violet.

But she had some stuff to deal with back in Illinois apparently. A house to sell, but the rest she was pretty private about. So, maybe a former beau? We weren't sure and tried to keep our noses out of it. Fortunately, whatever it was remained in Illinois for the time being. Her plan was to get healthy here and then return there to deal with things. We hoped she would come back to Cypress Bayou to live once that was done.

I'd bought the property in Bywater down in New Orleans after a full inspection. It was in decent shape but would require a good amount of work to create my vision, so it looked like I would be traveling back and forth for the foreseeable future. Jake was breaking ground this month on our house on the bayou. The one we'd planned years before.

Blake, Jake's roommate, after living and working together for ten years, had decided to return to England to help with the care of his dying mother, leaving a space for me to move in with Jake in his loft apartment, which I thought was extremely sad but fortuitous on our parts.

Carly would stay at Nana's for now, since her house was giant and having Carly there was a fantastic idea. Now, Carly would need to find a job at a local law office, of which there were surprisingly many in such a small town.

Tanner was the only one who hadn't benefitted from our almost-storybook happy-ending-for-now. He was still trying to wrestle his way free from Carson and start his own law firm in town, but Carson had him over the legal ropes to prevent it. We looked forward to a day when he could find happiness in his own story just like Jake and I had in ours...

The End

Don't miss the next book in the Louisiana series,
Secrets in Cypress Bayou!

Join Tule Publishing's newsletter for more great reads and weekly deals!

Red Beans & Rice (with smoked sausage)
Susan Sands's Recipe

Red beans and rice are a staple in most parts of Louisiana. There is a story behind this: Historically, Mondays were wash days on the bayou. The leftover ham bone from Sunday's dinner was used to simmer most of the day with a pot of red beans and spices on Mondays, when the women were busy doing laundry. So, Mondays are still red beans and rice days in Louisiana. It's often a special at restaurants every Monday.

Beans:

1lb. dried red beans (I prefer Camellia brand. Check the date for freshness.)

1 Tablespoon minced garlic

1 yellow onion finely chopped

1 green bell pepper finely chopped

2 stalks celery finely chopped

½ stick salted butter

1 quart chicken broth

2 – 3 Tablespoons Creole Seasoning (I use Tony Chachere's brand.)

2 lbs. smoked pork sausage cut in rounds and/or a ham bone for smoke flavoring.

Rice: 4 cups long-grain white rice. A rice cooker works best. Don't use converted rice.

Method:

*Heat beans in a large pot barely covered in water just until boiling. Let sit for one hour. This decreases the amount of gas in the beans.

*Dump water and re-rinse beans, then refill bean pot with one quart of water and one quart chicken broth. Set aside.

*Sauté onions, celery, bell pepper, and garlic in butter in a separate pan for about 10 minutes. *Add ½ lb. of the sausage rounds until sizzling, or for another ten minutes. Add ½ Creole seasoning and stir.

*Add sauté to large bean pot.

*Stir in the remainder of Creole seasoning and another ½ lb. of sausage or add ham bone.

*Cook for 2 – 3 hours on medium heat, stirring occasionally, until beans are easily smashed. (There is a significant range here, depending on how fresh the beans are. Also, longer cooking times needed for high elevation.)

*When beans are cooked, add the remaining 1lb. of sausage and cook over medium heat for another twenty minutes or so or until cooked through. This sausage will be the tastiest because the sausage cooked for hours will lose some of its original flavor that went into the beans.

*Smash some of the beans with a potato masher to thicken and add creaminess.

*Serve beans over rice.

Note: The amount of Creole seasoning is to taste, so if more is needed, add more.

Note: This works great in an Instant Pot or comparable pressure cooker in a fraction of the time.

Enjoy!

Crawfish Etouffee Recipe

Buy your crawfish tail meat from Walmart (I know) in the frozen seafood section. They are the only place that sells the ones farmed in Louisiana and not China. And they taste way better.

You will need:

2 lbs. crawfish tails (Wash all the nasty stuff away and rinse through strainer with big holes to get rid of everything that falls off the tails. This keeps them from having a fishy taste.) Do this before you start cooking.

½ – ¾ sticks of butter

½ cup of flour (maybe more or a little less)

½ cup of tomato sauce or pureed tomatoes

1 bunch green onions (just the green tops finely chopped)

1 yellow onion (finely chopped)

1 green bell pepper (finely chopped)

2 celery stalks (finely chopped)

1 teaspoon minced garlic

1 teaspoon Tony Chachere's seasoning (to taste)

Chicken broth

Make a pot of long-grained white rice. NOT the quick rice. It takes about 20-30 minutes to cook. I recommend about three cups. A $20 rice cooker from Walmart works best.

Note: You can add ½ to 1 can cream of mushroom soup to make this creamier or to extend the amount you are making. It's good to have on hand.

Note #2: You can use the frozen seasoning blend in a bag that has onions, green peppers, and celery to cut down on time.

*In a large saucepan, melt butter and garlic together, add onions, bell pepper, and celery. Cook on medium heat until softened. (about ten minutes) Add a little Tony Chachere's to this.

*Add crawfish tails and cook until the mixture gets juicy.

*Sprinkle flour a little at a time and stir as you do so there aren't any clumps. The mixture will thicken.

*Let this sizzle a little for a few minutes then add about a ½ cup of chicken broth and stir. If it's too thick, add more chicken broth.

*Cook for a few minutes then stir in tomato sauce.

*Add remaining Tony Chachere's to taste. You might need a little more before serving. It's up to you.

*Finish by sprinkling green onions on top, or stir them into the etouffee for more of the green onion flavor. I do both because I like the taste.

Tip: This will feed 4-6 people. There are plenty of crawfish in here, so adding a little more flour and chicken broth and a can of mushroom soup can make more etouffee.

If you enjoyed *Home to Cypress Bayou*, you'll love the next books in the…

Louisiana series

Book 1: *Home to Cypress Bayou*

Book 2: *Secrets in Cypress Bayou*
Coming in August 2022

Book 3: *A Bayou Christmas*
Coming in November 2022

Available now at your favorite online retailer!

More books by Susan Sands

The Alabama series

Book 1: *Again, Alabama*

Book 2: *Love, Alabama*

Book 3: *Forever, Alabama*

Book 4: *Christmas, Alabama*

Book 5: *Noel, Alabama*

Available now at your favorite online retailer!

About the Author

Susan Sands grew up in a real life Southern Footloose town, complete with her senior class hosting the first ever prom in the history of their tiny public school. Is it any wonder she writes Southern small town stories full of porch swings, fun and romance?

Susan lives in suburban Atlanta surrounded by her husband, three young adult kiddos and lots of material for her next book.

Thank you for reading

Home to Cypress Bayou

If you enjoyed this book, you can find more from all our great authors at TulePublishing.com, or from your favorite online retailer.

TULE
PUBLISHING